ONCE A HERO

KATHERINE SUTCLIFFE

JOVE BOOKS, NEW YORK

ONCE A HERO

A Jove Book / published by arrangement with
the author

PRINTING HISTORY
Jove edition / June 1994

All rights reserved.
Copyright © 1994 by Katherine Sutcliffe.
Author photograph by Rob Hess.
This book may not be reproduced in whole or in part,
by mimeograph or any other means, without permission.
For information address: The Berkley Publishing Group,
200 Madison Avenue, New York, New York 10016.

ISBN: 0-515-11387-5

A JOVE BOOK®
Jove Books are published by The Berkley Publishing Group,
200 Madison Avenue, New York, New York 10016.
JOVE and the "J" design are trademarks
belonging to Jove Publications, Inc.

PRINTED IN THE UNITED STATES OF AMERICA

10 9 8 7 6 5 4 3 2 1

IN MEMORY OF MY PRECIOUS CHIA
I continue to miss you so much.
You will never be replaced in my heart.

I dedicate this book to my darling husband,
Neil, and my children, Bryan, Lauren, and Rachel.

A special thank you to those who understand
my love for my pretty Arabian babies:
Equator AA, MHR Noblesse, NapPoleone
PF Locomotion, Ra-Bon Perlagal, and
Neil's Creek Count
(Not to mention my eleven
wonderful bunnies which
bring me such joy and pleasure):

Tracy Wynne Caruth (and D.A. Napitov+)
Margie Tarkington
Debbie, Christy, and Wayne Higgins
Jo An Bixby
June Colbert
Heather and Ken Lameiras

And as always to
Carrie Feron and Berkley Books
Thank You!

A sure mark of good breeding is the suppression of any undue emotion, such as anger, mortification, laughter, or any form of selfishness.

— *The Illustrated Manners Book*
ROBERT DE VALCOURT, 1855

CHAPTER ONE

1858

AS ALWAYS, SHE WORE WHITE: WHITE HAT, WHITE GLOVES, white gown, white shoes. The color only exaggerated the porcelainlike quality of her skin—what little skin the men of New South Wales were allowed to see, as Bronte Haviland came and went about her duties as the warden's daughter.

Today, her India-purchased gown consisted of layers of bleached muslin that were sparsely adorned with lace, the wide apricot-hued sash around her waist the only hint of color on her person. The simplicity of the garment did little to diminish her tall, coltish figure, or to alleviate the "pig-stubborn" set of her slender shoulders—as her father so often described her pertinacious personality.

Her face was almost hidden by the swooping brim of her hat, which was made of tightly woven straw and bedecked with white silk daisies. It shadowed her eyes, hid her wealth of blue-black hair. In fact, little could be seen beyond her slender neck, delicately pointed chin (which her father termed obstinate), and a lush red mouth that curved with a natural bewitchment.

But this beautiful woman was not at leisure.

She stood in the searing sun and vaguely listened to her father's assistant, Arthur Ellison, an unspeakably tedious man, a former marine private whose sole aspiration was to win Bronte as his bride.

God help her.

As Arthur ran down the list of names on the hastily penned roster in his hands, Bronte's eyes were drawn from the respectful row of men to some commotion at the far end of the queue. But her posture did not betray her interest.

"Defiance. Pure and simple," Arthur muttered. "One would think the idiots would assume their best behavior when offered an opportunity to leave this hellhole. What's the problem?" he called to the guard. "If you can not control the men, sir, then perhaps we should find someone more capable."

The distressed guard threw Arthur a telling look. "This bloke refuses to lower his eyes in Miss Haviland's presence, Mr. Ellison."

"You know the punishment, man. Inflict it!"

Bronte raised her eyes to Arthur and said calmly, "Please. That won't be necessary."

"Of course it is. It's your father's rule, Bronte. The lot of scum are to show you respect at all times. If you allow the vermin to take the smallest liberty, then before you know it, they are out of control."

Bronte merely said, "Let us proceed."

Arthur Ellison offered his hand to Bronte as she stepped from the platform. She ignored it, as always, and moved by him, down the file of prospective servants. Twice a year she performed this ritual, choosing a select few to work outside the normal strictures of prison life—on her father's farm, or, if one proved himself trustworthy, helping build the new school and orphanage on the land her father had donated to the Sisters of St. Joseph of Cluny. They were Catholic missioners dedicated to giving the offspring of the unmarried female convicts a brighter future than their parents had bestowed on them.

She glanced at the line of men. By the time Bronte had "interviewed" the first dozen, she was drained. There were very few men who were truly redeemable. Even fewer she would consider allowing into her home or to work around the orphanage children. Today was no exception. The unmerciful heat made her head ache.

But she stood straight, determined to give every watchful and hopeful prisoner a fair hearing.

With a half dozen convicts remaining to be inspected, Bronte flipped open her cockatoo fan and fluttered it before her face, hoping the slight breeze would alleviate the heat. That was when she noticed the tall, dark-haired prisoner at the far end of the queue.

"John J. Madison," Arthur read from the roster, but he failed to divert Bronte's attention from the prisoner being flanked by two highly agitated guards. "Turn about, Mr. Madison," Arthur demanded, oblivious to Bronte's inattentiveness.

"Mr. John J. Madison was convicted for theft and received seven years, of which he has served two," Arthur read. "By trade, he was a carpenter."

Bronte was still distracted.

The prisoner at the end of the queue spoke quietly to one of the guards, and the guard's face turned beet red with anger. The prisoner had the audacity to throw back his head full of shockingly black, slightly curly hair, and laugh.

Bronte stared at the man a long moment.

Odd. He seemed almost . . . familiar.

It was the hair, certainly. It reminded her of someone's. And that profile—

She bit her lip and stared harder over the top of her fan. An unnerving emotion rolled over in her breast—that same emotion she experienced anytime she allowed herself to think of—

"Mr. Madison's record since arriving at New South Wales has been exemplary . . . Bronte," Arthur said in a lower voice. "Are you listening to me?"

"Of course," she replied, and snapped the fan closed, forcibly focusing her gray eyes on his. "How many positions do we yet have to fill, Mr. Ellison?"

Arthur's face turned pink at her usage of "Mr. Ellison" in front of his peers. No doubt he would again be the brunt of jokes from the other officers, who vowed he stood a snowball's chance in hell of marrying the warden's daughter—the "iron maiden," the "last virgin in New South Wales." When it came to charity, she was passionate. When it came to men . . . no one could live up to her ideals of perfection.

Arthur removed his straw hat and mopped his forehead with his coat sleeve. "We have one position yet to fill," he finally replied, with barely concealed pique. "As I was saying about Mr. Madison—"

"Who is that incorrigible creature there?" Bronte

interrupted, flipping open her fan again and gazing at the tall prisoner, who had a smirk on his lips. A nagging, troublesome little quiver had returned to her stomach. Focusing harder, she tried to imagine what he might look like without the scruffy beard stubble and with the month's worth of grime scrubbed from his sunbaked skin.

Scowling, Arthur glanced toward the end of the queue. His displeasure deepened. "Good God," he muttered. "What the blazes is he doing here?"

Apparently forgetting Bronte for the moment, Arthur stormed toward the two guards, who were growing more agitated at their charge by the second. "Here now," Arthur said. "What is this man doing here?"

The guards stared at Arthur sullenly before one responded, "Mr. Haviland himself ordered the bloke to be included."

With an audible sigh, Arthur slapped his hat against his thigh. Bronte did her best to keep her sights focused on her task. In truth, she could not place the reason for her skittishness. She wasn't one to become rattled. She'd been around the prisoners for years, but there was something about this one that unbalanced her.

He apparently cared little about prison protocol. His stance was almost arrogant, and he wore his shackles as if they were little more than accessories to his meager wardrobe of ill-fitting duck trousers and a cotton shirt open down his chest.

"Obviously, there's been some mistake," Arthur grumbled.

Bronte glanced again at the convict who, so far, had ignored her interest. "Who is he?" she said.

Arthur muttered again and looked perplexed, then agitated, then resigned. Meeting her gaze directly, he swallowed and said, "Tremain. Brandon Tremain."

Bronte dropped her fan. It landed on the tip of Arthur's boot and bounced into the sand.

Arthur bent and retrieved the plushly plumed fan, shook away the dirt, and placed the expensive piece on Bronte's open gloved hand.

She swallowed again and laughed thinly. "I do beg your pardon. How clumsy of me. It's just for a moment I thought you said that his name was Brandon Tremain."

"I did."

Closing her fingers tightly around the fan, Bronte turned her eyes toward the line of fidgeting, sweating recruits who wished to work her father's farm for the next year. They appeared totally oblivious to the fact that, beneath her pristine white skirts, her knees had turned to aspic.

In a voice as dry as Australian dust, she said, "How very ironic. As you well know, Arthur, there is a national hero by that name. This . . . this man . . . of course, is not that Brandon Tremain. Not Captain Brandon Tremain of Her Majesty's Royal Marines. That Brandon Tremain is a much decorated icon of bravery. The very epitome of uprightness, as evidenced in his shining character and unflawed actions."

Arthur raised one eyebrow and looked disgusted. "Good God, you sound like one of those bloody articles from the *London Times*—"

"This man is obviously a disgrace, and I pity the good Captain who is forced to share his unblem-

ished name with such a reprobate." She usually was
not so harsh, but somehow she couldn't control her
tongue. Clutching the fan even tighter, Bronte stared
harder at the prisoner's profile, feeling her knees
grow weaker, and weaker still as her eyes returned
again and again to the crop of thick, black, curly hair
spilling over his back collar and the patrician brow
that in other circumstances might have passed as
noble . . .

"My dear Bronte, the cad in question is none
other than Captain Brandon Tremain, of Her Majesty's Royal Marines," Arthur said blandly.

She turned on him so fast and furiously his face
went sheet white. She slapped his shoulder with
her fan and said through her teeth, "How dare you
slander Captain Tremain with such a villainous lie.
I demand that you retract the falsehood this moment."

The convicts stared, as did the guards. No one
had ever seen the warden's daughter quite so
agitated. Arthur took a deep breath, ran his hand
over his brow, and said, "I cannot retract it, Miss
Haviland, because the man standing yonder truly is
Captain Brandon Tremain."

"Captain Tremain is my— is a hero," she stressed
more forcefully, aware that the edge in her voice
stemmed from fear now, and less from anger.
"You're simply jealous, Arthur. You've always been
jealous of the fine Captain because he was so
celebrated and decorated, and because I admired
him—"

"Admire is an understatement," he muttered
beneath his breath, then he spoke louder. "My dear
Bronte, everyone in this country has listened to you

recount each and every story printed about him in
the *London Times* for the last ten years." Arthur's
expression became almost smug. "I truly hate to
topple your hero from the pedestal on which you
have placed him, but the foul-smelling creature
there is—I repeat—is Captain Brandon Tremain."

She thought she might hit Arthur—just on prin-
ciple. Instead, she stepped away, aware of a sick-
ness that felt like disappointment and outrage
squirming in her stomach. For the first time since
her sojourn that morning to New South Wales
Prison outside of Sydney, she acknowledged the
unbearable heat by removing her hat.

Only then did she allow her gaze to slide back to
the prisoner called Tremain.

Her knees felt horribly weak as she moved up
before him—the man—the convict—the impostor
who would dare pass himself off as England's cham-
pion. In an instant the dozens of articles regarding
Captain Brandon Tremain that she had neatly clipped
and saved through the years of isolation from her
beloved England flashed before her mind's eye—all
those yellowed, sea-soiled newspapers with their
poor ink drawings that only vaguely captured the
likenesses of their subjects.

Throughout the lonely years Bronte had spent in
Australia, she had allowed her imagination to in-
grain the Captain's image on her dreams, and as
she cautiously moved before him and stopped,
forcing her gaze to climb up and up his tall body to
his face, she did her best to fight back the frantic
feeling that threatened to overwhelm her.

If indeed this were Captain Brandon Tremain, he
was much taller than she had imagined; the papers

had only mentioned "a man of supreme stature." This man stood at least four inches over six feet.

If indeed this man were Captain Brandon Tremain, his shoulders appeared extraordinarily wide—much wider and stronger than the papers' "slender and dignified carriage" had portrayed.

Frantically, her gaze traveled over his unrecognizable bearded face to his hair—the thick, black curls that she'd previously only seen as faint lines in a sketch.

"Are you Captain Brandon Tremain of Her Majesty's Royal Marines?" she heard herself ask in a hollow voice, suspecting, even before he looked at her, that she would not like his answer.

At last, his dark head tipped and his startling blue eyes met hers. For a long minute, he did not reply, but met her direct appraisal unflinchingly, his eyes lowering only briefly as he appeared to regard her person with flagrant appreciation.

"Spanish," he murmured.

Bronte frowned. "I beg your pardon?"

The prisoner raised one eyebrow and looked at her again. "Your mother was Spanish, yes?"

Mesmerized by the velvet inflection of his deep voice, she nodded, finding she could not look away from his vivid blue eyes, no matter how she tried.

"I thought so. 'Tis a well-known fact that some of the most beautiful women in the world come from Spain. Your mother must have been exquisite."

"Sir," she managed to breathe, "I could have you whipped for such impertinence." Lowering her lashes, she shook her head almost angrily. "Need I remind you who I am?"

"I know who you are. I knew the moment I saw

you. Odd. You don't look the least like an 'iron maiden' to me."

Arthur stepped between them. Shoulders back and square chin jutting, he glared up at the convict and said, "One more word out of you, Tremain, and I'll have you flogged." He nodded at the guards, and they grabbed the prisoner by each arm, planting their batons against the back of his neck.

He didn't flinch, but regarded Arthur with a look of blatant amusement.

"Release him," Bronte ordered. Arthur swung around with an expression of amazement.

"My dear Bronte, I needn't remind you of my feelings for you. However, I must insist that you not interfere with my authority. This . . . fiend is a prisoner and should not be encouraged."

"Are you finished?" she said.

Drawing himself up, he offered her a sharp nod.

"Good. Then if you'll kindly step aside, I shall continue my interview . . . Mr. Ellison."

Stepping around her father's abashed assistant, Bronte stood toe-to-toe with the prisoner, who had the audacity to continue smiling at her although the guards had yet to release their obviously forceful hold on his arms.

"I will ask you once again, sir—and this time I expect a direct answer or I will order these men to drag you kicking and screaming to the triangles."

"Sweetheart," he drawled, bringing a gasp from the guards and some unintelligible mutter from Arthur. "Heroes don't kick and scream."

She stared up into his eyes. The terrible reality clashed like cymbals in her ears, and for a brief moment the earth felt as if it had turned to a crashing, turbulent sea beneath her feet.

"Then it's true," she finally said. "You're Captain Brandon Tremain."

"At your service, m'lovely lady."

The heat seemed suddenly too wicked to endure. Bronte turned and walked some distance away, her eyes scanning the terrain that had been her home for the last ten years. There were paperbark trees scattered about the yard, ghostly in their silver blue hue, as if moonlight were spilling over them instead of the harsh afternoon sun.

Arthur moved up behind her and put his hand on her shoulder. She shrugged it off. "Is my father aware of this man's identity?" she demanded in a voice void of the emotion she was feeling.

"Yes."

"And he said nothing to me about it," she said more to herself than to Arthur.

At last, she replaced the hat on her head and faced Tremain again. Gloved hands clenched, Bronte set her shoulders and said, "Mr. Tremain, step forward."

The guards released their grip, and the prisoner stepped forward.

"Balance on your right leg," she demanded.

He did so effortlessly, and for the first time Bronte noticed that he was shoeless. The idea occurred to her that the hot sand must surely be burning the bottoms of his feet.

"Now on your left," she snapped, furious that she should care whether or not the sand was burning his feet. "Show your teeth," she said.

He flashed her a brilliant white smile that seemed as caustic as it was charming.

"Turn around."

Obeying, he offered his back as the guard at his right took hold of his shirt and yanked it down to his lower spine. His sweat-moist skin appeared as dark as his face. The last weeks of hard labor had defined each and every muscle beneath the taut flesh.

At her nod, the guards turned him back to face her. The fact that he continued to brandish that appallingly arrogant grin—despite her attempt to humiliate him—brought hot color to her cheeks.

Stepping nearer, so that again she stood toe-to-toe with Tremain, and bringing an agitated reaction from Arthur, Bronte focused on the prisoner's sky-blue eyes and asked unemotionally, "Have you any diseases that we should be aware of, Mr. Tremain?"

"Why?" he replied smoothly, "Interested in a little hanky-panky under the wattle tree, Princess?"

Her eyes widened briefly, then narrowed. Ignoring the guards', and Arthur's, outraged babblings, Bronte lowered her voice to just above a whisper. "If you believe that I would bring such as you into my home to work, you are sadly mistaken. And furthermore, I wouldn't 'hanky-panky' with you if you were the last man on the face of this, or any other, continent." More loudly, she called out, "Mr. Ellison, send this detestable prisoner back to the fields. I find him of unsuitable character."

"I beg your pardon, Bronte," Arthur said softly. Bending nearer her ear, he whispered, "I fear your father has decided otherwise."

She continued staring up into Tremain's eyes, the

realization that this fallen hero was far more beautiful than she had ever allowed her imagination to believe making her light-headed with disappointment. His reputation had been built on lies.

Or had it? Perhaps there had been some horrible mistake. Some error in judgment that had committed an innocent man—

"I appreciate your feelings in this matter," Arthur said, "but your father had already told me Tremain is to be involved in this work-leave program. In fact, he should have been sent on directly instead of being here today."

A smile inched up one side of Tremain's mouth. The very essence of it challenged her.

Very slowly, Bronte forced herself to turn, to fix her gaze on her father's distant brougham, which had become blurry behind the thin film of water covering her eyes. Forcing her feet to move, she slowly walked toward the conveyance, pausing only briefly to shut her eyes against the brilliant white sunlight bleaching the color from the world around her.

She longed, as she had for the past many years, for the sanity of England.

"Perhaps there's been a mistake," she said aloud. "Perhaps he's innocent—"

"No," Arthur replied, dashing her last thread of hope. "He was tried and found guilty by his peers."

"And what was his crime?" she asked, facing her father's assistant again, appalled that he was witnessing this crumbling of her world. "What violation of law could Captain Brandon Tremain have committed that would warrant his being sent to New South Wales?"

"Treason, for one," he replied. "Although he was never actually tried for that crime. There was inconclusive evidence."

Treason.

"And?"

Arthur took a deep breath and replied, "Murder. He was found guilty of cold-blooded, ruthless murder."

As we look, so we feel, so we act,
and so we are.
—*The Illustrated Manners Book*
ROBERT DE VALCOURT, 1855

CHAPTER TWO

EACH YEAR BRONTE CELEBRATED HER BIRTHDAY IN THE SAME
manner. She shared dinner with her father—always a
feast fit for the Queen, consisting of all of Bronte's
favorites: almond soup, pomplet, and croquettes of
sweetbreads; a grand cake decorated with marzipan flowers would follow. Afterward, they would
ride their hunters down to the river, well out of
sight of the rest of the world, and race the waves as
they washed ashore, not returning home until well
after dark. Then her father would shoot off fireworks, shipped all the way from China just for the
occasion.

This year, however, was different.

The cargo ship from India had not arrived the
previous week as anticipated, so Bronte had had to
settle for a steak from the leg of an emu, and rice
pudding.

If that wasn't disappointment enough, she was
forced to eat alone. She had held dinner for nearly

an hour, sitting in the high-ceilinged dining room at a table covered with a heavy white cloth, decorated with ivy twined with flowers and ferns, and littered with the brittle, crumpling newspaper articles concerning Brandon Tremain she had dug out of her scrapbook. She picked at the emu while overhead the punkah shushed back and forth, barely disturbing the hot air. It wasn't like her father to be late. Always, no matter what crisis might arise, William Haviland celebrated his only daughter's birthday with her.

And today was her twenty-seventh.

What a ghastly birthday it was!

Twenty-seven and unmarried.

Normally, she wasn't bothered by the idea of remaining a spinster. Certainly none of the men who had paraded through her house with courtship on their minds had tempted her. After all, she carried on a full life—running her father's house was a pleasure; discussing the problems at the prison was a stimulating challenge. Her days spent planning the school and orphanage were rewarding.

Still, these thoughts were not in her mind tonight.

Somewhere—in her deepest, most private thoughts—she imagined, as she had for so many years, being courted by her hero, Brandon Tremain.

With her gaze wandering over the untidy heaps of *Times* essays detailing the heroics of the young, handsome captain, Bronte tried her best to recall a time—aside from the night her mother died— when she had experienced such a shattering shock. Captain Brandon Tremain was no hero. He was no better than the other flagitious fiends in Australia.

Murder and treason.

Two of the most heinous acts a man could commit. What could the courts have been thinking to send him to Australia? Blazes! The man deserved execution.

Pushing away from the table, Bronte wandered the halls of the spacious house, searching for something—anything—to divert her. To make it seem as if her world still made sense.

Evening shadows stretched across the rugless floors and crept in ever-deepening darkness through the open window jalousies.

Oh God, it was simply too much to bear.

The very man who exemplified truth, honor, bravery, and loyalty to his queen and country had become a cold-blooded killer.

Brandon Tremain had become a fallen hero.

She wanted to cry.

The clock in the hallway struck ten as William Haviland glanced, appearing chagrined, at the china plate his daughter extended in one hand, filled with birthday cake sprouting a marzipan flower and a single skinny, slightly warped candle.

"By gosh, I've hurt your feelings," he muttered. "Problems with the convicts. But still, what a cad. An imbecile. I should be thrashed, I admit. Do you forgive me, Pumpkin?"

Obviously, he was trying to make up. Calling her "Pumpkin" didn't help. As a chubby child she hadn't cared for the sobriquet. As a woman who wished she had retained a smidgeon of that padding in certain areas, she found the endearment silly.

"Forgetting my birthday is beside the point. There is a business matter we should discuss."

"That's my lass. Business first. By Jove, you're a chip off the old block."

"Don't try to change the subject."

William plucked up his burning cigar from a clay ashtray shaped like a kangaroo and puffed on it, wreathing his handsome face in smoke. He had changed from his business suit into an emerald-green smoking jacket of raw silk. Even at leisure he radiated power that could set most men back on their heels—which was why the Queen herself had chosen Bronte's father to head New South Wales Prison.

He waited for her to continue.

"The matter concerns a certain convict," she began.

"Tremain."

Bronte took a breath and slowly released it. She forced a smile onto her face. "Why wasn't I informed about his situation, Father?"

"I knew you would be upset. And you are. I fully intended to speak to you on the matter before we brought him here, but there have been so many problems at the prison . . ." William sighed and glanced thoughtfully around the parlor. "A truly sad error on my part, Pumpkin, and I hope you forgive me."

"Just two evenings ago we sat in this very room discussing the success of his campaign in Delhi last year, speculating about what daring escapade he would launch next. Now I learn that the man is a traitor and that he's been residing in chains on this very soil for the last three months!"

William had the good grace to look discomfited. "He wasn't convicted of treason, Pumpkin."

She picked up a glass of vintage port and plunked it down before her father. With her hair wisping out of its coiffure, she almost shook with anger. She leaned toward him and narrowed her eyes. "Can you imagine that the very man about whom we once conversed in tones of idolatry has stooped as low as a man could get? Treason, Father!"

"Not convicted," he reminded her.

"Why, we used to sit yonder in the conservatory and read aloud the articles from the papers concerning his heroism. I lay in my bed at night imagining him as some gallant knight swashbuckling his way across stormy, war-infested seas in honor of God and our Queen Victoria."

William sampled his cake and grunted in approval. "Reckon his swash got buckled all right," he said.

"How can you make light of this . . this catastrophe, Father? One of the greatest heroes of our time is nothing more than a murderous traitor. He should be transported to Norfolk Island with the rest of the totally damned and doomed malefactors, yet you had the extreme poor judgment to consider bringing him to Haviland Farm. Father, I fear you're becoming senile."

William sat straight and raised both dark eyebrows. "Senile! By God, lass, I'm forty-nine years old. And I judge every man on his actions once on this island—never on hearsay. So if I desire to bring Atilla the Hun here to prove his mettle, by God, I'll do so."

"I would rather live with Atilla the Hun than with a traitor."

Slowly rising from his chair, William said, "No one asked you to live with Tremain, m'dear, only to treat him as you would any of the other men working and residing on this farm. Which brings me to the matter of assigning him his job . . . I'm considering stable work. He might prove quite good with the horses."

"I don't want him within five miles of my horses!" she replied hotly. "He's not worthy!"

William cleared his throat. "As I said, he's to be treated like any other man working this farm."

Bronte slowly straightened, feeling as if she were one hundred and twenty-seven instead of twenty-seven. Disappointment lodged in her breast like a stone. "But he's not like any other man, Father. For half of my life I have lived in New South Wales at your side. My only connection to England—my home, which I left behind when I was a child— were the few material treasures we brought with us and the occasional trinkets we purchase from the merchants in Sydney. For the last seventeen years I have lived for the moment the ships arrive from home. I immerse myself in the news and dream of one day returning. Meanwhile, the only English people I meet are men and women of the lowest moral standards."

She took a long, shaky breath. "But I always believed that there was such a thing as an incorruptible being, a true hero."

In a raspy voice, she said more softly, "Aside from you, he was . . . my only hope that gallantry

still survives somewhere. Now I learn he is nothing
more than—"

"A man, Bronte. Nothing more. Nothing less."

A knock at the door interrupted.

"What is it?" William barked.

Murray Grant, a stout Scot who'd long since
earned Haviland's trust, glanced nervously from
Bronte to William before announcing in his heaviest
brogue, "Sir, Mr. Ellison has arrived."

Bronte groaned and fixed her father with an
accusatory stare just as Arthur elbowed his way
past Murray into the room. He gave a flourishing
bow to Bronte and offered her a prettily wrapped
gift and a smile.

"The happiest of birthdays, m'dear Bronte. I trust
you're in a better frame of mind this evening?"

"Not particularly," she retorted as she regarded
the sizable package in her hand.

"Go ahead and open it," Arthur encouraged.

Sighing, Bronte sat down in a chair and tugged at
the satin ribbon and blue tissue surrounding the
prize. When the gift lay bare in her lap, Bronte
forced her eyes back to Arthur's and cleared her
throat. "How very . . . thoughtful. Another emu-
egg arrangement, Father."

"I say," William said noncommittally as he puffed
on his cigar.

They all stared momentarily at the five eggs
grouped together as a centerpiece, the middle consisting of a native—spear in hand—and a kangaroo carved from wattle wood and surrounded by
palms, ferns, and cockatoo feathers.

"It'll look smashing among the other eggs you've
given us," Bronte managed.

"I know how much you like them," Arthur replied, appearing smug.

Sweeping aside the tissue and ribbon, Bronte carried the atrocity to Murray. "This will look marvelous on the dining room table."

Murray's dark eyes grew round and shifted to William, who crushed the cigar stub out on the clay kangaroo. Bronte only smiled. "We were growing weary of that old Worcester porcelain tureen taking up space on the table, weren't we, Father?"

"That tureen was my mother's," he replied through his teeth.

Bronte retrieved the centerpiece and exited the room. It served him right. Every year for the last five years he had invited Arthur Ellison to join them in the shooting off of birthday fireworks. Her father maintained that all men had their good points— and that in time Bronte would come to appreciate Arthur's.

Once out of sight, Bronte placed the centerpiece on a side table and left the house, pausing on the veranda long enough to gaze toward the barns and paddocks, and beyond that, to the distant twinkling lights of the workers' barracks.

Perhaps it was just as well that Arthur had interrupted them. She had been on the verge of losing control of her emotions—and that was never good. It simply wasn't proper, and besides, she had been too close to revealing the idiotic, fairy-tale fantasies that had occupied her long nights alone.

Closing her eyes, turning her face into the warm south breeze that toyed with the chimes hanging above her shoulder, she wondered, with a growing sense of despair, what new dreams would occupy her empty hours now.

Wang Cho, once a master rabbit breeder for some Far East potentate—and who now took immense delight in caring for Bronte's growing warren of pet rabbits—appeared from around the corner of the house, his queue hanging like a beautiful silken rope down his back. Seeing Bronte leaning against the porch column, he paused at the foot of the steps.

"If you please, Missy Bronte not be sad on birthday, yes? Wang says everything will be fine soon. Not to worry. Nothing is ever as bad as it seems." He flashed her a smile. "Hurry! Wang will make a big boom for you, yes? Make Missy smile again. Hurry! Boom boom!"

Despite herself, Bronte smiled and slowly descended the steps, her stride lengthening as she hurried after Wang, holding up her skirts slightly so she didn't trip. This was ritual, this space of time, when her father allowed her the privacy to watch her fireworks alone—to lose herself in the bursts of color and sound. Tonight was her time to feel seven years old again and flushed with the anticipation of witnessing the breathtaking fireworks spectacle.

She would not admit to herself that on her twenty-seventh birthday she now knew she would remain a spinster—that her last phantasms of swashbuckling heroes and knights in shining armor had suddenly vanished. This was her birthday, and she would live it as if it offered her everything her heart had ever desired, she told herself as the first rocket shrieked into the night sky and exploded into a thousand pinpoints of red and blue fire. Another fired off, then another—*Boom! Boom!*—with ribbons of dancing fire flowing out over the lush pasture. As always, the solitude of the moment, and of the night, filled her with euphoria and brought with it a soaring sense of freedom.

On and on went the rockets, turning the night into day, until, swept up in the excitement, Bronte spun round and round, her head thrown back while her dark hair flowed like an ink-black river behind her.

This moment felt so perfect she thought she must be asleep, dreaming.

She fell to the ground. Lying on her back, she watched the black, smoky sky change patterns like the glass of a kaleidoscope, until her mind whirled dizzily, and she closed her eyes.

The finale was coming; she could feel it, the rhythm of the rockets growing, building.

Bronte opened her eyes to watch again. But though the thundering noise continued, she saw only darkness. Then she realized that a man was standing over her, and focusing her eyes harder on his features, she felt her heart turn over. Oh yes, she must *certainly* be dreaming.

"Surprise," Tremain said, and she watched his dark face crease in a slow smile.

"Oh," her lips said.

Brandon Tremain watched the yellow, blue, and red sparks overhead reflect in the warden's daughter's dark eyes. Where was the prim and proper "iron maiden" he'd met that afternoon? A virginal spinster with nary a hair out of place and revealing no slight glimpse of feminine flesh that could, even remotely, be deemed sexual?

As he watched this wild, beautiful creature from

across the lawn, she had reminded him of a gypsy, with fire in her eyes and her skirt twisted around the tops of her exquisite shapely legs—long, slender, pale as cream—her arms above her head, hands tangled in her hair, mouth slightly open, eyes sleepy with the passion for life. Looking at her, he thought he recognized a kindred spirit, and he had dared to approach her.

"Captain," she murmured.

"Again at your service."

Then her surprise seemed to vanish.

Her eyes closed and she smiled. A rocket burst overhead, flushing her complexion with streaks of hot light. "Captain Brandon Tremain at my service. This is a dream."

"No dream," he replied, taking a quick look around to make certain they were unobserved. He eased down to one knee beside her. She smelled of lavender and sweet crushed grass. A long time had passed since he'd last been so close to a woman— and Bronte Haviland was one hell of a woman. A woman much different from her public facade.

"Isn't it magical?" she said. "The rockets. The fire—red and gold like dragon's breath. It's like a fairy tale or a heroic legend." Looking up at him again, her smile less vibrant, a shadow of poignancy, she whispered, "Have you come to my dream to slay my dragons, sir?"

"Show me your dragons and perhaps I'll consider it," he said, responding to her whimsy.

She sat up, her shoulders back and her small, oval face tipped up toward his. A breeze teased the fine dark hair at her temples, and an exploding rocket painted her lips succulent red.

He could think of nothing to say. In truth, he could think of nothing but how beautiful she was. There was something mesmerizing in the way she held him prisoner with her presence—her very being a lure and temptation.

"I'm twenty-seven years old tonight," she told him matter-of-factly, her sweet, warm breath touching his cheek, so close was she. "Most women would have parties on their birthdays, lawn parties, hunts, soirees; dozens of their friends would attend, lavishing the lady of the hour with gifts. Who attends mine, I ask you?"

"I do." He smiled. "Although I fear I come empty-handed, m'lady. All I can offer you is a dance."

She eyed him a little suspiciously. "But there's no music."

"There's the music of the wind. The rockets. The stars. Pretend you're back in England and you're surrounded by friends."

Offering his hand, he helped her to stand.

He bowed slightly.

A moment's hesitation, then she curtsied.

He slid one arm around her narrow waist, and felt her tense, heard her catch her breath. She quivered against him like a tender leaf in a wind, then slowly, slowly began to relax. They moved into a waltz, her inexperienced steps at first awkward but her lithe body lightly falling into step with his, until they were both spinning round and round while the lights flared above their heads and sprayed like flowing water toward the ground.

Little by little, their steps slowed, and as they

gazed up into the night sky, he heard her sigh. "Have you ever seen anything so lovely?"

"Not since this morning."

"This morning?" She sounded a little confused.

"When I saw you at the prison."

The almost dreamlike quality of her face dissolved in an instant. Like one coming out of a trance, she looked at him hard a long while, her features a riot of conflicting emotions.

The prison.

Her fantasy world disintegrated with a shocking impact that left her trembling.

The prison.

She had just danced with a prisoner. Touched him. Laughed with him. Forgotten.

Forgotten that he was Captain Brandon Tremain— once a hero.

Backing away, closing her eyes, she shook her head and angrily cried for the guards.

Only the acrid smell of exploded rockets remained in the night sky as the guards hauled Brandon to the "sweatbox"—a cramped cubicle serving as punishment for any workmate who misbehaved—and shoved him to the rock-littered clay floor. They slammed the door shut behind him and locked it.

Lying in the dark, he looked up through the tiny barred portal in the door and watched the eerie gray clouds of spent gunpowder shift over the stars. Outside, he heard the guards say, "That should do 'im, Miss Haviland. Locked up tighter'n a spinster's drawers, I wager. Beggin' yer pardon, ma'am. Will there be anything else?"

"Nothing," came the cold reply, then silence.

Inside the box the air smelled foul. Breathing through his teeth, Brandon thought of telling Miss Hellcat that her housekeeping left a great deal to be desired; she, no doubt, would arch her back and inform him that traitors of the motherland deserved worse . . . then she would make good on the threat.

Best to leave well enough alone. Obviously, the beautiful, foul-tempered little chit was more than a little temperamental: one minute a temptress with the fire of desire and longing burning in her incredible eyes—certainly beautiful enough to tempt him into forgetting his good judgment—the next a spitting feline bringing guards running from every direction.

At least the chains were gone. Since his arrival at New South Wales Prison three months before, he'd continually heard the other prisoners discuss their desire to be accepted for the work-leave program. Usually the process took two years. His being chosen for the program after only three months had almost caused a riot. Glancing about the stinking, pitch-black cubicle, he would have gladly traded places with any of them at that moment.

Climbing to his feet, forced to duck his head due to the low ceiling, he looked out the window. Bronte Haviland stood in the distance, her white dress a pale glow in the darkness. Her skin looked as white—what he could see of it, of course. Just her slender hands, with their long, graceful fingers that should have been fluttering over harpsichord keys back in England instead of drying up in this clime. And her face—a waxen but perfect oval amid her tumble of blacker than night hair.

He had heard the men talk, of course.

They called her eccentric, but kind. Singular, but fair in her dealings with the men who worked her father's farm. They informed him that there was nothing that went on on this farm that she did not know about—or would not find out about. They also said a great many other things about her under their breath.

But they had never mentioned that she was this beautiful—or tragic.

Yes, "tragic" was the perfect word, he thought, as he watched her continue to stand still as a statue and stare at him through the dark. Tragedy had been reflected in her eyes that afternoon as she stood on a platform in front of the sweating line of convicts. She was made for an easier life. Alas, there would be no teas on misty verandas for her. No passing idle gossip between giggling, tittering lady friends. Those eyes, a few years past their prime, had reflected her resignation and, sadly, her acceptance.

But her behavior just moments before had driven home the sad truth of her circumstances.

"I could use some company," he said aloud to the shimmery image, and was not surprised that she did not reply. The temptress who had lured him into such rash behavior might never have existed. "Do you always treat your new employees so warmly, Miss Haviland? Or is this box simply a special treat for me? Come, come, this really isn't necessary. Contrary to what you believe, I wasn't attempting to escape. And I wasn't attempting to seduce you. I simply thought to wish you a pleasant birthday, considering we'll be working so closely together for the rest of our lives—or at least the rest of mine."

At last, she moved. Brandon watched Bronte Haviland gracefully, but slowly, advance until she stopped only inches from the door—surely close enough that he could easily detect each gentle contour of her face, the perfectly molded nose, the deepset eyes, shadowed by long jet lashes.

Christ, she had an incredible mouth. He wished now that he had kissed it those minutes ago.

He thought of a dozen remarks to further tease and taunt her, to put back in her features that spark that had changed her into the fire nymph dancing among the streamers of colored lights.

But all thoughts of flippancy evanesced the moment she wrapped her fingers around the corroded cell bars and, pulling herself up onto her tiptoes, stared unblinking into his eyes and whispered, "In case you weren't informed, Captain Tremain, there are certain rules you must abide by while living and working off the prison premises. One: you are never to leave your barracks after curfew—which is sundown. Two: if you attempt to harm a freeman, you will be immediately returned to the prison, then deported to Norfolk Island, a place worse than death, I assure you. And three: associating with a free woman is against the rules of this farm— indeed, this entire country. If we allowed the sentenced riffraff to seduce free women, we would have no end of problems. Therefore, if you are caught in any compromising situation with a free woman, you will be rewarded with one hundred lashes across the back, then you'll be deported—"

"Don't tell me. To Norfolk Island, where the closest thing to a woman is a six-foot jailer with arms the size of ship masts. Tell me, Miss Haviland, what happens to the 'free woman' who seduces a prisoner? Could it be that she, too, enjoys the bite of the cat-o-nine? Seems to me that would be just."

"You speak of just? You are beneath contempt, Mr. Tremain. You are not worthy even of this horrible, stinking hole where you will remain for the next three days. You will learn the meaning of rules and justice, Mr. Tremain. I promise you."

He said nothing as she stepped away from the cell. "Enjoy your stay with us, Mr. Tremain," she called back, then she walked off into the dark.

Brandon slammed his hand against the door and kicked at a bucket. He sank against the wall and closed his eyes, listened to the unharmonious choir of night birds and insects filling up the ensuing silence . . . and he waited. He was here because he never could resist a risk—and speaking to Bronte had seemed worth it. He closed his eyes, his mind on Bronte—her flashing eyes and warm body lightly pressed against his as they danced. He tried to ignore the tedious passing minutes.

Finally . . .

"Welcome to Haviland Farm," a muffled voice said from the dark outside Brandon's cage.

"Some welcome."

"You've met Bronte, I see."

"Is our hostess always so gracious?"

"Obviously, she doesn't like you."

"An eloquent understatement."

"She's very fair . . . as long as you abide by her rules, and her father's."

"Which are?"

"Never be caught lying, cheating, or stealing. Work hard. Don't complain or cause trouble for your companion prisoners; she will eventually get around to reminding you that this isn't White's Men's Club in London."

"That predictable, huh?"

"Far from it, my good man. Bronte Haviland is the most unpredictable female you are ever likely to meet. Not that she would admit to it. Not our Bronte. She does try terribly hard to act the paragon to the female convicts, no doubt hoping that they will learn by example. But she is vulnerable when it comes to her father, children, and animals—specifically her horses and rabbits," the voice added amusedly.

"But when it comes to men and business—"

"Let's just say she could hold her own against the lot of Norfolk convicts if she was forced to."

Leaning one shoulder against the door and crossing his arms over his chest, Brandon gazed out toward the house in the distance, the image of Bronte Haviland's face painted with rocket fire and outraged surprise bothering his memory. There had been nothing demure or retiring in those smoldering eyes, or in those full red lips that had parted in surprise the moment her eyes met his. If the population of New South Wales looked upon Bronte Haviland as some straitlaced, puritanical, stuffy little maiden, they had sadly underestimated her.

And it appeared she had fooled herself into believing it as well . . . What a bloody shame.

"You'll get me out of here, of course," Brandon said.

"*Au contraire*, my dear friend, I'm sorry to tell you. You see, Miss Haviland's word is law. She can be as stubborn as a rock."

Brandon continued to stare off into the dark.

"You must admit," the voice said, "she's most intriguing."

"The more beautiful they are, the more treacherous."

"And you consider Bronte beautiful? Of course you do or you wouldn't have done something so stupid. But remember, time is precious. Shenanigans such as this will hardly help our cause. Do try to keep your mind on the business at hand and less on the pretty young lady."

"I know what the hell my business is."

"Arthur Ellison isn't pleased that you're here. Haviland will have some explaining to do," the voice said more quietly. "You'll have to be very careful, Captain. Many will be suspicious. Others will be envious of you. While the lot of these convicts were little more than petty thieves in England, they've found that their survival in New South Wales depends on striking the first blow. And as we all know, most will do anything to gain a way out of this sorry situation. They harbor a great deal of resentment toward the empire. Because of what you represent—or once represented—you may well find yourself disliked and/or distrusted by every man here."

"Thanks for the encouragement."

"Have you a plan?"

"That would depend on how much you can

educate me on the problem. I, of course, know my role."

"I'm sorry to say there is little to tell. There have been few prisoner disappearances recently, but that stands to reason. There has not been a ship from Calcutta for several months. The last time the *Sirius* docked, however, four convicts went missing on the evening of her departure. They were never discovered."

"Presumably because they were buried up in the bowels of the *Sirius*."

"Precisely. Would you care for a smoke, Captain?" A hand appeared at the window, offering Brandon a lit cigar. Brandon accepted.

"Any idea how they manage it?"

"The river. There simply is no other way. While it's not wide or deep enough for a ship, it could easily manage the smaller skiffs. They must rendezvous at some point along the river, then, very easily, sail back to the harbor and slip on board the *Sirius*. Of course, the work-leave program, with its fewer restrictions, offers the perfect opportunity for the men to slip away almost undetected."

"I imagine if the one arranging all this owns the property along the river, it would be easier still."

Silence then, "Yes."

Brandon smoked. "I assume that would narrow down the options."

"Yes."

Frowning, he looked back toward the stone house that stood strong as a fortress in the dark, each window brilliantly lit.

"Something else," the voice said. "We've recently learned that whoever is supplying these men is receiving a great deal of money for his—or her—effort. We're beginning to suspect that not all of the escaped prisoners or so-called 'mercenary volunteers' have enlisted willingly."

"Shanghaied."

"Exactly. A word of advice, Captain?"

"Why not?"

"Suspect everyone. These men and women hold no loyalty. Any one of them would applaud the opportunity to raise arms against the Queen. If we don't act swiftly, we may well see an uprising in Calcutta and Bombay that will rival those of Meerut and Delhi, thanks to these butchering mercenaries who were once our own countrymen."

Brandon tossed away the last embers of his cigar. He felt weary suddenly. Sleep offered little respite these nights. His mind was still burdened by the memories of the Delhi massacre. The terrible dreams still racked him at night.

By the grace of God, he'd survived. But many of his trusted men had been butchered in their beds. The memory of their young souls continued to haunt him, to drive him, which was why he'd volunteered for this "suicide" mission—as his commanding officers had termed it. Why he had willingly blackened his name as a disguise until he had searched out, and discovered, whoever was selling Australian prisoners to underground Indian forces. When he'd uncovered the source, he would have begun to make reparations to his men.

There came an audible sigh, then, "I do hope your resolve stems from loyalty to our country and not from some lingering need to avenge a certain Indian woman's treason."

Brandon frowned and stared harder into the dark. His motivation was nobody's business but his own.

"Captain Tremain, I will kindly remind you that while your reputation has been built on audacity, your present assignment requires patient, quiet skill. Take a good look around you, my young captain, and remind yourself why you are here. Already you've risked something to see Miss Haviland. I urge you to use caution. Always be on your guard. Please remember what I said: Trust no one."

"You suspect the Havilands."

Silence.

"Of course you do. Quite obviously whoever is behind the smuggling must be in a position of authority—someone close to the prisoners."

Continued silence.

Brandon realized that he had been left alone in the filthy, stinking pit. His contact had gone.

He'd been warned against recklessness, the quality that had brought him such acclaim and then such misery. And left with the memory of Bronte Haviland's face lit by rocket fire . . . and the realization that she, or her father, might well be the enemy he had been sent here to crush.

To your equals a tranquil nature and
manner should always be shown, no
matter how trying the position.
—*The Mentor*
THOMAS EMBLEY OSMUN
A.K.A. ALFRED AYERS, 1884

CHAPTER THREE

SMILING, BRONTE GAZED DOWN INTO A SLEEPING INFANT'S
pink, wrinkled features as she tucked the light-
weight bunting about it and shifted it more securely
in her arms. The past sleepless night was forgotten
the instant the baby turned its head toward her.
Though this hospital and orphanage was solely for
female convicts and their children, for Bronte it was
an oasis.

Instead of the nagging, dull listlessness she'd felt
since her birthday, she experienced the blossoming
of warmth, and the sweet exhilaration of love for
the innocent child in her arms. Her father would
again warn her about becoming "too involved"
with the bairn she had named Lisa; she, of course,
would assure him that she wouldn't.

But they both knew she would.

For the next few years Bronte would sing to Lisa,
play with her, read to her; but when the child
turned six, Bronte would be forced to watch the

government take her away to a home in Sydney, where she would reside until adopted, or transported back to England for adoption.

The light breeze through the open window cooled Bronte as she turned toward her companion, Pilot Crenshaw. As with most officials here, she did not trust him. The lieutenant governor of New South Wales was a pompous little man with a bulbous nose and bloodshot eyes, and he always smelled of rum.

Not decent rum, mind you. He was too cheap to put out money for the good stuff that occasionally found its way into Sydney Harbor. Instead, he purchased the inexpensive type, the sort the convicts stewed up in the backs of their rank little cells. In New South Wales, convict rum flowed freely as water.

As pleasantly as possible, Bronte said, "She's the third child born in the past month."

"Beautiful children," Crenshaw responded absently, his focus on the long line of unoccupied beds running the length of the room. "By golly, your father has erected a superior facility. He's to be commended. The building would make a fine lockup in case something were to happen down at the prison—not that anything will," he hurried to add. "But one never knows, does one? It pays to be prepared. That's my motto. You never know when the lot of villains will decide to revolt—perhaps burn the entire prison down and kill everyone they can get their hands on."

A quiet gasp sounded and Bronte looked around. Sister Elizabeth Clore stood at the door, her eyes like little dark blue buttons in her round face. Sister Beth was well known for her nervousness.

"I shouldn't think we'll have anything to worry about," Bronte replied pointedly, more for Elizabeth's sake than for Crenshaw's. "Once my father was put in charge, trouble subsided. I feel our concerns should be devoted more to the problems at hand now."

Noting Crenshaw's obvious disinterest, Bronte frowned. "Such a facility as this wouldn't be necessary if you would only discontinue your support of The Rocks in Parramatta," she pointed out. "The filthy bordello is little more than a breeding ground for these helpless, parentless children, not to mention disease and crime."

Crenshaw, apparently lost in his own thoughts, shook his head and proceeded to examine a collection of vials and instruments on a chest against the wall.

Raising her voice, Bronte said, "A young woman was brought in only last evening with unmentionable injuries perpetrated by a drunken convict. Turning a blind eye only compounds the problem."

He glanced at Bronte and the child. "My dear Bronte, this is hardly a topic for a young lady such as yourself. Leave the running of the prison—and other establishments—to the men."

"But you aren't dealing with it—obviously."

Crenshaw removed a handkerchief from his coat pocket and mopped his brow as, moving before the window, he peered off into the horizon.

He waited until Bronte had handed the newborn to Sister Elizabeth before speaking again. "I hesitate to insinuate my opinions on certain matters, however, I should remind you that a great deal of this sort of trouble stems from you and your father's zealous following of Alexander Maconochie's Mark System. You simply cannot control convicts with a system of rehabilitation, or, God help us, one in which they are rewarded with an early release for good behavior. Wait and see. These policies will lead to disaster. Take Tremain, for instance."

Bronte felt her body stiffen. "Did you come here to complain about my father's decision to employ one prisoner, or did you wish to discuss the problems concerning hundreds?"

"I only wonder why your father would break one of his own hard-and-fast rules and bring Tremain to the farm. If that wasn't questionable enough, I see you have him working at the orphanage."

Despite her self-control, Bronte allowed her gaze to shift from Crenshaw and out the window, to the building site in the distance. She easily spotted Tremain. Among the half dozen other men, whose lethargic laboring left a great deal to be desired, Tremain moved graceful as a gazelle along the roof ridgepole. Because she refused to allow the miscreant to tend her horses, her father had sent him here, to help with the building, thereby reminding her every hour of the day of his presence in New South Wales.

Hearing the door open behind her, Bronte looked around to discover Crenshaw leaving the building. She followed close on his heels as he moved toward his buggy and occasionally glanced toward the children playing ring-around-the-rosy. Several had broken away from their mates and were rummaging around the fresh-cut lumber in hopes of discovering building blocks.

"Mr. Tremain is not important," she announced

in a slightly raised voice as she caught up to Crenshaw. "It is the circumstances facing these children—their futures, sir, are in jeopardy if we are not allocated more money for the completion of the orphanage and school. As it is, the bricks the convicts have supplied us with are pitifully poor. The majority of them disintegrate before we can slap them in mortar. The walls will no doubt crumble in the first high wind."

Crenshaw's stride lengthened. Again, she was forced to run to catch up. "If you would only speak to the local merchants, explain what their donations of lumber, shingles, and nails would do to help these children. Already the children are sleeping five and six to a room, and if you continue to deny them their rights to an education—menial as it may be—you will soon find yourselves with a second generation of felons."

Pilot climbed aboard the carriage, then looked down at Bronte. "We've been over this problem a dozen times, my dear. The merchants barely have enough supplies to *sell* the local business establishments, much less *give* their inventories away to a lot of . . . orphans."

"Sell? Sell to whom? New building is practically nonexistent in Sydney and has been since most every freeman rushed off to the hills to hunt for gold!" she shouted, then caught herself, glanced around to discover several wide-eyed children peering at her over a bush. She felt her face turn warm as she discovered Tremain, having stopped his work, standing slightly spread-legged on the ridgepole, weight resting on one hip, his attention on her.

Taking a deep breath and mentally counting

backward from ten, she slowly turned back to Crenshaw, who regarded her somewhat disapprovingly.

"You're doing a fine job, Miss Haviland. If you'll just continue to be patient, I'm certain things will work out for the best. Please give my best to your father."

The lieutenant governor nodded at his driver, and the carriage wheeled down the road, stirring up a cloud of dust in its wake.

"Oh!" she cried, and stomped her foot, chastising herself even as she did it because undignified behavior was hardly an example for the children. But just how much more of this lackadaisical attitude would she be forced to endure?

Turning back toward the building, she stopped short, again finding her gaze drawn toward the roof, where Tremain continued to pose against the blue sky, dark hair rising and falling in the breeze, loose shirt fluttering, his sights fixed on her. She couldn't be certain from this distance, but she thought he was grinning.

"Buffoon," she muttered under her breath, and marched back into the hospital.

She spent the afternoon planting peas with some of the children. With small spades, the children dug into the soft dirt, squealing with delight each time they unearthed a worm or bug. With their tiny fingers, they poked little craters in the soil and plopped a pea in each, tamped the dirt down over their buried treasure, then sprinkled water on it from a bucket. Sister Elizabeth suggested they say a prayer over each prospective plant—which they did, crusty hands clasped under their chins and their angelic faces turned toward Heaven.

It was times like this that strengthened Bronte's resolve to give these children a fair chance. On her knees in the cool dark soil, Bronte turned her face up to the sky and, closing her eyes, prayed—in French—for more than just a bountiful pea crop.

"Hey," came a little voice behind her. "They's prayin' again. Sisser Lizbeth says prayers make the peas grow bigger and faster. That's why I don't pray. I don't like them bloody peas."

Bronte opened one eye, then the other. Red-haired, freckle-faced Sammy Newman flashed her his snaggletoothed smile from atop Tremain's shoulders.

She swallowed and tried to breathe.

His nose slightly sunburned, his once white shirt stained with sweat and dirt and drying mortar, Tremain stared directly at her, his mouth tilted in that infuriatingly familiar grin. To Sammy, he said, "They make you eat peas here?"

"Uh-huh." Sammy scratched his ear, streaking it with dirt.

"But I don't like peas."

"Don't matter. They make us grow 'em and eat 'em. If we don't eat 'em, we don't get no puddin'." Dropping his head and shoulders over the top of Brandon's head, staring upside down into his eyes, Sammy declared, "I'd rather take a whoppin' than have to do without me puddin'. How about you, Misser Tremain?"

Coming to her senses at last, Bronte scrambled to her feet. Not bothering to knock the dirt from her skirt or from the gloves on her hands, she leapt over

the row of freshly planted peas and hurried to
Tremain. "Put that boy down this instant," she
ordered him, grabbing Sammy as he slithered off
Tremain's shoulders and threw his arms around her
neck. She gently dropped him to the ground and
watched as he, as well as the other young planters,
dashed away toward their peers, then she turned
on Brandon again.

"What can you be thinking to leave your position
as if you have every right to come and go as you
please?" She looked around almost frantically for a
guard. "Mr. Tremain, there are *rules*!"

"Why do I have the feeling you're more concerned with my speaking with a child than you are
over my straying from the work site?"

"We do our best to protect these children, Mr.
Tremain. To shelter them from the brutal and ugly
realities that await them out there. They are very
impressionable, and subjecting them to your less
than desirable company can only hurt them."

"Sorry. I didn't realize giving him a ride on
my shoulders would impair the quality of his
character . . . any more than your making him eat
peas when he doesn't like them."

She narrowed her eyes. "I doubt eating peas
would make a murderer out of a child."

"Depends on how badly they were cooked, I
imagine. Tell me, Miss Haviland. Is knowing all the
rules and regulations your only talent, or can you
cook?"

"That is none of your business."

"Ah. Then I suppose you can't. I never met a
woman yet who could cook who didn't like to brag
about it."

"Stay away from the children," she stated pointedly, then turned on her heels and began collecting the spades and buckets, doing her best to focus on her task and not on the fact that Tremain continued to watch her.

"Stay away," he finally said. "Has it ever occurred to you, Miss Haviland, that your highbrow idealism is doing little to help these children cope with their circumstances?"

She glared at him, feeling her face grow hotter.

His eyes vivid blue and his hair windblown, Tremain continued unemotionally, "You cloister them away from reality like they were china puppets. Reality is New South Wales, Miss Haviland. They should learn to survive here. Whether you want to believe it or not, the majority of them will grow up to live and die here. Reading them fairy tales and filling their young minds with your own unrealistic stories about England is unfair. Sammy's not interested in parroting a lot of French phrases. He's interested in picking up a hammer. That's why he strayed over to the building site. An interest in hard work and practical skills should be rewarded, even if it isn't in the guidelines, because that's what's going to make this country: a future generation who is strong enough to build something out of nothing."

"It will be a cold day in Hades before I ever allow these precious children to emulate a miscreant such as you, sir. Now, get to work before I report you."

Head up and shoulders back, she marched into the yet to be finished section of the orphanage, her spades and pails clattering as she maneuvered over and around crudely hewn planks of sap-seeping lumber. Flinging the buckets aside, she stared at the rafters overhead and refused to cry over the shoddy materials, Crenshaw's unwillingness to help, and Tremain's infuriating arrogance.

Then the realization occurred to her that the skeletal structure of bare posts and joists and studs and cripples did nothing to hide her, and turning her head, she discovered Tremain standing exactly where she'd left him, staring at her through the window frame, his eyes deep velvet blue. Only this time . . .

He wasn't smiling.

Bronte had just slid from her horse onto the veranda of the house when her father exited through the nearest door. "There you are," he declared. "By Jove, I was about to send Wang out to find you. Where the blazes have you been the last three hours, Bronte?"

The lathered bay hunter pranced in place, nostrils flaring as Wang appeared from some niche and took the reins from Bronte.

"I sent word to the hospital that I wished to speak with you on a matter of extreme urgency. That was three hours ago. I've been half out of my mind with worry, Pumpkin."

"Sorry, Papa," she muttered almost absently. Bronte walked by him and into the house, her footsteps ringing on the hardwood floors, her boots dusting the planks with dry mud. Catching a glimpse of herself in a mirror—wind-whipped hair, torn sleeve, and scratched cheek—she frowned and did her best to tuck her hair back into the tortoiseshell combs that held the mass of dark curls on the back of her head.

She feared that her riding habit was beyond repair, however—too many mad rides through the underbrush and gum trees had taken their toll on the once much-cherished habit ordered from London.

She looked around as Murray Grant, carrying a tray laden with raspberry tarts and lemonade, scurried out of her way and headed for the veranda outside the parlor French doors. She followed, listening to her father's footsteps ringing through the house like drums as he hurried to join her.

The sunken veranda offered a haven of coolness during the miserably hot afternoons. Bronte always took her tea there, enjoying the little beds of African marigolds and rudbeckias that bloomed in brilliant yellows and golds surrounding the cozy porch. She hoped that someday the partially constructed shallow pool in the center of the porch—modeled after a seventeenth-century carp pool stocked with golden orfe she'd seen once as a child—would be completed. The image of the sky reflecting upon the water and the backs of the gilded fish remained with her even now.

Bronte managed to smile at Murray as he handed her a glass of cool lemonade and a plate piled high with pastry.

Her father joined her. "That blasted horse has thrown you again, Bronte. Don't deny it."

"I rarely deny the obvious, Father."

"She's too much for you, dammit."

"She's simply spirited."

"She's full of the devil." Preferring port or brandy, William frowned at the glass of lemonade Murray offered him, but accepted it anyway. "Are you hurt,

Pumpkin?" he asked, his frustration and anger briefly giving way to concern.

"A bruise here and there. Nothing more. We eventually come to terms once we decide who's in control. She's such a baby . . ."

"A spoiled, ill-tempered child is more apt," he muttered.

"Which is why Cytduction and I get along so famously. We're two peas in a pod, so to speak." She manufactured a smile for her father's benefit, only to have him stare back at her. She felt foolish suddenly. Mean-spirited and lunatic to have frightened him in such a manner. What could she have been thinking?

"I'm sorry, Papa. I should have known you would have become worried when I didn't return home for tea."

He put his lemonade aside. "I didn't bring you here to discuss that bloody horse."

"No doubt."

"I understand you spoke to Crenshaw this morning."

In the process of spreading her lace-edged and monogrammed napkin across her knees, Bronte paused, feeling her stomach knot. "Yes. Seems he's not overly thrilled that you've brought Captain Tremain to Haviland Farm. But then . . . ," she smiled, "who is?"

Somewhat cautiously, William leaned toward her with his elbows on his knees, his hands clasped gently in a show of patience. "I thought it only right. I'm surprised at you, Bronte. You are usually more than fair with the prisoners."

Bronte briefly met her father's concerned eyes.

She left her chair and paced the floor, her riding skirt making shushing noises around her long legs, her lithe body throwing shadows upon the bricked floor. "He has no business being at Haviland Farm," she said at last.

"That was my decision to make, Bronte."

She spun on her heels to face him. "When Mother died, you gladly gifted me with the responsibilities of running this farm, and of selecting the men whom I wish to work it. Until now, those men have been nothing more than a lot of petty thieves who wouldn't harm a mosquito if it bit their arm. Now, suddenly, you bring a convicted murderer, not to mention a suspected traitor, into our company without consulting me."

"Regardless of his crimes, Brandon Tremain is hardly the sort of man who should be confined with common cutthroats. He has achieved much that is commendable in his life. He's a natural leader; he can be useful to us as an example, not only for the prisoners, but for the children as well. I understand from Sister Elizabeth that many of the children are becoming quite fond of him."

Recalling her heated debate with Tremain regarding Sammy, Bronte frowned. "The man is arrogant."

"Be that as it may, Bronte, it is my policy that every man working this farm should be treated with respect and consideration—if they are so deserving. Your behavior toward Tremain—locking him in that box—was inexcusable. And frankly, I don't believe your charge that he tried to escape."

She turned for the door, feeling frantic suddenly. She couldn't breathe. Couldn't shake the intense anger she experienced every time she allowed herself to acknowledge his existence here, in New South Wales. Why couldn't her father understand?

Without a word, she exited the house through the front door, refusing to look back or stop as her father shouted her name. Few heads turned as Bronte moved down the walk, past the small rich beds of imported earth erupting with sunflowers, dahlias, and delphiniums.

Her father's prized peacock, Hiawatha, strutted off the path as Bronte swept by, scattering the petals of a rugosa rose flowering in a lichen-covered urn. Wang came dashing from the straw-thatched hut toward which she was headed. The Oriental flashed her a smile and thrust a bundle of fur up to her. Bronte grabbed it, cradled the long-eared gray rabbit she called Dusty against her bosom, and sank in despair onto a wrought-iron bench.

If her father had turned against her, she'd lost her only ally.

When a woman abandons herself to terrible
fits of anger with little or no cause, and
makes herself a frightful spectacle, by
turning white with rage, rolling up her
eyes, drawing in her lips, gritting her teeth,
clenching her hands, and stamping her feet,
depend on it, she is not of a nervous, but
of a furious temperament.

—*Miss Leslie's Behaviour Book*
ELIZA LESLIE, 1853

CHAPTER FOUR

HEAT SHIMMERED FROM THE GROUND IN WAVES, AND MOP-
ping his face with his shirtsleeve, Brandon glanced
at the sun. White. Spherical. Radiating like a fur-
nace on his shoulders. Men had a tendency to go a
little crazy in such heat.

He knew all too well about such heat from India.

Ross Rodale, a small convict balancing on the
beam next to Brandon, shook his head and finished
driving a nail into the green timber. "I don't mind
tellin' ya I never had no aspirations of becomin' a
bloody carpenter."

Tim Hawcroft, a fellow prisoner, frowned at
Rossie and whispered, "Yeah, well, you'd better
hop to it, laddie, before the beast sees ya. You'll only
make it harder on yourself by lollygaggin'."

"Rodale!" Johnny Turpin shouted. "Get to work,
ya grizzly little weasel!"

Turpin, a guard standing six-foot-six with arms
like tree trunks, swung a club at his side, his face

reflecting malice as he eyed Brandon and Ross. A convict himself, Johnny Turpin had attained guard status due to his keen ability to scare the hell out of any man who crossed him. "Somebody give you leave for the day?" he shouted at Brandon.

Glancing at Rossie, Brandon grinned. "His middle name wouldn't be Bronte would it?"

The lad chuckled and grabbed a handful of nails from the bucket between his feet. So far Brandon had found that the other convicts accepted him without question, once they saw that he did his fair share. The men all worked on until Turpin turned his attentions on a pair of squabbling prisoners on the ground.

Squatting alongside the collar beam, Brandon focused on the distant activity. In the shade of a wattle tree a half dozen children, sitting on a lush patch of grass, encircled the warden's daughter. She was reading from a book—as she had every morning for the last four days. Back and forth she paced, punctuating her words with an occasional thrust of her fist, a dip of her knees, a rising upon her toes. And with each exclamation point the boys and girls let out a squeal of delight, covered their eyes and ears and mouths, and every now again, collapsed in a feigned faint.

He watched Bronte laugh.

Watched how she infrequently paused long enough to touch her kerchief, with delicate white lace edges, to the sweat at her temple and the soft hollow at the base of her neck.

"I wouldn't if I's you," came Rossie's voice close behind him.

"You wouldn't what?"

"Even think about her. You know what happens to prisoners who cause that kind of trouble to free women. If yer randy, take it up with the whores at Parramatta. That's what they're there for."

"I'm not in the habit of frequenting bordellos, Mr. Rodale. Never had to."

Story time apparently over, the children jumped to their feet and dashed away, leaving Bronte under the tree with her book.

"Mr. Tremain!" came the little voice from beneath him.

Brandon looked down. Sammy beamed up at him, his freckles bright red in his hot face.

"Can I come up?" the lad shouted.

"No."

"But I know how to hammer."

"No."

The lad's mouth screwed to one side.

"Sammy!" Bronte dashed toward the boy like a hen with her feathers ruffled. "Come away from there this moment."

"Ah, criminy," Sammy uttered.

Brandon grinned and raised one eyebrow at Bronte, who protectively gathered the boy in her arms and flashed a speaking glare up in his direction.

"Morning, Miss Haviland," he said down to her. Then, slightly raising his voice, he replied for her, "'Why, good morning, Mr. Tremain, how delightful to see you up there sweating your brains out and smashing your fingers.' 'It's delightful to see you, too, Miss Haviland. You're looking enchanting as always. Just like an angel, all in white. Have you ever considered the stage, Miss Haviland? Your readings are quite animated.'"

For a long moment, she didn't move so much as a finger, so much as an eyelash. Her hand remained lightly on top of the boy's head while the intensifying heat turned her cheeks, on her otherwise pale face, the color of burgundy.

Finally, she said, "If you're overly warm, Mr. Tremain, we'll be glad to supply you with a hat."

He thought of telling her that after spending years in India he was somewhat accustomed to the heat—that it wasn't the sun that was making him feel overly warm. Not by a long shot.

But he hadn't come all the way to New South Wales merely to flirt.

He watched as Bronte escorted Sammy toward the others. She looked back once, just a barely detectable glance over her shoulder, but enough for him to note the flash of annoyance in her eyes.

"Ever get the feelin' she don't like you?" Rossie said with a snicker.

Brandon didn't really hear. He stared off: could that protective lioness be sacrificing prisoners in the hope of bringing some benefits to the children?

Bronte hurried the children into the school and proceeded to the hospital, where she tried her best to ignore the fact that Brandon Tremain's presence had begun to bother her more than she cared to admit. She couldn't concentrate on the daily task that brought her such pleasure—cooing to and caring for the infants. Unconsciously, she found herself straying to this or that window and gazing out at the building site.

"Sammy loves that man," the nun declared. "I fear our Captain Tremain can't take a step without trodding on the lad."

"You really should be calling him Mister," Bronte corrected. "Perhaps I should speak with him."

"Mr. Tremain?" Elizabeth looked around at her with wide blue eyes slightly blurred by her thick-lensed spectacles.

"Sammy," Bronte said.

The enthusiasm slid from Elizabeth's face. "Leave the lad alone, lass. Poor little tyke. He's found a friend."

Moving up beside Elizabeth, Bronte watched Sammy meander through the wood shavings and lumber refuse, occasionally glancing up to watch Tremain leap from timber to timber, driving nails, flushing and leveling the lumber, while the other workers dawdled about and caused Johnny Turpin to roar like a lion and threaten them with his club.

"Look at the lad." Elizabeth beamed and pressed her chubby hands to her breasts. "Have you ever seen him so enthused over anything? Why, he mimicks everything the Captain does. The Captain drives a nail, so does Sammy with his pretend hammer."

"Yes . . . I know," Bronte said softly, her gaze traveling from Sammy up to Tremain, who balanced on the beam as confidently as a rope walker. He had removed his shirt, and his skin had grown dark as mahogany from the sun. Every movement brought a tensing and flexing of his hard arms and back, which shone in the sun like wet copper. No doubt another woman would have considered him spectacular, Bronte thought. A god. The very image of physical human perfection. But certainly not her. Not anymore.

"Still," she murmured, more to herself than to Elizabeth, "a felon is hardly a role model for a vulnerable child like Sammy."

"But the point is," Elizabeth said, "that because of his encouragement, Sammy's shown interest in something for the first time. A man such as the Captain will set a fine example for the young ones to follow, I think."

"My dear Elizabeth," Bronte muttered, "you're beginning to sound exactly like my father."

Bronte left the room and tried her best to focus her mind on her work, on her duty to the orphans. But her mind fixed on one question: how could people she respected hold a fallen hero in such esteem? Respect, she mused as she went to draw water from the well, knowing as she did so that Tremain was watching.

She didn't have to look. She felt it—those eyes. Blue eyes. Set in his sun-darkened face. No doubt if she allowed herself to look up, she would find him grinning that smug lopsided smile that made her want . . .

What, exactly, did they make her feel?

The bell tolled musically in the late afternoon air, calling the children in for their nap. They scrambled out from under bushes, from behind trees, swung from branches, leapt, tumbled, jumped imaginary obstacles in their mad dash toward Sister Frances, who continued to ring the bell with enthusiastic energy.

Having finished the washing of bed sheets at last,

Bronte stiffly climbed to her bare feet, which were mired in the cool mud surrounding the washtub, swept loose hair from her brow, and released a weary breath.

"Need some help with that?" came the deep voice behind her.

"No, thank you, Mr. Tremain," she replied properly without turning, and quickly unrolled the sleeves of her blouse and buttoned the cuffs at her wrists. She clutched at the open collar of her blouse and buttoned it as well. "I can manage nicely without your help."

"No doubt."

He moved by her anyway, his naked arm brushing hers—it looked even darker up close, and oh my, but it was hard as the trunk of a red gum—and caught the edge of the heavy washtub and, with a grunt—and a rippling, flexing display of his biceps and shoulders, whose color reminded her again of the cook's shiny copper pots—tipped it onto its side, spilling mucky water over the ground. He didn't so much as look at her as he easily grabbed up the heavy straw basket of wet sheets and started for the clothesline, down the path toward the gurgling stream of water, rushing toward the river that would, eventually, empty into Sydney Harbor.

"I assume you have permission from Johnny to be away from your assigned task," she called after him.

"No."

She looked around at Johnny, who watched Tremain with the hooded eyes of a hawk, thumping his stick against his leg in apparent aggravation, no doubt waiting for a signal from her before he unleashed his unsavory forms of punishment on his rebellious worker. Bronte shivered, not caring much for her father's most feared sentry. With one nod from her, she knew he would gladly pounce on the opportunity to inflict punishment on Tremain.

Not that he didn't deserve punishment for leaving his duties without permission.

But she hadn't looked forward to hauling the heavy linens to the line. Her back was aching, and there was still the task of refilling the tub for the children's baths.

Wiping her hands on the towel she had tucked into the front of her skirt like an apron, she hesitantly followed Brandon down the well-worn path, stopping as he stopped, raising her chin as he deposited the basket next to the clothesline and turned back toward her. Only it wasn't her face that caught his attention and held it.

"Nice toes," he said, flashing her an indolent smile. "A smidge dirty, perhaps, but nonetheless lovely. One can tell a great deal about a person by examining their toes."

Bronte curled her toes under so they dug into the dirt and focused her eyes on a pink Leadbeater's cockatoo perched on the line near Tremain's head.

"Need some help with those?" He thumbed at the sheets.

She opened her mouth to decline his offer to help, but before she could utter so much as a sound, Tremain bent to the task of grabbing up a sheet and flinging it over the line.

"Actually, as a child this was one of my favorite chores," he explained, smoothing the wrinkles from the sheets and anchoring them with wood pins he dug for in a pouch hanging from the line.

As a child? Bronte glanced nervously back at Johnny and ran her drying hands up and down the towel tucked in her skirt. Surely all the papers had claimed he'd come from an aristocratic background. Why would he be hanging sheets?

"There was something about burying my face in the clean sheets that I loved, Miss Haviland. Especially after they dried in the sun. Have you ever stopped to smell the sunshine, Miss Haviland?"

Chewing her lower lip, Bronte eased a sheet from the basket and flung it over the line, which was no easy feat, considering how heavy the cotton became when it was wet. In truth, she was only helping out today because the laundress was sick. She'd never hung sheets before.

Realizing that he would no doubt stand there and stare until she responded to his idle chatter, she said, "I wasn't aware that one could smell sunshine, Mr. Tremain."

"That doesn't surprise me."

"What is that suppose to mean?"

"You're too intent on rectifying the wrongs of the world to stop and acknowledge all the things that are right."

He offered her a clothespin. She snatched it from his hand and jammed it down onto the line.

"There is very little to find in this place that is right, sir. The heat is appalling, the soil is deficient, and I'm surrounded by human failures." She glared at him pointedly. "Besides, I can hardly imagine what you could find so wonderful about this place, considering you've been sent here to toil away the rest of your miserable life."

"One can find pleasure in almost any circumstance if one's outlook be healthy." Tremain crooked his finger at her and backed toward the copse of trees crowding the stream. "Come here, Miss Haviland."

"Don't be ridiculous."

"I dare you."

"You're being absurd. I shouldn't be speaking to you like this, much less frolicking in the wood—"

"Just for a moment."

Crossing her arms over her breasts, Bronte turned her head and stubbornly set her jaw. "Sir, you are half-naked."

He laughed softly, deeply, jarring her to the tips of her muddy toes.

"What can I do?" he said. "One peep from you and our friend Mr. Turpin will peel my skin off with his whip." His smile far less challenging, he said, "You won't regret it, I assure you."

The fact that she would consider, even for a moment, leaving her chore undone, stepping toward the trees with Tremain, was preposterous. Yet her feet began to move of their own accord. Giving Tremain a wide berth, she moved cautiously toward the copse.

The trees offered her deep shade, a cool, welcome respite from the intense heat. The stream gurgled, forming mirrors of silver water that slid from pool to pool, leaving beards of rusty algae on their sandstone lips. Here and there were banksia bushes, their sawtooth-edge leaves and dried seed cones like multiple, jabbering mouths each time a breeze disturbed them. Within the bushes poised a pair of kangaroos, their kind faces regarding her with mild interest, and no fear.

She looked around, amazed.

"Deny this is beautiful, Miss Haviland, and I'm afraid I would be forced to call you a liar."

Bronte said nothing, just focused her attention on the kangaroos across the stream and did her best to quiet the riot of nerves winding her body tight as a bowstring. She was fraternizing with a prisoner. And not just any prisoner.

"Go ahead," came his quiet words. "Try out the stream. It's warm, Miss Haviland. Like bathwater. Your dirty toes will love it."

She shook her head and centered her attention on the stream, listened to it babble amid the smooth, polished stones. Before she realized it, she had slightly lifted her skirt to the tops of her ankles and stepped into the shallow, rushing stream, just where the sun formed a shaft of butter-yellow light that spilled through the overhead eucalypts and flowed over her head and shoulders.

Oh, he was right! The water felt warm and satiny. For a long moment she stared down at the tiny bubbles rushing around her feet, and before she realized what was happening, the tension in her body had dissolved, leaving her with a languid feeling.

How odd that she had never considered doing such a thing as wading in the luxurious stream. She turned her face up toward the sun spilling through the leafy roof and noted the towering red gums— the eucalypts with their strings of hanging, half-shed bark. There were cabbage-tree palms as well, their limbs supporting hosts of ferns and mosses that spilled toward the streambed like flowing water. The occasional sprays of yellow mimosa flashed with spears of light, setting the dim interior aflame with bursts of color. In truth, the setting reminded Bronte of an English deer park. If she closed her eyes . . . she could almost imagine that she were home again . . . in Kent.

"My, my," came Tremain's gentle voice, dragging her reluctantly back to the present. "Is that actually a smile I see on the dour Miss Haviland's face?"

"I have been known to smile occasionally," she retorted without looking at him. But the mood was lost.

"Not nearly enough, I imagine."

"It's not your place to imagine anything concerning me, Mr. Tremain." Casting a last look around her, Bronte waded from the water, immediately dropping her skirt in a belated attempt at modesty. Still, she refused to allow her gaze to drift to Tremain—where he leaned against a gum tree, his arms crossed over his chest—but hurried back to the line of sheets flapping in the breeze, her step hesitating as she discovered Sisters Elizabeth and Frances poised at the well some distance away, their attentions focused on her, then Tremain as he exited the copse behind her.

She felt her cheeks pinken as she sensed him standing near. "You seem quite familiar with the area, Mr. Tremain." Snatching at a clothespin, she flashed him a quizzical look. "Perhaps I should remind you that the prisoners are never to leave Johnny's sight."

Tremain tipped his dark head slightly to one side; his look became intense.

Intrigued despite herself, Bronte raised one eyebrow. "How well acquainted are you with Haviland Farm, Captain?"

"Not nearly as well as I would like to be. Perhaps you would care to give me a tour? A morning ride, perhaps?"

"I fear the heat has affected you." She jammed the pin onto the line, pinching her finger in the process. "Have you any legitimate questions about the farm, I will happily answer them." She sucked her finger until the throbbing stopped, then looked back at Tremain. "Well?"

He regarded her a long minute without replying. Then, quite abruptly, he asked, "The river runs along the boundary of your property, yes?"

She frowned. "Yes."

"Do you go to the river often?"

Bronte, one hand on the taut clothesline, watched the blue of his eyes turn black. His entire bearing appeared to change, albeit subtly—just a tension across his shoulders and a wariness to his countenance that seemed strangely foreign to the devil-may-care scoundrel.

"I can not imagine why it should concern you," she finally managed in a dry voice.

Little by little, his tension eased and his old smirk returned. "Need a hand with the rest of that laundry?" he finally asked.

"No, thank you."

"Have it your way," he said with a shrug, then walked past her without so much as giving her a glance.

"Mr. Tremain."

He walked on a short distance before stopping and turning.

Fixing her sights on the cockatoo, which cocked its head of splayed feathers and pinned her with one round beady eye, she said, "A word of advice: such curiosity about the boundaries of this farm could prove dangerous. One might construe from such questions that you've given some thought to escape. I wouldn't advise it. And furthermore, from now on you will keep your shirt on when you work. Your immodesty is an affront to the moral and righteous women residing on these grounds . . . not to mention the children."

He made no reply, just pivoted on his bootheels and sauntered back to the building site. As Bronte yanked up a sheet and tossed it over the line, she peered over it to watch Tremain swiftly climb the ladder to the orphanage roof and, once again, take up his hammer—without his shirt.

A loveless marriage is an unchaste union.
—*Common Sense for Maid, Wife, and Mother*
AUTHOR UNKNOWN, 1882

CHAPTER FIVE

WHERE WAS HE, EXACTLY? CHILLIANWALLA OR GUJARAT? Canton perhaps?

Concentrate. Escape if you must into your mind. But don't lose consciousness. Wars had been lost due to the ramblings of semiconscious soldiers.

Brandon forced open his eyes and, breathing heavily, stared up at the dimly lit ceiling. His body felt raw, on fire, and he couldn't move. For an instant the memory of his two hellish months of incarceration in a prison camp rushed at him like floodwaters through a crumbling dam.

Managing to turn his head slightly, Brandon squinted to better see the misty image in the shadowed corner of the room. He couldn't quite make it out, so vague was it, and still. Then soothing undertones, hushed encouragements, touched his ear. Cool hands brushed his cheeks.

"Mr. Tremain? Open your eyes, sir, and look at me."

He did his best. His eyelids felt like lead weights.

"My name is Sister Elizabeth, Mr. Tremain."

He tried to move again; the manacles around his wrists would not allow it. Just as well. He hurt too damn much.

Odd that there was no memory of why he was here, only still images of a woman's face with wide, anguished eyes and her lips parting in a silent cry of alarm. Ah, but it had been a beautiful face, full of fire and compassion and . . . what else? Something . . .

Think.

When he opened his eyes again, the first streak of gray dawn had begun to creep across the horizon outside the window by his bed.

If he lived to be a hundred, he would never forget the instant he recognized the figure in the distance as Bronte's. In the garden outside the room where he lay, she sat on a tree stump facing the rising sun, black hair flowing down her slender back, her elbows resting on her knees and her head bowed wearily.

Around Bronte frolicked a half dozen children, some toddling, others joining hands and forming a circle around her as they sang in disjointed harmony into the cool morning air. She looked up at them and smiled, and the love and devotion Brandon saw reflected in her face made his chest ache.

It was a look of selfless duty.

He knew that look . . . that feeling only too well.

"Good morning, Mr. Tremain. I'm Sister Elizabeth."

He turned his pounding head. A round-faced nun stood over him, her visage dimly gray in the half-light of early morning. Looking like a chubby cherub whose cheeks were lit by a sort of sweet mischief, she glanced out the window and a faint smile crossed her lips.

"I was here during the night to relieve Bronte," the nun said. "She'll be in soon."

The nun gently raised his head and pressed the rim of a glass to his lower lip. He gulped at the cool water thirstily. "How long have I been here?" he whispered, his thoughts suddenly disturbed by the realization that he had lain here vulnerable for hours.

"Two days."

"Damn." He looked toward the window again, but Bronte was gone.

What the blazes had happened to him? Why did it feel as if he had broken every bone in his body?

Brandon caught his breath as the sister carefully removed the layers of sodden bandages from his wounded leg. Body breaking out in new waves of fire, he shut his eyes and did his best to focus on something other than the excruciating pain. It all came back to him then—the reason for his being here—wherever here was. The images of Sammy, having scrambled up the ladder unbeknownst to Brandon, and tottering helplessly on the ridgepole atop the orphanage, flashed like lightning before his mind's eye. The memory of yelling the boy's name, then diving to catch his little hand before he spilled to the ground, made him break out in a new wave of sweat.

"The boy," he whispered in a dry voice.

Her face beaming with satisfaction, Elizabeth smiled. "True to your legend, sir, you saved him. Broke his fall. He got nothing more than a scratch or two." Her eyebrows knitting, and with a defiant nod, she added, "The way you grabbed him in that last moment, clutched him to your chest and tumbled backward into that heap of lumber was enough to make me weep a tear or two of pride, yessir. I'll be on me knees for the next month thanking our Father for your unselfish bravery. You're a true hero, sir."

Glancing around the comfortable room, he quickly ascertained that he wasn't occupying a hospital cot, but a bed . . . a real bed. Not prisoner's rags on an army cot. God, how long had it been since he'd last slept on a feather mattress with clean sheets . . . that smelled like sunshine.

"Sister Elizabeth?" came the voice from the door, and Sister Elizabeth jumped as if goosed, spinning around to look wide-eyed at Bronte, who watched her with a raised eyebrow. "I trust that the muttering I hear is prayer and not gossip."

Bronte carried in an armload of bandages and a bowl of steaming water. Her face seemed masked with the indifference she always bestowed on him. Yet there was a difference. Somehow she looked almost fragile.

"Well, well," Brandon said. "At last we meet again. Pardon me for not rising in the presence of a lady." He flashed her as belligerent a smile as he could manage.

Raising one finely arched brow, Bronte eased into

the room, her look going briefly to Sister Elizabeth.

Bronte reached for the sheet covering Brandon from the waist down, nudging it aside slightly so she could easily see his bandaged leg, and nothing more.

"I understand the injury is deep," she remarked unemotionally. "It pains you?"

"Obviously," he replied through his teeth.

"The doctor fears there's muscle damage."

Brandon stared at the ceiling, the idea occurring to him that the rumors of Bronte Haviland's stoicism had been understated. He'd been in and out of hospitals a dozen times throughout the last years, and never had he looked into a less sympathetic visage.

"Why do I get the impression that you don't like me, Miss Haviland?"

"You exaggerate your esteem in my eyes, Mr. Tremain. I don't care about you enough to dislike you."

Elizabeth moved around the bed, fetching a cloth from a side table and handing it to Bronte. "He'll need bathing. The physician left a bit of salve that's to be applied to his wounds three times a day . . . or was it four?" One pudgy finger poised on her lower lip, she looked toward the ceiling as if waiting for God to instruct her. "Yes. Yes, of course. Five times. How could I have forgotten? Oh my, my memory is so dreadful. I apologize," she added, bending so near her nose nearly touched Brandon's. The nun with the glowing cheeks smiled at Bronte. "You're on your own, lass. Make certain his wounds are cleaned well before you rebandage."

Bronte looked surprised, then unsettled. "Surely you would rather do it."

"Sorry, love. I've a meeting with Father Clarke in ten minutes."

"Then perhaps one of the others—"

"Busy, I'm afraid. They've all got their duties, you know. I'm certain you'll manage fine."

Following Elizabeth to the door, Bronte caught the sister's arm. "But I shouldn't—"

"There's naught that he can do, my child, if that's what you're concerned about. He's much too weak and sore."

From his bed Brandon watched as Bronte's spine went rigid. She remained at the doorway a full minute after Sister Elizabeth had vanished before slowly turning back to the room.

She took a long, slow breath and appeared to hold it. Then she advanced, slowly.

For a long moment she stood by the bed, hands fisted at her sides. At last she reached for the sheet, reluctantly tugging it down slightly to expose his belly. Watching her eyes, the way her lashes were lowered, the way her lips were slightly parted, he said in a much softer, teasing voice, "This is rather sudden, isn't it, Princess?"

"I don't find your ridiculous remarks the least bit amusing." Appearing a bit white-lipped, she flung a soiled bandage to the receptacle on the floor. He caught his breath, and she jerked her hands away, her gaze coming back to his at last while the sheet settled low. Her cheeks looked flushed suddenly.

"Your fingers are cold," he told her.

Her face flushed even more, until it shone with moisture. Brandon frowned suddenly and tried to concentrate on the pain that, moments before, had filled up his body to pathetic extremes. Instead, he fixed on her eyes, which had yet to leave his. He saw something in those turbulent depths. Disappointment?

He frowned at the thought. He wasn't accustomed to confronting such an emotion in a woman's eyes. Even in his youth, he'd basked in his mother's and sisters' pride and adoration . . . struggled to live up to their lofty ideals of what a son and brother should be. He'd succeeded, of course. Built himself into a legend that his beloved England would be hard-pressed to forget. Occasionally, the weight of it had threatened to break his back, and he'd wished, more than once, to feel human, to be looked at as flesh and blood, not an icon.

So why, then, did he feel so disturbed that a prim little miss looked down her nose at him? The idea unnerved him in a way his injury did not.

Without a word passing between them, Bronte efficiently administered the salve to his leg, keeping her eyes focused on her duty, never once looking up. Just as well, he thought.

Having finished the bandaging of his leg at last, Bronte collected her washbasin and gauze and turned away.

"Mind telling me what's happened to my leg?" he said through his teeth.

"When you fell into the lumber, a sizable sliver of wood pierced your leg."

"Sliver? It feels like an entire bloody tree has amputated the damn thing."

Raising one eyebrow and looking back over her shoulder, she said, "Profanity isn't necessary. Had you been more careful—"

"Had I not dove off that roof in an attempt to save Sammy, I wouldn't be in this predicament now."

The look of irritation on her features vanished like vapor—at least for a moment. Her cheeks gradually flushing with color, she chewed her lower lip and said nothing for a tense moment. Then, almost begrudgingly, she said, "Point taken, Mr. Tremain."

She raised her chin.

"Your show of appreciation moves me, Miss Haviland."

This time she didn't reply. With the water in the basin sloshing on her dress, Bronte moved out of the room and shut the door behind her.

Alone, Brandon closed his eyes and allowed the sudden quiet to relax him little by little, until the pain in his leg eased.

Then he looked around and truly studied his surroundings.

He obviously was not at the hospital. The room in which he resided was far too pristine and pretty—a portrait of English civility with an overstuffed chair and oil portraits on the wall. Next to his bed were two ivory portrait miniatures—one woman with dark hair and gentle black eyes, with Bronte's sultry mouth and obstinate chin. A tamer version of Bronte—Bronte's mother, no doubt.

But it was the miniature of Bronte that caught his eye and held it. The image of the warden's daughter, reposing in a garden of blooming flowers, stared

out at him from a frame depicting cupids in flight.
Lonely and tempting and dangerous, he thought . . .

Very dangerous.

William sat on a wrought-iron garden bench,
drank his brandy, and occasionally cast a reluctant
look at his daughter, who continued to lecture him
even while she dug around her plants in the
garden, her sunbonnet dangling down her back
from a ribbon around her neck.

"I beg you, Father; for the good of the household
send him away. I cannot conceive of why you
insisted on bringing him here, to our home. We
have a perfectly respectable hospital—"

"St. Cluny's is a woman's birthing hospital, Bronte.
You know it's against the rules to keep a man there."

"It was also against the rules to allow a prisoner
on the work-leave program before his two years
hard labor were up. You are picking whichever
rules are expedient."

Frowning, William tipped up his drink. "I simply
believed Tremain wouldn't survive being wagoned
into Sydney to the prison hospital. Perhaps when
he's stronger . . . perhaps." He paused. "Bronte,
he saved that boy from a fall at great personal
expense. Surely he's shown himself to be commendable in his actions."

She stayed silent.

"He'll be no trouble at all, Pumpkin. I'll post a
guard outside his door at all times, and if it makes
you feel more secure, I'll ask Sister Elizabeth to
send over some extra help."

"Elizabeth has her own duties, and the hospital is
already short on staff."

"On the other hand, your time is valuable, too. You have your obligations here as well as to the hospital and orphanage—"

"That's not my greatest concern," she declared. In a patch of cool, dark earth, a long furry caterpillar wiggled. Bronte gently eased it aside before plunging her spade into the ground.

William shifted uncomfortably on the seat and continued to drink, his silence growing longer and longer still, until Bronte was forced to look up, her hands pausing in their busywork as she met her father's bothered eyes.

William put down his empty glass. "Blast it, I can not help but like the man, Bronte, and admire what he stood for, the character he has shown this far. It's not often that a man of his caliber finds his way to Haviland Farm. I'd like to become acquainted with the man—to be allowed the simple repast of pleasant, congenial conversation with a fellow countryman; to discover the truth behind the heroic stories as well as his crime. But listen to me wax on like an old fool. Tremain should be the least of my troubles."

Putting down her spade, removing her soiled gloves, Bronte moved over to her parent and went to her knees beside him. She took his hand. "There's been trouble again?"

"Ten more escapes last evening. A guard killed."

"You've sent out a posse, of course."

"For whatever good it will do. We haven't managed to track down a single escapee in the last year. Damn me, but it's as if they vanish. No doubt I'll be hearing from the governor again. Or Crenshaw.

They are all breathing fire, demanding explanations for our apparent lack of security. If that weren't enough, I have no idea if the escapees are lurking about out there waiting for an opportunity to harm you or any of the other families. You'll take care, Pumpkin, won't you? No more daring solitary rides on Cytduction. No more walks alone. Or venturing down to the cottage."

Thinking of the little stone, thatch-roof cottage down the lane that had been their first house in New South Wales before the larger one was built, Bronte mistakenly allowed her disappointment to show.

"I know how you love it there," William said kindly, and sadly. "I loved it, too. But I simply can not take the risk of your coming to harm."

"I know. But I sometimes feel as if we're the prisoners in this godforsaken place."

Noting her father's pained and disturbed expression, she squeezed his hand harder. "Forgive me."

"There's nothing to forgive," he replied wearily, and smiled. "This has hardly been the sort of life a beautiful, vivacious young woman such as yourself should lead. I don't know what I was thinking to have brought you and your mother here. I thought that eventually the conditions would improve. But they seem only to grow worse. You deserve better."

"I've managed, Father. After Mother's death, there's been the sisters and the children . . . not to mention you."

He shook his head and pulled his hand away, left the seat and paced the neat garden, where tiny green sprouts would soon burst open with riotous color. "You're twenty-seven years old, dammit. And you won't consider any of the men here."

Bronte climbed to her feet, dusted the dirt from her skirt, and slapped her gloves together. Replacing the straw bonnet on her head, tipping it at an angle over her eyes, she shrugged. "I suppose I'm a romantic at heart, Father. Too much like Mother, I fear. I expect to be in love with the man I marry. I want to experience a little of the romantic passion that I read in those books Mother used to keep tucked in the lower drawer of her wardrobe."

William looked around, both eyebrows raised. "Bronte!"

Laughing, going up on her toes, she pecked his cheek with a kiss. "Not to worry. I'm content."

Bronte gathered up her spade and gloves while her father, his hands in his pockets, watched her closely.

"What about Tremain?" he asked, and Bronte spun around to face him, her mouth slightly open, her heart racing erratically.

"Tremain?" she managed, but barely.

"Will you allow him to stay—just until he's strong enough to endure the trip into Sydney?"

"Oh. Oh, of course. I thought you meant . . . Oh. Well. Never mind. I mean, I suppose I have little choice."

Her father regarded her with a contemplative expression before turning back toward the house and pausing in the doorway long enough to say, "I don't think we have to worry too much. Mr. Tremain wouldn't take any foolish action that would risk his position here."

"Yes." She forced a smile onto her face and thought of reminding her father that Tremain's entire legend was built on taking risks. He was as drawn to danger as a moth was to a flame. No doubt about it . . .

Captain Brandon Tremain would be trouble.

If an emotion be dwelling in
the heart, agitating and disturbing
it, it is physically impossible that
it should not be visible in the
features . . . A man might gain a great
command of countenance by acquiring
a great command of passion.

—*Advice to a Young Gentleman*—
An Etiquette Manual
AUTHOR UNKNOWN, 1839

CHAPTER SIX

HER SHOULDERS HUNCHED AGAINST THE DARK, HER HANDS
fumbling with the tattered material that she held to
the dim light of the flickering lantern, Bronte wove
the blunt needle in and out of Captain Tremain's
shirt—the one he had been wearing when he
toppled with Sammy from the roof. She'd managed
to scrub out the stains. The rips, however, posed a
greater problem.

Stiffly, she sat back in her chair and glanced at the
clock. Ten-fifteen. Her father should have been
home long ago.

She frowned and rubbed her aching eyes with the
back of one hand. She heard a door slam, and
watched through her open window as Cook, a
burly, straw-haired bear of a man, lumbered down
the path toward the barracks, a dish towel flapping
like a flag in his back pants pocket. He would be
leaving in a few weeks. His seven-year prison term
having been fulfilled, he planned to return to

England, where he had left his wife and six children in charge of a tavern house in Yorkshire. His life would go full circle.

She sighed. Stitching done, Bronte bit off the needle and thread and put them aside.

The quiet set in again, seeped into every dim nook and cranny in her comfortable bedroom. With the shirt balled up in her lap, her fingers twisted into it almost nervously, she watched a moth dart in and out of the smoke from the lantern flame.

Normally at this time she would have fallen into bed, her favorite pet rabbit sleeping peacefully on her pillow. But she was wide awake.

For a moment she considered flipping through the well-worn pages of Flora Tristan's *Memoires et Peregrinations d'une Paria*. But she didn't have the heart to occupy herself with Madame Tristan's forbidden writings on the emancipation of women.

Her hands smoothed the wrinkles from Tremain's mended shirt, spread it across her knees, a fingertip tracing the uneven row of crisscrossed threads holding the ragged rip together. The seam would hold, but the cloth would always bear the evidence of mending. She placed it carefully on the pile.

She stood and walked around her room. In her chemise and drawers, her thin, finely spun silk dressing gown open down the front, Bronte reluctantly allowed her gaze to travel to the cheval mirror in the ill-lit corner. The hazy image of herself stared back at her, although her reflected face was partially hidden by her sunbonnet dangling from the knob at the top of the mirror frame.

She stared at her image—her lips, her throat, the

V of white skin above the lace edge of her chemise. Very slowly, she allowed the dressing gown to slide off her shoulders, hardly noticing as it spilled to a filmy puddle around her ankles.

Scandalous girl, regarding her body in such a way.

What could she be thinking? A lady's body and mind should, at all times, reflect a demure and chaste mien—never, under any circumstances, acknowledging the base instincts of the iniquitous women who had fallen into despairing moral ruin.

Yet, the thoughts clamoring around in her mind were sexual. How could she deny it when the images flashing before her mind's eye were of a man's eyes and body—his shirtless body—revealing every defined muscle beneath taut copper-colored skin. How ironic that, during all the years of fantasizing about Tremain, she had never thought of him in that light—only in images of a dashing hero, in a uniform flashing with medals, plying her with poetry, charming her with compliments and promises of undying devotion. He had not been an infuriating beast of a man who found humor in shocking her.

She should detest him.

And she did.

She not only detested his character for its criminality, but also despised the flagrant manner in which he sauntered about life.

Decorum, she'd always supposed, was a virtue.

But acting decorously, at least in his eyes, seemed ridiculous.

. . . And she wondered if he could be right.

She should rail against the fact that his presence had apparently brought her to a point of moral degeneration. Look at her, for heaven's sake, standing here before a mirror, staring at her own reflection as if she were an actress or a dancer—or a writer of those questionable romantic novels.

Slowly, she raised her hands and loosened her hair, watching as the dark coils slid down over her white shoulders, and over her breasts, which were pressed tight against the confining strictures of her buttoned chemise. With her slightly trembling fingers, she undid the top three buttons, allowing the white cotton material to flap open, releasing the pressure on her breasts so the soft, white swells spilled forth, forming a surprisingly adequate display of cleavage.

Her eyebrows went up. She almost giggled, then reminded herself that she was too old for such girlish shenanigans. Still, the picture of her with her hair down, her chemise open and hanging partially off one shoulder, made her feel . . . vibrant. Flushed . . . and . . .

Was she wicked at heart?

A knock sounded at the door.

Gasping softly, Bronte quickly grabbed up her dressing gown and clutched it closed around her throat.

Jumping as if she had just been discovered peeling off her clothes in a room full of sailors, she spun toward her closed bedroom door and stared at it forever it seemed before the knock came again.

"Who is it?" she demanded in a tight, dry voice.

"Leaving for the night," came Wang's voice. "Is there anything Missy wants before I go?"

"Nothing, thank you."

"Should I bring rabbit?"

"No."

Silence, then she heard him shuffle off down the corridor.

Again, the silence settled in, and with it, Bronte's reasoning. Snatching a lap blanket from a chair, she flung it over the mirror. She grabbed Tremain's shirt. It was the reminder of him that made her feel so unsettled.

She eased from the bedroom and up the hallway, her bare feet soundless. She would give the shirt to Murray, Tremain's night guard.

But Murray apparently was asleep, his chin resting on his chest as his chair leaned back against the wall.

"Protection," Bronte muttered to herself, her gaze going to the closed door briefly before she tiptoed by the sleeping Scotsman and turned the knob, gently shoving open the door.

A lantern hissed on a table near the bed, where Tremain appeared to be sleeping peacefully.

Good. Leave the traitor's shirt and escape.

But now that she was closer, she could tell that his forehead was beaded with sweat and his lips looked dry as parchment.

She bent nearer. Pressed her cool hand to his hot brow.

His eyes opened.

Bronte jumped back, the first rush of embarrassment paralyzing her. At last, she managed to turn on her heels and start for the door.

"Wait," came his soft voice.

Her step slowed, then stopped. Heart thumping, hands twisting into his shirt, she stared at the door while reason and judgment floundered around in her head.

"Miss Haviland," he said more loudly.

Slowly, slowly, she turned back to face him.

"I'd like some water, please."

"Water. Yes. Of course." She grabbed for the pitcher of water, splashed a measure into a cup, and with halting steps, carried it to him. Hesitantly, she slid one hand under his head and pressed the cup to his lips.

He drank deeply, thirstily, until the last of the water was gone. With a sigh of relief, he lay back on the pillow. "Thanks," he mumbled.

No sarcasm.

Her shoulders relaxed.

Brandon remained silent for a long moment, as if the effort of drinking had completely drained him of energy. Then, "What have you got there, Miss Haviland?"

"Here? Oh. Yes. Your shirt. I mended it."

He smiled. His look riveted her, made her feel conspicuous and all too aware that she stood before him in such a shocking manner, with her hair down—as she had so often seen her mother do before her father.

She took a deep breath and slowly released it. "I thought that perhaps we would be forced to issue you another, but I think I managed to mend the rips well enough. Money is tight, you understand. We're often forced to make do with inadequate supplies."

His eyes watched her. She noted in the dark room they were the color of the midnight sea. He had incredibly long lashes.

"I see you didn't eat this evening." She pointed to the tray of cold food by his bed.

"Not hungry."

"You really should try. It's imperative if you wish to regain your strength."

"Make you a deal," he said. "If you stay and keep me company for a while, I might consider eating."

"Stay?" She swallowed and hugged his wadded shirt tighter against her. "No. I . . . couldn't. It's late and . . ." She chewed her lower lip and stared at the tray of food—mutton broth, custard, warm milk, and stale bread. Hardly appetizing fare. "No," she said, more to herself than to him, then flung the shirt down on the bed and grabbed up the tray, causing the dishes to bounce and rattle.

Without another word, she hurried from the room, casting an annoyed glance at a snoring Murray, and rushed, with her gown hem flapping around her ankles, to the kitchen, where she slammed the tray down on the countertop, spilling the milk into the soup and the hard bread to the floor.

She heard the words "Make you a deal." Just who the blazes did he think he was to believe that she would simply sit at his side like some adoring puppy there for his amusement?

No doubt he was accustomed to women stumbling over themselves for the opportunity to spend time in his company.

Perhaps once, but not now. Not ever again, thanks to the English court system.

And thanks to the English court system—and her father—Brandon Tremain was now *her* responsibility . . . whether *she* liked it or not . . .

* * *

"Mr. Tremain."

The words were softly, hesitantly, spoken, teasing at his dream-sleepy consciousness like a vague breeze. Despite the increasingly painful throbbing in his leg, he'd finally managed to doze, focusing his mind on the memory of the warden's daughter standing over him in the dark.

"Mr. Tremain."

With an effort, he opened his eyes to find Bronte at his bedside—again—face painted pale gold in the lantern light, her hair a luxurious mass of waves spilling over her shoulders, her spine stiff as a ramrod, and her chin set at a stubborn *I dare you to comment* angle. She held a tray of steaming broth, toast, and water.

"I'll stay until you've eaten," she announced. "No longer. That is the deal."

He nodded.

Bronte put the tray on the table. A wave of scents washed over him—feminine smells, soap, lavender toilet water . . .

She pulled a chair up by his bed. He watched her eyes as her hands took the bowl of soup and the spoon and stirred the flavorful concoction round and round, her lips lightly blowing the mixture to cool it.

Her eyes—silver and sparkling as dew—met his briefly as she raised the spoon to his mouth. Her own lips parted as she waited for him to eat. Her expression was strange, almost calm—much more serene than he had ever seen it.

Of course. She was in her element now, submerging herself in her martyr's role. He was no longer a danger or threat, but an invalid in need of patience, understanding, and care. He was a bit player in her drama.

"Eat." She coaxed him.

At last, he did so, closing his eyes as the warm, flavorful broth trickled down the back of his throat. The toast followed. Then water. And all the while he continued to watch her features, how the shadows enhanced the contours of her face, the shape of her lips, the paleness of her neck.

A drop of soup trickled down his lip. As her attempt to catch it with the spoon failed, she pressed her finger to the errant drop and swept it away, as she might have with a child. He realized in that moment that against logic, against his better judgment, he would shake her out of her prudish, conformist role.

He wanted to unleash the passion he saw roiling behind those stormy eyes. He wanted to turn her apathetic *you can drop dead and I couldn't care less* expression into one of awakening. Or even anger. He wanted to see the same pleasure on her face as he had during the fireworks.

And he knew he was foolish enough to risk everything—his pride, his countrymen—for a woman again.

Her eyebrows drew together as he turned his face away, refusing further sustenance. "Eat," she said.

"I'm not hungry. Take it away, for God's sake. It's turning my stomach. I don't want that bloody toast, either. Or that water. I want a drink. A real drink. And some decent goddamn conversation with a flesh and blood woman who can look at a man as if he's something better than a slug under a rock."

Her back turned more rigid, if that were possible, her lips pressed. "Obviously," she said in a wooden voice, "you're in no mood for food *or* company."

"Oh, I'm in the mood for company," he remarked with heavy lids and a smirk. "I've been in the mood for the last miserable months I've resided in this hell-hole. Only my kind of company has soft gentle hands and breath as warm and sweet as cinnamon—"

"Are you insinuating, sir, that my hands are not gentle?"

"Gentle as a blacksmith's maybe," he said to her wide eyes, then winced for effect as he shifted his leg, exposing his knee from under the bed covers. "But never mind, love, some women are born with the ability to please a man and some women aren't. It's probably best that you've chosen the life of a martyr; you wouldn't know what to do for a man if you had one."

She glared at his face, her cheeks flaming, then glanced at his knee, which looked large and dark against the clean white sheets. Obviously, he'd hit a nerve—a very sore nerve and he considered backing down, of apologizing, but his mood was raw. And besides that . . . he wanted to toss her onto the bed and teach her exactly what it was that men expected from a woman as beautiful as she was . . . a woman who glided in and out of his range of vision wearing nothing but a skimpy little night rail and her magnificent hair down like some evil angel sent here to seduce him, when he imagined she had no inkling whatsoever what it felt like to seduce a man—as if she ever would . . .

Very slowly, Bronte put down the spoon and carefully left her chair, putting the tray on the nearby table next to the miniature of her posing in flowers. For a long while she stood there, staring down at the image of herself. Brandon cast cautious glances at her stiff, straight little spine and rigid shoulders. Silent women made him nervous. *Angry* silent women terrified him.

At last, she turned—little by little, hardly causing a ripple of her thin white gown as it slowly slid around her body, smooth as water around a pale stone. The light from the kerosene lamp on the table behind her shimmied a little, appeared to catch fire on her blacker-than-night hair that tumbled over her slender shoulders. She stared down at him with dark, dark eyes. She was lit with purpose.

"You're right, of course," she stated in a soft, matter-or-fact voice, totally void of the anger he had anticipated.

"I am?" he replied wryly, and not a little suspiciously.

Bronte moved toward him, white hands clasped before her loosely, the silhouette of her perfect body a shimmering glimmer through the transparent gown. He could see every detail: the fullness of her breasts—even the coin-shaped nipples that swung seductively from side to side when she shifted her weight from one curvaceous hip to the other. And there was that other place—there between her legs—where the gown clung just slightly to the shadowy recess at the juncture of her thighs.

Bending over him, sliding the sheet back from his leg with the cool tip of one finger, Bronte regarded his injured leg that was beginning to throb annoyingly—then on second thought, he realized that it wasn't his leg . . . exactly. "I suppose I've spent all these many years doing my best to make those I care about as comfortable and happy as possible." She glanced up at him, her long black lashes shadowing her eyes briefly.

Her cool fingers touched his thigh and he flinched. And frowned.

Her red mouth pouted slightly. She tipped her pale chin and peered at him from the corner of her eye.

"Your fingers are cold," he said tightly.

She blew at her fingertips. He watched her mouth, slightly parted lips, forgetting to breathe as she laid her warmed hands back on his tender thigh.

"Better?" she said softly.

He made a sound that caught in his throat as her hand slid up his thigh, and he shifted, hitching up further on his pillows and glancing repeatedly toward the closed door.

"Perhaps I've been remiss with you," she continued, both hands gently massaging his leg that was now on fire which had nothing to do with the heat of his injury. "It's just that . . . relax, Mr. Tremain, you're terribly tense . . . there—my, you do have muscular thighs. They're so very . . . hard. But this swelling . . . tsk, tsk, sir, if you aren't careful you'll find yourself without your . . . is something wrong, Mr. Tremain? Am I hurting you? Just tell me if I am. But it's occurred to me suddenly that therapy will help more than broth and bread."

With her hands on his thigh, he groaned despite his attempt to swallow it back.

"As I was saying," she continued, ignoring his

reaction, "I suppose I've been so involved with bettering the plight of the orphans I've not given much thought to what it must be like to deal day to day with the normal musings of girlish fantasies. Perhaps had I had friends my age to conjecture with I might possibly be more learned when it comes to . . . flirtation and seduction . . . what it takes to win the admiration . . . or desire of a particular man as you said."

He grabbed her wrist—couldn't help it. He was on to her now—she was teaching him a lesson and she was doing it pretty bloody well.

He could see it in her eyes, dancing there in smoldering sparks of fire as her luscious little mouth curved up in a go-to-hell smile.

"What's wrong, Mr. Tremain?" she asked innocently. "Perhaps you're not up to therapy tonight?"

"Oh, I'm up to it," he said, grinning. "The question is, are you, sweetheart?"

She stared at him, unblinking, her perfect face looking as if she had suddenly turned to marble. She smelled of lavender toilet water. Of talc powder. Of fresh, clean cotton that had dried that morning in the sun. He had challenged her. She had met the challenge. They both knew it. And it suddenly occurred to him that for her to flee now would be, in her own eyes, her conquest. He admired her pluck, and decided to let her emerge the victor.

He pushed her away, catching her off guard, causing her to step on her gown hem and trip slightly. Straightening, her eyes flashing, she glared at him with her hands in fists and her cheeks flaming.

"I've changed my mind," he announced. "I don't want any company. Just let me die in peace."

"You aren't dying," she snapped. "And further-more, this isn't your room. If I had my way I would have incarcerated you out back of the barn with our pigs. No, on second thought, I wouldn't subject the dear swines to company such as yours. Very well, Mr. Tremain. Starve if you like."

She grabbed the tray and headed for the door, slamming it behind her so loudly Murray came awake with a grunt as his chair banged onto the floor. Staring at the closed door, doing his best to ignore the lingering trace of her perfume teasing his nostrils, Brandon laughed.

The hour was nearing noon, and the heat in the room in which Brandon lay was oppressive. His head and every bone and muscle in his body throbbed. For the last few hellish days he'd done his best to suffer silently like any dignified hero who was no longer a hero, yet he was concerned.

He'd been in and out of enough hospitals during his military career to know that infection was a threat. Also, he needed exercise. The fact that the doctor who occasionally wandered in to check his wounds was usually cockeyed with homemade rum didn't help his peace of mind—nor did the fact that every time he struggled even to sit, a rough-hewn guard would push him back onto his pillows. Consequently, he felt that his health was at a low ebb.

Bronte entered the room, her arms full of linens. "Good morning," she said in a maddeningly un-emotional voice, moving in front of the open window, flashing a look toward the garden where she had frolicked with the children those many mornings ago, then dropping the linens on a table against the wall. Facing him again, she placed an envelope on the bed beside his hand. "From the post."

He didn't look down. He watched Bronte walk around the bed, almost nervously rearranging the sheets as she went, tucking here, smoothing there as she refused to meet his eyes directly.

"You seem to be popular with someone back in England. Now that you're more aware, perhaps you would like to read it." She glanced at the letter, then away.

She poured water from a crude pottery ewer into an equally crude basin that was decorated with childish smears of blue paint.

Her back to him, Bronte proceeded to dip a cloth into the water and wring it out with her pale hands. "The doctor feels certain that you're healing nicely."

"He's a drunk," he finally managed.

"You exaggerate, sir . . . Besides, Dr. Symms is the only physician available to us. I fear England's more prominent physicians would rather remain in England."

"So what's he here for?" Brandon asked in a piqued tone. "Murder? Theft? Blackmail? No. Don't tell me. I'd rather ponder on the subject."

Bronte turned back to the bed, avoiding his eyes. "Elizabeth tells me that you continue to refuse your meals." She measured a length of gauze against her outstretched arm, peered down it with one closed eye, then snipped it in two with a pair of blunt-nose scissors. Then she measured a second length. "Do you think that's wise, Mr. Tremain?"

"I've tasted better food from Canton swills."

"I suppose you could do a better job of it." She clipped the gauze with relish, as if it were his throat.

"Yes, as a matter of fact."

She glared at him.

He glared back. His leg throbbed. His head pounded.

"I'm hot," he snapped.

"Aren't we all."

"How about opening a bloody window so I don't asphyxiate?"

"And have you slither away at the first opportunity?"

"Slither?" He choked back a laugh. "Lady, I'm weak as a kitten. I couldn't *claw* my way out of that window, much less slither. Now get me a goddamn decent doctor before I—"

"Before you what?" she replied coolly, almost amusedly, her cheeks going from pink to red then almost purple. But still she didn't so much as quiver with an outward show of anger.

Exhausted, Brandon fell back onto his pillow, eyes on the ceiling as he did his best to focus his mind on something besides his startling desire to shake her. Today, it seemed, he could not get under her skin.

Bronte continued collecting medicinal staples, humming to herself as she efficiently went about her business of ignoring him completely. Finally, having arranged then rearranged the supplies on the table by his bed, she turned back and rewarded him with a stiff-as-a-board little smile that she no doubt saved for convicts on the eve of their hangings.

"Sister Elizabeth will be here soon to change your dressing. Unfortunately I can not stay as I am waiting for Mr. Ellison to accompany me to the orphanage."

He groaned under his breath and said, "Spare me the details. Just help me sit in the chair."

She stared at him speculatively. "First you'll swear to me that you won't try anything funny."

"As if you could take the word of a murderer. Very well, Miss Haviland, on my word of honor as a convicted murderer, I promise."

Again, she hesitated. She glanced back at the door, hesitated, took halting steps to the doorway, and gazed down the corridor. "Wang?" she called. "Are you there?"

Nothing.

"Mr. Grant?"

Still getting no reply, she rubbed her hands up and down her white skirt, her booted foot tapping her impatience on the floor. "Very well," she muttered to herself. "I suppose I have little choice but to do it all myself."

With a fresh sense of duty and determination, she stepped away from the bed and looked at the overstuffed chair in the corner covered with worn flowered cotton material.

"Right." Lips pressed, body stiff from lack of mobility for so many days, Brandon attempted to push himself up. Wobbled. Swayed. Clutched at the bedsheets while his head began to swirl like a whirlwind.

With all his effort, he attempted to stand. The

world careened. And though he did his best to focus on Bronte's face, and not the room spinning around him, the attempt was all for naught.

"Oh!" she cried, and as he began his slow spiral toward the floor, she flung herself against him, slender arms wrapped around his waist while her light weight struggled to keep him afoot. "Careful!" she panted. "Put your arms around me. There! Yes, that's it. Why didn't you tell me you were feeling so ill? Wang! Murray! Someone help! Mr. Tremain! Don't you dare pass out on me now."

But his feet gave way.

They spilled onto the bed, she clutching his hot body against hers, his long arms wrapped around her slender shoulders, hands tangled in her spilling hair. The bed ropes creaked. The mattress sagged. The letter she had earlier delivered floated like a feather to the floor.

Neither of them moved.

Brandon lay with his eyes closed, face buried in her lavender-scented hair, feeling her surprisingly pliable body molded against his while her hands continued to grip his gown as if she were afraid of tumbling down some bottomless hole.

For an instant, he forgot where he was. When, at last, she began to squirm to free herself, he continued to hold her tightly—forcing her to struggle harder, to wedge her elbows between them and shove herself away. In a panicked voice, she demanded, "Let me go. Let me go."

"Shut up," he growled and twisted his hands in her hair, cutting off her desperate babbling, making her body go stiff again with fear or anger—he couldn't tell which.

Didn't much care. Didn't care about anything but losing himself in the softness of her body, the scent of her skin.

Her eyes met his at last.

In an instant he felt as if he were drowning. He tried to ignore it, but it wouldn't go away. His attempt to fight it was futile. Perhaps the voice that had welcomed him to Haviland Farm the night of his arrival, and incarceration into solitary, had been right. Too many months had passed without the companionship of a beautiful woman. There was simply no other explanation for this urgent desire that could overwhelm even his pain—and his better judgment. He had come to New South Wales to inflict vengeance and vindication upon the bastards who had murdered his entire regiment of young soldiers during the uprising in Delhi and Meerut. She was the enemy. She was not to be trusted. He'd learned from experience—the more beautiful and brilliant a woman was, the more deadly.

But his mind only focused on his desire to destroy her composure—and regain his own.

Again she struggled, and he held her tighter, pinned against his chest with her nose an inch from his, his fingers pressed firmly into the soft, moist skin at the base of her small skull. Again he was swallowed by her eyes, almost drowning in their depths of intelligence and resolute independence. She didn't so much as squeak in alarm, as most women would have, just returned his appraisal with a look as unreadable as a stone.

Her nostrils flared—her only show of alarm. He could feel a slight escalation in her heartbeat, and her red mouth parted, as if she were unable to breathe properly. The tip of her tongue toyed a moment with her lower lip before she said, "If you'll release me immediately, I won't scream for the guards. We'll forget this ever happened."

He tightened his hold on her nape, just enough to bring about a soft inhalation from his captive. Vainly, she tipped her head back in an attempt to escape the pressure. The movement exposed her ivory throat, and the butterfly flutter of her pulse racing there.

She was beautiful. Too damn beautiful not to be trouble.

He squeezed again, this time harder, rendering her incapable of moving so much as an eyelid. Sweating heavily, he stared down into her flawless face, the shape of her mouth that seemed so familiar, because its lush redness had bothered him every minute of his confinement in that hot, black cubicle of a punishing room she had confined him to upon his arrival to Haviland Farm—not to mention the many long hours he had lain in this bed watching the door, hoping for her entry. The realization occurred to him at that moment that he wanted to rape her mouth with his own—to discipline it for affecting him to this point of fury and frustration. For continuing to regard him so unemotionally.

"Good God!" came a cry from the door, and suddenly someone was frantically pulling at his hands, which continued to pin Bronte to him. The girl, however, didn't flinch, just pinned him with her inscrutable mist-colored eyes as if she were some damned sphinx.

"Release her!" Arthur Ellison shouted, and leapt to Bronte's rescue.

Bronte scrambled to her feet, shoving Arthur away as he attempted to force Tremain further into the bed, roughly knocking her aside in the process.

"Stop it," she declared in a surprisingly strident voice. "Take your hands from this man immediately!"

Arthur stood away as she rose and regained her composure. "Mr. Tremain, are you all right?"

"No. I've obviously died and gone to Hell at last," he mumbled.

"That's it," Arthur snapped. "I'm going outside to fetch the guards."

"You won't dare." Bronte's look stopped him in his tracks.

"I beg to differ," Arthur argued. "That man was caught red-handed in his attempt to abuse you."

"What are you insinuating?" she said.

"I am insinuating nothing. This is fact. That the man there"—he pointed at Brandon with a shaking finger—"was assaulting you. My dear, you know the ramifications of such an action."

"Don't be ridiculous." She looked at Arthur, shaking partly with fright and partly with rage. "What you saw, Mr. Ellison, was my attempt to help the man who saved Sammy Newman's life." Drawing herself up, she forced control back into her voice. "Get out of this room this instant. And send Dr. Symms to see me as soon as possible. Quickly!"

Arthur glared at Tremain. "It is beyond my ability to understand why your father brought this man here in the first place. Then to bring him into your home to be pampered as if he were a guest—"

"You should discuss the situation with my father."

"Rest assured that I will." Pivoting on his heels, Arthur stalked to the doorway, where he paused long enough to collect his hat, which had spilled to the floor during the struggle. Only then did he look back, face pinched, mouth a thin, tight line. "I suppose this means I will not be accompanying you on your excursion today?"

"No, Arthur. This wouldn't be an appropriate time."

"Perhaps later."

She looked away, focused her attentions on collecting the scattered linens from the floor.

"Bronte," Arthur said more softly, his voice annoyingly supplicating.

Frowning, Bronte looked to the floor and counted to ten.

Finally, when she looked toward the door again, Arthur was gone. Dropping a pillow to the floor, she hurried from the room, down the corridor, and into the parlor, where she peeked through the white lace curtains and watched as Arthur, having boarded his carriage, rode off down the road.

Bronte closed her eyes and willed her heart to stop beating so furiously and her breathing to return to normal. Only then did she allow herself to return to Tremain's room, stopping just on the other side of the threshold because her wobbly knees would not let her go any farther.

Her body shaking, Bronte leaned against the door frame, eyes closed, forehead pressed against the jamb so fiercely it hurt. Released at last from the necessity of keeping her features composed, she gradually

felt the tight band, which had seemed to hold her
lungs in a grip, begin to relax, allowing her to
breathe normally again. She lightly touched the
tender, throbbing muscle at the base of her skull.

She wanted to cry. But she did not cry. She looked
around the high-ceilinged room with its white-
washed walls and portraits and wondered why she
had never, ever felt the surge of thrill over Arthur's
presence as she had in those moments Brandon
Tremain had forcibly pressed her body to his.

She should feel outrage, not this sense of excitement. God help her, but there was no telling what
might have happened had Arthur not come barreling in to remind her just how close she had come to
disaster.

Closing her eyes, she reluctantly allowed herself
to feel his hands on her again. Her arms tingled
still; the back of her neck burned where his fingers
had gripped her. His scent of hot musky flesh
pervaded her nostrils every bit as potently as it had
during those eternal seconds he'd held her fiercely
against him.

Without thinking, she touched her hair, which
had come loose from its ivory combs during her
tussle with Tremain, then she frowned at her show
of vanity.

God, but she suddenly felt desperate. And afraid.
And foolish for wasting the best years of her life
infatuated with a man who had turned out to be
nothing more than a figment of her imagination.
How many men—decent, trustworthy men like
Arthur, like the dozen or so others who had worked
for her father, admirers—had she turned away

through the years because they could not measure up to Captain Brandon Tremain?

All this time she had waited—prayed—for that special something—that touch, that kiss. She wanted fireworks, dammit. Fireworks! Shooting rockets, streaming ribbons of red and blue light to turn her body into pinpoints of energy, and her heart into a wild thing that romantic novels promulgated with such terms as "roused to passion" and "swooned with the heat of his fervent kiss."

She was twenty-seven years old, and she had never been kissed.

Just minutes before . . . if Arthur hadn't come charging in like one of Tremain's regiments with an eye for blood, she just might have . . .

No. Reason tapped at her conscience.

She had broken two of her father's hard-and-fast rules: never, under any circumstances, find yourself alone in a room with an untrustworthy prisoner, and never put yourself in a position of having to defend yourself, for any reason, against him, against yourself.

Never trust a prisoner—this prisoner, this man who had annihilated her nerve and self-control with a simple grip of his hand on her head. Never. Never.

Even if he was once a hero.

No girl should permit a boy to be
so familiar as to toy with her hands,
or play with her rings; to handle her
curls or encircle her waist with his
arm. Such impudent intimacy should never
be tolerated for a moment. No gentleman
will attempt it; no lady will permit it

—*Good Morals and Gentle Manners*
AUTHOR UNKNOWN, 1873

CHAPTER SEVEN

MARGORIE FISH WAS ACCUSTOMED TO LUXURY. OR SHE HAD
been before moving to New South Wales with her
much older husband, the once honorable Lord Fish
of Balmoreland Hall in Essex, a title which, it was
whispered, had been bought with the tidy sum of
ten thousand quid in order for Lord Fish to more
successfully woo his beloved, status-greedy inamo-
rata, Margorie Goodhue. Five years later, he'd sold
Balmoreland to close-residing gentry, packed up his
belongings and his recalcitrant, philandering wife
practically overnight, and beat a hasty retreat from
the country on the first available ship to anywhere.
Rumor had it that his lordship's quick exit had
something to do with choosing not to meet his
wife's lover on the dueling field. Bronte didn't
doubt the rumor.

She placed the china tea service emblazoned with
faded red roses on the table by the parlor settee.
Taking a moment to collect herself, she inhaled a

much needed breath and briefly cast a cautious glance at her uninvited guests, thinking such an impromptu visit would be considered poor etiquette back in England, even for Margorie Goodhue Fish. Then again, nothing that Lady Fish did would ever surprise her.

Clearing her throat, focusing on the rich golden brew she poured into matching cups, she said, "You were saying, Lord Fish?"

Pacing the sparsely furnished room, wearing a faded red hunting coat with a frayed black lapel, Lord Fish appeared more than ordinarily agitated as he cast glances at his disinterested wife. The man's bedraggled appearance never failed to stir Bronte's sympathy. Like so many others who had journeyed to New South Wales in hopes of establishing themselves a prosperous empire, only to find themselves rapidly sinking in the quicksand of failed hopes and dreams, Lord Fish did his best to put forth the false image of success and prosperity— fooling no one but himself.

"We were distressed to hear that recently a young woman died in childbirth. Of course, Margorie and I felt it imperative that the child be given every opportunity to experience the closeness and security of a loving, happy, and successful home."

"I understand your great desire to have a child, sir," Bronte replied softly and as compassionately as possible.

Turning his aging face to her, he offered her a thin smile. "No, my dear, I don't think you do. Not completely. I'm not exactly a young man any longer, Miss Haviland. I've long since given up any hope of having my own son . . ." Again, he glanced at his wife, who, by now, had moved to the window, where she looked out on the goings-on in the yard. Bronte suspected Lady Fish found more entertainment in the working convicts than she did in the frolicking children.

"The infant is only days old, my lord. You realize that I could not consider your request until the child is past the customary waiting period—which is six weeks. Perhaps if you come back then . . ."

She would not consider his request regardless of the child's age, and Lord Fish knew it. While most homes much less respectable than St. Cluny's would welcome any opportunity to "farm off" the parentless children, Bronte was well-known for her strict obedience to the prescripts her late mother, who had worked faithfully to better the plight of the orphans, had issued on the children's behalf before her death.

Without exception, no child would be offered for adoption to a family whose ability to provide financial security and a stable loving environment was questioned.

Alas, Lord Fish was one of the many gentlemen farmers whose lofty aspirations for success in New South Wales had eroded to the point of struggling to survive—and it didn't take much to see that when it came to providing a stable loving environment, Lord Fish and his wife would prove to be total failures.

But that wasn't the only reason. While Lord Fish, on the surface, appeared more than a little controlled and manipulated by his wife, Bronte was well aware that his tolerance ended when it came to dealing with his workers. He was a severe master.

She simply would not allow a child to be brought up in that environment.

At last, Margorie turned from the window and offered Bronte a flat smile. "While my husband's focus is on the child, I confess I am more interested in hiring more men for the farm. Your father mentioned there were inmates available for work leave."

Lord Fish made a grunt of disgust and exited the room, slamming the door behind him. Margorie shrugged, and gathering her lavender satin skirts with one hand, she moved across the room to another window, where she watched the workers like a cat contemplating a field mouse. Her chestnut hair pinned in coils atop her head looked like flames in the afternoon sunlight spilling through the window. As always, the scent of violets clinging to her hair and shoulders filled the room like a bed of spring flowers. And her clothes . . . Bronte suspected that Lady Fish's exquisite wardrobe robbed her husband of every spare pence—few as there were.

"I understand your husband's need for help, Lady Fish. However, at present it is very difficult—"

"There is one man in particular who interests me." Lady Fish touched her hair lightly and smiled at her reflection in the window glass. Even before Margorie spoke again, Bronte sensed what she would say. "Brandon Tremain," Margorie said smoothly, as if speaking his name were as easy as saying her own.

"Impossible," Bronte replied, startled and slightly embarrassed by the vehemence of her response.

Margorie's eyebrows arched and her jaw became tense. For a long minute she contemplated Bronte.

"He's very ill," Bronte rushed to explain. "It simply wouldn't do for him to be reassigned . . . at this time."

"I see. He'll soon improve, of course."

"We're doing everything humanly possible." Bronte swallowed and glanced at the door, nagged by the infuriating knowledge that he lay only doors away.

Her gaze locked on Bronte, Margorie moved to a chair opposite, spreading her skirts around her feet.

Bronte handed her a teacup and saucer, and the woman relaxed further into the ornate chair. "Imagine Brandon being here. I can hardly believe it to be true. When your father told me—"

"My father?"

"Last evening . . . He stopped by the house to see Giles, of course—something about those horrible little men who escaped last week. But never mind. I can't tell you how stunned I was. Such misfortune! I was even more stunned to learn that you are keeping him here while he recuperates. How very convenient . . . for everyone."

"I hardly call murder and treason misfortune."

Margorie looked thoughtful. "I cannot imagine his committing treason. Murder, on the other hand . . . Let me just say that his nature has always been . . ." She searched for the proper word, looking as if she found amusement in the idea of Tremain's transgression. "Volatile," she finally supplied. "Combustible. I think our Queen and country should thank God he turned his rather explosive energies on the enemy. But treason . . ." She waved the idea away. "I'm certain he must have had just cause."

"Obviously the courts didn't agree." Bronte

poured another cup. "About the idea of your adopting a child—"

"What a dreadful shame, and a waste of such a magnificent specimen of a man," Lady Fish interrupted. "Don't you agree, darling? You of all people must be devastated."

"Oh?" With the posture and uniform of a stiff-backed majordomo, she rearranged a bronze rabbit card holder stacked high with calling cards, moving it to the edge of the table beside her chair.

"You've been so vocal about your admiration. As I recall, there were numerous occasions when you occupied a dinner party with tales of his escapades and heroics in some country or other—stories fresh from the *London Times*. Your father mentioned once that you kept a scrapbook—"

"I was a child, Lady Fish. All children have their heroes. I simply respected and admired him—as did all of England—once."

"All the ladies of England, certainly. I did mention to you that I have known the good Captain for some time?"

Bronte frowned and fidgeted with her lace-edged napkin. She did not want to be here, trapped in the company of a woman she neither liked nor respected. But according to custom the woman should pay a half-hour call.

"Yes, we met some years ago at a ball. What a scandalous flirt! Aside from battle, I'm certain Brandon took nothing seriously. Not even his mistresses."

Bronte left her chair. "Obviously you know him quite well."

"Very well." Shrugging, Lady Fish stood and

moved toward the door, pausing only long enough to look back and flash Bronte an emotionless smile. "I really wouldn't bother any longer with my husband's tedious and rather annoying wish to adopt. You won't, of course, tell him I suggested such a thing."

"Certainly not," Bronte replied. "Since I never entertained the idea even for a moment."

Margorie's eyes narrowed slightly, then she smiled again. "Enjoy the good Captain, my dear Bronte. I do so envy you." Then she was gone, leaving a wave of perfume behind her.

To your equals a tranquil nature and
manner should always be shown, no matter
how trying the position.
—*The Mentor*
THOMAS EMBLEY OSMUN, 1884

CHAPTER EIGHT

*Therefore, Mr. Crenshaw, I feel it imperative that
strict measures be elected as soon as possible to
confront the unseemly situation of The Rocks. To
neither forbid nor prevent—indeed to applaud and
excuse—the use of these havens of foul corruption
upon the human spirit is a crime in and unto itself.*

Bronte dipped her peacock quill into the inkwell.
With her hand poised above the letter, she gazed
toward the flickering sconce on the wall and the
scattering of English mementos on the table beneath it.

Her favorite and most cherished was a pink
lusterware saucer honoring the wedding of Victoria
and Albert. With the Queen draped in her wedding
veil and sitting on her throne, and Albert dressed in
his royal uniform with epaulets and sashes, they
looked the perfect bride and groom. Victoria's love
for Albert was widely acknowledged, and every

young woman throughout the civilized world dreamed of being so lucky.

Bronte dipped her quill again and did her best to focus on her business and not on thoughts of England or love matches.

If there ever was a time she allowed herself to feel a sense of melancholy, it was now—when she thought of all those young women back in England who were no doubt waiting impatiently for their beloved to saunter up the walk with his arms full of flowers. For the next couple of hours they would sit on opposite ends of a settee and pass polite conversation. Perhaps they would study the young woman's collections of engravings, maps, and architectural or botanical prints. And, of course, she would astound and impress her beloved with her ability to master the piano or harp.

Bronte didn't own a piano or harp. Such musical instruments were far too great a luxury to be purchased and shipped all the way to New South Wales—at least for her father.

She shook her head. All this was folly.

In my opinion, sir, the reformation of these pitiful women, not to mention men, should begin with intense concentration on the education of their minds and the teachings of social graces. Most women, regardless of their unfortunate backgrounds, would welcome the opportunity for self-improvement and to overcome real or imagined disadvantages of birth, class, and training. I highly suggest that these women be given the opportunity to study with extreme dedication the Guide to Good Behaviour, *written for the instruction of the young, as well as for those*

*who neglected to avail themselves of refinements
within their reach. I suggest to you, sir, that by
enforcing the laws of good and appropriate social
behavior we (people as a whole) shall find radical
change in this disquieted time. Manners are of more
importance than laws, for upon these in a great
measure the law depends.*

Bronte put down her pen, waited until the ink
had dried sufficiently, then tucked the letter to Pilot
Crenshaw into the top drawer of her writing desk.

Duty number one finished. Then to duty number
two: deliver the supper tray to the prisoner.

She exited the room and moved steadily to the
kitchen, where Cook had prepared a tray of lamb
chops and chutney, fresh baked bread, and lemonade. Bronte thanked him, mentioned that she and
her father would surely miss him when he left, and
swore they would be hard-pressed to find another
cook so talented as he. Squaring her shoulders, she
marched down the corridor to Tremain's room.

And paused.

Closed her eyes.

Took a deep breath. "Duty," she murmured to
herself.

Balancing the tray on one hand, she shoved open
the door with the other.

Tremain appeared to be sleeping.

Good. She would leave the tray.

Yes, she would put down the tray and leave
directly.

Right now, she would leave it.

She tiptoed across the room and placed it on the
bedside table, next to the miniature of her in the

pewter frame. Brows knitting, Bronte took the paint-
ing and placed it back on the table across the room,
near the window, where it had resided for the last two
years.

Had Tremain moved it? Surely not . . . why
would he?

"Hello," came his voice behind her, and she
jumped and spun, knocking the table so the miniature tumbled onto the Clones Irish lace tablecloth.

Tremain regarded her with sleepy eyes.

"You're awake," she said.

"And hungry."

"Do you like lamb?"

He nodded.

"And chutney?"

"My favorite."

She chewed her lower lip.

Pushing himself up on his elbows, Tremain clumsily attempted to right his pillow. Bronte hurried to
his aid, poking and prodding the goose-down pillow while she did her best to force her eyes away
from the thick dark hair growing long on the back
of his neck.

Stepping away, she watched as he lay back again,
a look of relief on his tired features. "Dr. Symms
says your leg is healing nicely," she finally said.

"We discussed the incompetent Dr. Symms during your previous visit."

Awkwardly, Bronte stepped away.

Bronte regarded the food in silence. Then he took
the napkin from her fingers, offering her a casual
smile in return.

"I think I can manage from here."

She nodded. Then, slowly, she turned for the door.

"However," he said, stopping her in her tracks. "You never know. Perhaps if you'll only stay a moment . . ."

"Well . . . I . . ." She cleared her throat. "I suppose a moment won't matter. We'll simply leave the door open if you don't mind."

Bronte moved to the chair across the room and sat on the lip of it, knees pressed tightly together, hands clasped and lying tensely in her lap.

Brandon drank his lemonade and wiped his mouth with a monogrammed napkin. With his attention apparently focused on his food, Bronte could regard him more closely, her attention going again and again to the shock of dark, untamed hair that spilled profusely over his brow.

"I can't stay long," she finally announced.

"No?"

"I have plans for the evening."

His blue eyes looked up. "Don't tell me. You finally agreed to see him again."

"I beg your pardon?"

"Ellison."

"Oh." She unclasped her hands, stretched her fingers, noted that her palms were sweating, and then clasped them back, more tightly. "No. It's not Arthur."

"Then someone else?"

She shook her head.

"Surely there's someone special. Why else would you look so pretty tonight?"

A flush of heat rushed to her face. She stared at

him like a mute while his intense eyes studied her over his quickly disappearing meal.

"So tell me, Miss Haviland, how do you normally occupy your evenings?"

"I read a great deal." She cleared her throat. "Or Father and I discuss business."

"Prison business, I assume."

She nodded.

"You and your father seem very close."

She nodded.

"And your mother?"

"She's dead."

"But you were close."

She nodded.

"You look a great deal like her."

She raised her eyebrows.

He pointed the fork at the miniature.

"Oh. Yes. Only she was far prettier than I."

"I don't think so."

Bronte smoothed back an errant strand of hair spilling around her temple, and tucked it behind her ear.

"Tell me about her," he said.

"They were very much in love. She was brilliant, kind—"

"And spirited."

"Yes."

"And a lady, no doubt."

". . . Yes."

"Would she approve of Arthur?"

"Arthur? What do you mean?"

"He wants to marry you . . . I sense your father wants to see you happy—"

"I am happy, Mr. Tremain. I needn't marry to attain that."

"I can't imagine anyone being happy who hasn't ever smelled sunshine or wiggled their toes in the mud."

Shifting on the chair, Bronte lowered her gaze to the floor. What on earth was he doing? she wondered. Taunting or simply teasing? Was he intentionally attempting to disconcert her with his mildly flirtatious manner, or was this merely another one of his ploys to lure her into a state of gullibility?

Frowning, she looked down at her slippered toes and spied the envelope beneath the bed. Grateful for an excuse to divert his attention, she leapt from the chair as if goosed and dove for the letter, recognizing it immediately as the missive she had delivered to him the day before.

He raised his eyebrows as she thrust it at him, dropped it on his tray, and again backed away. For a long moment, he didn't move, just stared down at the stained, yellowing envelope, slowing chewing, swallowing, gently putting the fork down by his empty plate on the tray.

"I brought this to you the other day," she hurried to explain. "I suppose in all the . . . um . . . excitement it was lost and forgotten."

He picked it up. Bronte found herself somewhat mesmerized by his dark, hard hands as they gently turned the article over and over while he contemplated opening it. The seal had been demolished long since, as had most of the inscription addressing the parchment-thin envelope, the ink no doubt washed away by sea spray and the dampness found in the dank belly of a ship.

Still, Bronte had noted that the script was decidedly feminine.

Finally, she lifted her eyes back to his.

She felt herself growing limp, a weakness sliding through her blood like slow quicksilver. There was something in the lines of his face that bespoke sadness . . . and regret.

Removing the tray from his lap, she set it aside. In the space of seconds, it seemed, night had crawled silently into the room, cloaking their faces in deep shadows. Fumbling with a box of matches, she struck a lucifer once, twice, three times. As the little flame sent a stream of spent sulfur into the air, she touched the match to the wick of the lantern.

In the orangey glow of the oil lamp, Tremain's face looked crimson with heat, his hair a blue-black cloud swirling with copper fire. The realization occurred to her that, once again, she was breaking the rules, dallying in the company of a prisoner whose hands and legs were no longer bound. Why not leave that moment? Return to her room, her books, her rabbits, and count the minutes until her father returned home, so she could bore him with monologues on the world's great need to liberate women through etiquette and education.

But the thought of returning to her room filled her with a restlessness.

Instead, she moved to the window and gazed out over the garden, watching the white moon creep over the tops of the eucalypt trees.

"Miss Haviland," Tremain said.

"Sir?" She focused harder on the moon.

"It seems I'm suddenly not feeling so well. Would you mind?"

"Oh. Certainly." She hurried to the bed and retrieved the tray, started for the door.

"That's not what I meant," came his voice, stopping her abruptly. Looking back over her shoulder, she watched as he held up the letter. "Would you mind reading it to me?"

Oh, she thought. Somewhat reluctantly, she set aside the tray and, haltingly, returned to the bed, eyes focused on the letter in his hand, and not on his face, his eyes, his mouth, which continued to carry a singular sort of smile that made her feel as if butterflies had suddenly taken flight in her stomach.

Gently, she took the envelope from his fingers, careful not to touch him. Oh no. That wouldn't be at all appropriate.

Letter in hand, bending nearer the light, she did her best to concentrate on the mostly indecipherable script swirling before her eyes. She cleared her throat. Took a breath:

"My Darling Brandon," — her face flushed — "A fortnight has passed since I last bid you adieu." Her voice began to quiver. "I cannot relate how my heart grieves with the thought of never seeing you again."

Hands beginning to tremble, Bronte squinted her eyes and tipped the paper toward the candle flame, hoping to better read the faded, blotched meanderings of Tremain's . . . what? Friend? Lover? Mistress? *Fiancée?*

"Closer," he said, and, mistakenly, Bronte allowed herself to look up. His features appeared smoldering in the dim gold light. "I'd like to read along with you," he explained, then reached for the lantern on the table and dragged it closer to him.

She blinked and breathed and flipped through the sadly decomposed papers, coming to the final page, where the writing was not so illegible. Forced to move nearer the bed, she bowed into the light, sharing the letter with him so they were practically cheek to cheek, their eyes focused on the paper that was, by now, shaking so badly the words were little more than a jumble.

Tremain gently caught her wrist in his fingers and, without looking up, said, "Relax, sweetheart, I won't bite . . . I promise."

Bronte closed her eyes as every nerve seemed to concentrate on the feel of his warm hand on her arm. A moment passed before she was capable of even breathing.

"And therefore, despite your desires that I should not involve myself in this tragic matter, I do so with every fiber of my being, and will continue to do so until I have exhausted every source of aid on your behalf. I will not rest until I learn the truth, until I have declared the truth to all of England, indeed to all of the civilized world. I will fight until my dying breath to prove you are innocent. Soon, I vow, you will return to us. Until then, I am devotedly yours, Clarissa."

Bronte took a breath. Long. Deep. Drawing in the still silence and holding it there until her lungs began to ache. Continuing to stare down at the weathered page, she tried to imagine what sort of woman had written the words, had so bravely voiced her continuing belief in Tremain's innocence.

She would be beautiful. Properly educated. Undeniably feminine. A perfect English rose who was accustomed to dancing and dining with royalty: the expensive, fine-grained linen stationery was proof enough of that.

And, most obviously, she was loyal. And thought he deserved loyalty in return.

What most women admire most in men is
gallantry; not the gallantry of courts
and fops, but boldness, courage, devotion,
decision, and refined civility. A man's
bearing wins ten superior women where his
boots and brains win one.

— *"Titcomb's Letter to Young People,*
Single and Married"
1858

CHAPTER NINE

BRONTE GAZED OUT THE SCHOOL WINDOW, VACUELY HEARING
the hammering and sawing, the occasional voices of
the workmen, not to mention Johnny Turpin's barks
of reprimand. Even the children's tittering and
whispers had become little more than an insect's
hum as her occupied thoughts toyed with the
previous night's memory.

The letter.

And the unsettling emotion it had provoked in
her.

Surely that emotion had not been jealousy. Or
envy. Or disappointment.

"Bronte?" Someone tugged on her skirt. Bronte
looked down. Sammy beamed her a freckle-faced
smile. "When is Mr. Tremain comin' back?" he
asked.

"Soon, I hope. He's much improved."

He offered up a dried clay miniature of a wombat

he had finger painted with blue dyes. "I made him somethin'," he said.

Smiling, Bronte went to one knee, cradling the wombat securely in his hand. She kissed the lad's dewy cheek, and he nuzzled against her.

"I don't ever want to leave you," he said. "Promise me that you won't let them take me. Promise!"

She hugged him close and kissed the top of his head, loving the scent of his skin and carrot-red hair. Loving even more the feel of his little arms holding her so tightly. "Oh, my darling," she whispered in his ear. "Wouldn't you rather have a nice home—"

"This is my home! I don't want no place else. Please don't send me away. Please!"

Frowning, Bronte looked into his frightened eyes. "Sammy, what has you so suddenly concerned about leaving?"

"They always leave when they get big like me. Always. That bad man always comes and takes 'em away and they don't ever come back. I don't want to leave. I won't!"

"Shh." She hugged him again, rocked him, kissed him until his trembling subsided.

"What's wrong, Sammy?" Bronte asked. "Please tell me."

He sniffed and rubbed his nose on her shoulder. "Ever'body I love always leaves."

"Who has left you, Sammy?"

"Mr. Tremain."

Elizabeth peered at Bronte over the top of her spectacles.

"He was my friend and now he's gone," Sammy explained.

"He hasn't gone far. You'll see him again."

"Promise?"

"As soon as he's better."

Sammy held her fiercely again. "Know what?" he said.

"What?"

"I wish you were my mummy."

Bronte smiled and squeezed him back.

"Know what else I wish?"

"Tell me."

"That Mr. Tremain was my papa."

Brandon watched her walk down the road—a leisurely glide, skirt lazily swinging from side to side as her feet kicked up small puffs of dust in the late-afternoon air.

She was a vision, all right. All in white. Long, graceful limbs moving freely, her face protected from the sun by her bonnet, which was tied with a pale blue ribbon at her jaw.

The moment she saw him, her step slowed, then stopped. With not so much as a blink, she stood in the middle of the rutted wagon path, the wild-flowers lining the road bowing their heavy heads by her feet.

Grimacing, he stretched his leg down the steps, and leaned back on his elbows on the porch.

After a long moment, Bronte moved forward, though not as freely. Her body had taken on a rigidity that was noticeable even from his distance. Brandon did nothing, said nothing, just fixed his sights on her, wondering how she could remain so bloody fresh and cool-looking in the ungodly heat.

Finally, she reached the porch.

"Welcome home," he said in greeting.

"You're up." She took note of his legs—his bare legs, and his bare feet. He had cut off one leg of his trousers because it would not fit over his swollen, bandaged thigh. He'd cut off the other to even things out, grinning as he did so because he knew already what Bronte's reaction would be when she saw him.

Still, she surprised him by saying nothing. Ah, what sweet disappointment. He'd looked forward all day to her disapproval.

"Difficult day, Miss Haviland?"

Her face remained passive, if not remote. "Yes," she finally replied.

"I assume all is going well with the building."

She nodded and tugged the ribbon at her jaw. It fell free, and she swept the hat from her head and used it to fan her face. Finally, she replied. "The building is going very well. Or as well as can be expected under the circumstances."

"And the circumstances . . . ?"

Glancing toward the low sun, Bronte narrowed her eyes. "This bloody heat." Her voice sounded weary. "It hasn't rained in months. And the men . . ." She shook her head. "They really don't care." Her eyes came back to his. "For them, Mr. Tremain, the building of the orphanage is simply a punishment. A duty. A way to force them to give something back to the society from which they took. They haven't the slightest idea what it means to the children."

"And what does it mean?"

"Permanence, sir. Home. Or as permanent as it can be, considering the circumstances."

"Which are?"

"That they will leave soon enough. When they turn six. Then they'll be shipped like little loaves of bread back to Sydney or Melbourne, or perhaps even London, to be displayed before prospective parents. They'll be lined up like little soldiers attempting to pass inspection as the well-meaning couples parade by them searching desperately for the perfect child. I don't think you, or even I, can comprehend the sense of disappointment which must surely go through their little minds and hearts when they are passed over."

The intensity of her features made Brandon frown. Bronte looked off, back down the road toward the orphanage. Her jaw tensed. Her hands fisted.

Murray appeared at the door, tray loaded with pitcher and glasses and freshly made tarts. Wang hurried around the corner of the houses, a black-and-white lop-eared rabbit in his arms. Brandon knew that every evening Bronte played with her pet. It seemed to be an attempt to lighten her burden of sadness and responsibility.

Murray poured her a glass of lemonade. At her nod, he poured one for Brandon. Surprising him she sat down on the step beside him, placed her hat aside, and spread her skirt down over her dusty boots. A light wave of lavender touched his nostrils. For a moment, he studied the delicate shell of her ear, and the tiny pearl stud in her lobe, then he forced himself to look away.

Wang handed the rabbit to Bronte. Its normally floppy ears twitched with enthusiasm, its puffy tail wiggled. Bronte laughed.

Just a throaty, soft little sound.

He felt his body stiffen, while Bronte's appeared

to relax. Her eyes closed, face tipped up so the
mellowing sun shimmered upon her moist features.
She allowed the rabbit to lavish her with affection,
then she buried her face in its luxurious black-and-
white fur and hugged it back.

Brandon drank his lemonade. He didn't have
much appetite for the tart drink, however.

At last, the rabbit scurried from her lap and leapt
into the nearby flowers, where it proceeded to
stand up on its haunches and sniff the air.

"Do you realize," Bronte said, "that this country
is one of the very few that offers no natural preda-
tors to the rabbit? Can you imagine living in a
world where you were totally secluded from danger? Did you also know that, aside from mine, there
are no rabbits in Australia?"

"No." He smiled. "I didn't know."

"You must think me odd to love them so—I
mean my rabbits."

"Perhaps a little."

She raised one eyebrow and ran a fingertip
around the rim of her sweating glass. "They are
silent, you know. Unless wounded or upset. They're
deliciously affectionate, and easily trained. Watch."

"Baby," she called softly and made a kissing
sound with her red lips. "Baby, come."

The rabbit came bounding through the flowers,
ears up, nose twitching, paused on its haunches at
her feet, and gazed up at her adoringly. Bronte fed
it a pinch of tart.

Brandon laughed. Bronte blushed.

They fell silent and watched the sun turn the sky
scarlet.

Finally Brandon asked, "What do you normally do this time of day, Miss Haviland?"

She shrugged and treated the hungry rabbit again. "Read. It helps me to relax. Or perhaps I walk."

"To where?"

"I have a place where I go . . . when I want to be alone."

"Tell me about it."

She nibbled the tart herself, spilling flakes of crust on her skirt. "A cottage not far from here. It's been deserted for years. We lived there when we first arrived. It was meant to be the overseer's cottage, but my mother insisted that she could run the farm as adequately and save money."

"And naturally you've followed in her footsteps."

"I've tried."

"And succeeded quite well, by the looks of it."

"Too well, I think." She did not look at him, but continued to pick at her pastry.

"Will you take me there?"

Bronte stared hard at her rabbit, which had begun to dig vigorously in the garden.

"The leg needs to be exercised," he explained. "So it doesn't get . . . stiff."

"That's impossible, of course." She flicked away slivers of crust from her skirt and dropped the uneaten portion of her tart on the plate. "You're a prisoner, Mr. Tremain."

"I could hardly escape. Not with this leg."

"The cottage is too far. You would reinjure yourself."

"I couldn't with your shoulder to lean on."

Dark color crept up her throat and into her face. "I'm growing bored, Miss Haviland. I'm not accustomed to a life of such ease."

"It's simply not possible," she stated firmly—almost angrily—her discomposure obvious. Suddenly she stood. Her skirt hem brushed his arm and shoulder as she whirled for the door, offering him a glimpse of ankle and shin. Pausing at the door, she announced, "You're a prisoner, sir. Never forget that fact."

He said nothing, just took up the tart she had been eating and flicked a portion to the rabbit sniffing at his bare feet. To the west the sun balanced upon the tips of the gum trees—a great orange ball of fire that turned the horizon into a black silhouette. Twilight was simply an illusion, however. Darkness, true darkness, was still two hours away.

Having finished his lemonade, Brandon put aside his glass and grabbed the porch balustrade in an attempt to stand. He winced, and wobbled, gritted his teeth, and broke out into a telling sweat, and, at last, he stood and leaned against the rail in an attempt to catch his breath and force the discomfort from his mind.

Glancing toward the door, he discovered Bronte in the threshold, bonnet in one hand at her side as she regarded him in silence.

"You see," she finally said in an emotionless voice. "You're not ready to walk."

"And I won't be unless I get some exercise."

The bonnet fanned against her leg, stirring the skirt of her dress. "Perhaps a short walk."

Bronte placed the hat on her head, tilting the

straw brim over her dark eyes, tucked an errant
strand of hair at her temple behind her ear, then tied
the sash at her jaw. Without meeting his appraisal,
she moved across the porch, took one of his arms
and lapped it around her shoulders, then slid one of
her own around his waist. Slowly, carefully, they
descended the steps and moved at a snail's pace
down the pathway.

"We shan't go far," she announced dogmatically.

"All right," he said.

"And you needn't begin your misguided attempts at wit."

"I wouldn't think of it." He grinned down at the
top of her bonnet, watched a black-and-white spotted bug light on the silk daisy at the brim, then take
off again in a whir of wings.

They walked, or limped, down the roadway, which
was little more than a sandy wagon path rutted by
wagon wheels and eroded by weather. The pain in
his leg panged, but he'd experienced worse—far
worse—and then he hadn't had Bronte Haviland's
shoulder to lean on.

And what a slender but strong little shoulder it
was, and doggedly determined. He wondered how
many others she had hoisted about the last many
years—men, women, children.

Occasionally, the plantations of stately trees were
interrupted by breaks of sprawling lush grasslands,
waist high with waving greenery. A mob of kangaroos, looking more like a group of fawn wraiths,
grazed there, pausing in their somnolent chewing
to look their way, to crowd close to the edge of the
lane and sniff and offer a faint bleat in greeting. But
it was the birds that filled up the silence: sulfur-

crested cockatoos, flocks of hundreds that settled on the dead limbs of gum trees, covering the silvery branches in what seemed to be a thick blooming of white flowers. Their hoarse, squalling voices vibrated through the woodland. The wind from their wings brushed Brandon and Bronte's faces with cool air and a snowing of white and yellow feathers.

As they rounded the farthest bend from the house, Bronte paused and shifted his weight more comfortably around her shoulders. She glanced toward a grotto-like clearing in the wood, appeared to hesitate, then carefully turned him back toward the house.

"Is that the way to the cottage?" he asked.

Bronte said nothing.

"Take me there," he said.

"No."

"Just for a moment. We won't stay."

"I . . . can't." She began to move.

He locked his good leg and refused. She turned on him swiftly, so swiftly her hat slid back on her head.

"You promised you'd do nothing foolish."

"No, I didn't." He flashed her a smile and limped toward the clearing. Without Bronte's help, he was practically forced to hop on one leg.

She moved up beside him and grabbed his arm. "You're incorrigible, you know."

"So I've been told . . . by you . . . a great many times."

"You'll probably be bitten by a tiger snake."

"Then you won't have to carry me home."

"That, sir, would be a great relief. But then, I'd be

forced to dispose of your body before someone realized that I'd brought you here—alone. I must be insane. My father would be furious."

"I'm certain your father's grown accustomed to you by now."

Her head came up; she stared at him, her eyes gray as gunmetal, her cheeks flushed with . . . what?

Even before they reached the cottage, he heard the river, rushing and roaring, filling the dim chamber of trees with a sort of mist that appeared to hang suspended in the air. The trees and flowers took on a vibrancy that hurt the eyes.

At last, she said, "There."

From a tangle of vines erupted the peak of the cottage. The leaded glass windows winked in the occasional shaft of failing sunlight. The walls were brown stone and mostly covered by lichen.

For a long moment, Bronte said nothing, just stared down at the quaint little abode, her face full of yearning. Finally, she said, "Are you happy now? Come along, Mr. Tremain. It's time to go back."

"Wait. I want to see the inside."

"No." She shook her head and tried to turn him.

He broke away, stumbled, ignored her furious countenance, and hobbled down the faint path until he stood in the doorway. A goanna lizard sat sunning itself on a windowsill.

He eased the door open with one finger. The rusty hinges creaked.

He'd hoped to see ruin. Perhaps moldy ceilings and walls—how could it be helped in this heat and humidity? He'd hoped to see emptiness and rot.

What he found was Bronte's touch apparent in

everything, from the frilly lace window coverings to the silk-fringed tablecloths. The little chamber was a sanctuary of comfort. For an instant, suspicion tapped at his conscience, and whispered that this lush little haven might be used as a hideaway for mercenaries.

"Come away," her soft, pleading voice said behind him. "I shouldn't have brought you here. It's against the rules—"

"Whose rules? Your father's or yours?"

"Both. Please. Come away before . . ."

He limped into the cottage, panting slightly, body breaking out in a sweat of growing discomfort. For an instant he tottered and grabbed for the back of a chair, tipping it, sending something—a book?—spilling to the floor.

Bronte gasped and rushed by him, falling to her knees as she grabbed for the littering of yellow paper clippings that had scattered over the floor. Brandon had seen enough scrapbooks to recognize one.

"Sorry," he said.

"You might try to be a little less clumsy, sir."

"Let me help."

Shoulders snapping erect, clutching a handful of brittle-looking papers to her bosom, she declared, "Absolutely not. You'll keep your hands and eyes to yourself, thank you very much. You've done quite enough already." She jammed the articles back into the well-worn, dusty book, collected the book against her, and climbed to her feet. She hurried across the room and shoved the book into the bottom drawer of a tiny desk. Only then did she turn back to face him. Her features were chalk white, her lips the color of ripe peaches. Her eyes were like onyx in the dim quarters.

"Relax," he told her in a quiet voice. "Believe me, Miss Haviland, I have no improper motives for coming here. I'm not in the habit of seducing virgins."

Her chin came up. Her mouth fell open slightly. And her eyes began to burn with their more recognizable fires.

He saw the truth—that this was as she had said, a private place. Even his presence unnerved her. He glanced around. "Very nice. I can understand your hesitance in bringing *anyone* here. Enchanting, to say the least. You want to keep its mystical qualities a secret."

Silence.

He ambled, limping, to the far window. Stretching out before him, beyond the break in the green brambles and stunted thorns, the river raged, crashing its way around upthrusting rocks and fallen tree dams. The dwindling sun, splashing upon the spray of water, painted a vibrant rainbow that rose up and over the distant treetops.

"Tell me, Miss Haviland, what do you do when you come here?"

He watched her reflection in the windowpane. She hadn't moved so much as an eyelid, her gaze riveted on him. Finally, she took a breath and appeared to hold it before replying. "I . . . daydream, mostly."

"Ah. A respectable pastime."

"Do you make light of me, sir?"

"Hardly. I did the same when at Salin Hall. That was my home. Where my mother resides. Only I

climbed into the attic. I always swore it was haunted."
He smiled at her reflection. She looked at her hands,
then removed her bonnet and toyed with the blue
satin ribbons and white daisy on the brim. "Do you
believe in ghosts, Miss Haviland?"

She shook her head and refused to look up. She
looked, he thought, like a child.

Finally, and without looking at him, she said,
"I've never brought anyone here before. Except my
father, of course. He used to come here with my
mother when they wanted to be alone. He won't
come here now because he says it holds too many
sad memories."

"He must have loved her very much."

"Yes. Very." She flashed him a glance and put on
her bonnet again. "We should go."

Turning from the window, Brandon rested back
on the sill, relieving the weight from his leg. "Could
I have a drink before we go?"

"I've not brought any fresh water recently. All
there is is . . ." She chewed her lower lip and still
would not meet his eyes. "There's brandy. I enjoy
an occasional tipple now and again, although most
polite life guides say it's improper for ladies."

"Brandy would be delightful."

"Only one, then we must return before someone
discovers we're gone."

Bronte dove into a drawer and dug beneath old
linens that released a flurry of moths into the air.
She waved them away nonchalantly as she turned
back toward a little shelf on which rested a pair of
teacups that matched the china at the big house. She
poured him a finger's depth, deliberated, then
splashed herself a portion in her own cup.

She carried his to him. He thanked her with a smile, his fingers brushing hers.

They sipped the potent liquor in silence while the river roared and the wood came alive with bird chatter. Finally, Bronte moved to the window and gazed out. Little by little, the brandy in her cup disappeared. Little by little, the obstinacy of her carriage began to relax. Almost languidly, she leaned her head against the window frame, briefly closed her eyes, and sighed.

"One cannot help but relax when coming here," she said, sounding sleepy. "My mother always swore that it was magical."

Brandon moved up beside her, careful to do nothing that would frighten her, break the mood of repose that had settled into each dimming corner of the little house. An oblique shaft of soft light found its way through the trees and filled her face with a glow that left him more than a little mesmerized.

Her hand slowly slid into her pocket and withdrew a clay figure—a very rudimentary likeness of an animal smeared in blue paint. She offered it to him.

"For you. From Sammy. It's a wombat. I might add that you should feel greatly honored. Sammy isn't one to reach out to just anyone. Seems you've become quite the hero to him. But then, I suppose you're accustomed to that."

"To war-mongering men and civilians who seem to think making war on others, and defeating them, is honorable."

"You don't?"

"No."

"But—"

"But I've devoted half of my life to the military? Men toy with war who haven't anything worthier to do with their lives than dying for questionable causes. For the most part, I never took pride in killing. I find it more honorable to stop the killing before it starts."

Her fine, dark brows knitted, and tilting her head to one side, she regarded him intensely. "And yet you're here, in this prison, for murdering a man."

He drank his brandy and continued to watch the river roil.

"Why did you do it?" her voice asked softly, yet urgently. "Why did you kill him?"

He looked at her—her eyes, her lips, the shallow, almost unnoticeable cleft in her chin, the tiny beauty mark at the corner of her mouth that he had not noticed before. Odd how the failing sunlight brought out even the tiniest perfections in her features.

Closing his fingers around the clay wombat, he put down the china teacup and moved away from Bronte, steadied himself on a chair, then limped to the door, hesitating, looking back briefly to find her silhouetted against the window, one hand poised on the sill as if she were willfully holding herself back. He considered telling her the truth—to discover if she was trustworthy. But all he said was "Coming, Miss Haviland?"

She put down her teacup and followed.

We are free to choose what course
we will pursue, and our bodies, our
brains, and our features readily adapt
themselves and clearly indicate the
lives we lead and the characters we form.

—*The Illustrated Manners Book*
ROBERT DE VALCOURT, 1855

CHAPTER TEN

BRONTE RAN DOWN THE LANE, TUMBLING HAIR AND BONNET
flying out behind her, while Sammy charged ahead
with his sister Pam close behind. Behind Bronte, the
church bells pealed while the congregation—of
nuns, children, expectant women, and new mothers, not to mention the convicts, who resented being
forced to attend church twice a week—spilled out
of the doors of the little chapel, hesitating as they
were struck by the midday sun.

Rounding the bend, Bronte paused, laughing,
bending double as she attempted to catch her
breath. Sammy raced toward the house, letting
loose a cry of pleasure as he saw Tremain sitting by
Bronte's father on the porch.

William left his chair and threw open his arms.
Sammy sailed by him and flung himself full tilt
onto Brandon, hugged him, and pressed kiss after
kiss on his bearded cheek. Pausing at the bottom
step, doing her best to catch her breath, Bronte

found herself imagining what Tremain would look like beneath the beard he had allowed to grow in the last weeks. Not that she didn't care for beards. She supposed it did his face justice. It certainly took nothing away from his appearance.

Nor did the cropped-off breeches he continued to wear. He had magnificent legs. Long and muscular and browned by the sun. His injury appeared cleaner every day. Soon he would return to the prison barracks, and work detail.

"Bronte." William tapped her shoulder. She looked around. "I'm afraid I've been called into Sydney. Seems there was trouble at the prison last evening."

"Nothing serious, I hope."

"An attempted escape. Foiled, however. Alas, I'm forced to fill out the necessary paperwork to send the man to Norfolk. Damned idiot. We learned he'd made plans to leave New South Wales with a free woman."

Bronte removed her hat and flung it into the chair her father had earlier occupied. She did not, however, look at Tremain.

There was no reason to.

Any more than there was a reason to experience the flutter of guilt and uneasiness she felt at the mention of the prisoner's involvement with a free woman.

"Forgive me, Pumpkin."

"It can't be helped." She offered her cheek for him to kiss. As he started down the steps, he hesitated and looked back.

"Arthur sends his regards and hopes to see you this week. What shall I tell him? Come, come, sweetheart, it's not as if he intends to go to his knee in marriage so quickly."

"Quickly? He's been interested in me for the last five years. Oh, very well, Father, if it'll please you. Tell him Wednesday night. We'll take dinner here."

"That's my lass." To Brandon, he said, "I'll have her married yet, Captain. Just you wait and see." Then he bounded off down the lane to fetch his driver and buggy.

Squirming on Brandon's lap, Sammy said, "Eww. I don't like Misser Ellison. You ain't gonna marry him, are ya, Bronte?"

Bronte grabbed the fidgeting lad and plunked him on his feet. "Do I look like a fortune-teller?" she asked him.

"You ought to marry Misser Tremain."

"Don't be ridiculous," she muttered under her breath, only then allowing her gaze to meet Brandon's amused eyes.

Losing interest in the topic, Sammy howled, "I want a picnic!" He leapt from the porch and into the flower bed. Pam popped her head up out of the flowers where she was playing and cried, "I want the bunny!"

Wang exited the house with basket in hand, and the children set up a squeal, jumping up and down and clapping. Sammy dashed up the steps and grabbed Bronte's hand, tugging hard, freckled face beaming with excitement. "I want to go to the river!"

"Me, too," Pam said to join in. Then they both set up a chant of "River! River!" until Bronte gave in with a laugh.

"The river it shall be, then. I'll race you."

The children spun and made for the road while Bronte replaced her bonnet. Then Sammy stopped abruptly, spun on his heels, raced again for the house, leapt the steps two at a time, and grabbed Brandon's hand. "You come, too," he panted.

"Sammy!" Bronte gently took the lad by his hand and attempted to pull him away, refusing to look at Tremain while her face turned into a slow burning heat. "That's impossible. Come away—"

"But I want him to come! Please!"

Bronte went to one knee and took his pink face in her hands. "Mr. Tremain's leg is frightfully sore—"

"I'm fit as a fiddle," Tremain informed her with a sleepy smile.

She glared at him before forcing her eyes back to Sammy's. "It's against Warden Haviland's rules, Sammy."

"What for?"

"Because Mr. Tremain is a . . . is a . . ."

"Pris'ner?"

"Yes! Yes, he is, and it's against the rules for a prisoner to associate socially with freemen. He could get into a great deal of trouble."

"Don't you like Misser Tremain?"

Her face grew hotter. Tremain watched her, she could feel it, as did Sammy and Wang, who waited at the bottom of the steps, the basket balanced on one shoulder. Only Wang gazed out over the flowers and pretended to be deaf.

"Sammy." Brushing the locks of red hair from his sweating forehead, Bronte smiled and struggled for some reasonable escape from the uncomfortable situation. Finally, she released her breath and shrugged.

"Of course I do. How could I not when he saved your life?"

"Then you'll let him come? I won't tell, I promise."

Bronte glanced at Wang.

"Neither will Wang," Sammy declared. "Will ya, Wang?"

The man flashed him a smile and winked.

"See." Sammy grinned.

"Well . . . we haven't asked Mr. Tremain whether he cares to join in our picnic. Perhaps he has something else he would rather do?"

He met her eyes with a lift of one eyebrow, acknowledging the query for what it was—an obvious invitation to turn their invitation down gracefully. To avoid a very problematical situation.

"I'd love to," he said.

Too busy chasing birds and annoying a platypus buried up to its bill in mud, the children barely touched their food. Wang chased after them.

Bronte, too, didn't have much of an appetite. She picked at the moist pink ham, poked at the baked apples, and fed the fresh bread to the birds.

Tremain, wearing nothing more than his cut-off trousers, lay back on the spread, his face to the sun, apparently sleeping. Bronte cast him a glance every so often—more often than she liked. In truth, she had trouble concentrating on the children at all.

She had never truly looked at a man's naked chest before, always choosing to avert her eyes as any decent Englishwoman should who was pure of mind and body.

There were a couple of minor scars here and

there, traces of war wounds, perhaps. And, as she had noted before, his skin, the color of old copper buffed to a dull shine, was tight, defining each rise and fall of his muscles. Her eyes took in each minute detail, from the coin-sized nipples to the tiny patch of dark hair swirling around his navel. The hair, she thought, was as dark as that on his head.

Oh, to touch that hair, as she had imagined doing a thousand times throughout the last years—when her empty hours were spent in the company of aging newspaper stories written by some fanciful writer who undoubtedly indulged in embellishing the truth, because he knew how desperately England worshipped valiancy. How pitiful had been the drawings in the brittle old newspapers! She had always imagined that the sketches of the handsome young hero, Captain Tremain, never could have done him justice.

And they hadn't.

Dare she?

Just a quick touch of his hair with her fingertips while he slept, just to discover whether or not it was as soft as it looked. Or as heavy. Or as thick.

What harm could come of it?

Who would know?

Why not satisfy her curiosity? Put the demon of fantasy to rest once and for all so she could return to her routine life, where all of her thoughts were occupied by the unselfish and Christian ideals of respectable women. Then, perhaps, she could rid herself of these absurd concerns—such as the smell of his body and the warmth and strength of his hands as they had embraced her those nights ago.

A touch.

A brush.

Light as air. Gentle as a breath.

A curl coiling around her fingertip. Springing with a life of its own between her fingers.

She closed her eyes and imagined, for a moment, that he awakened and found her with her fingers in his hair.

She imagined that she would not recoil and flee in humiliation and disgrace.

She imagined kissing him.

Oh God—to even imagine it.

Perhaps he should wake up—before she did something to totally humiliate herself.

She sighed.

So did he.

Frowning, chewing her lower lip, she leaned slightly toward him and whispered, "Are you awake, Mr. Tremain?"

"Yes," he whispered back.

Sitting upright, rigid all of sudden, Bronte grabbed for a slice of ham and tore it in two.

Brandon stretched and yawned, pushed himself up on one elbow, and looked at her sleepily.

"You're becoming a man of leisure, it seems," she told him. "I shouldn't get too accustomed to it."

"God forbid."

"I suspect Father will send you back to the barracks this week."

"Will you miss me?" He grinned.

"Certainly not." She licked ham juice from her finger. "Frankly, I'll be more than happy for things to return to normal."

"A direct hit."

She glanced at him from beneath her lashes. His eyes were bluer than the sky. They regarded her with an intensity that made her breathing run shallow. "What I mean is . . . my life has been so routine the last years, I find it difficult to go about my . . ."

"Routine."

"As I always have."

"I've always found routine to be quite boring."

"Routine is comfortable."

"But boring." Brandon sat up and eased his leg into a more comfortable position, which happened to be close enough to her that she could have touched him—had she wanted to. "I'll bet," he said, "that when you bring the children here on a picnic, you never join them in their games, never remove your shoes and wade with them in the river."

"I'm not a child any longer," Bronte pointed out. "I have a certain image I must maintain. As the warden's daughter I should exemplify the standards and morals which we are doing our best to teach the children."

"Why do I get the impression, then, that you don't always enjoy the role?"

"Don't be ridiculous. Of course I do."

"No, you don't, Miss Haviland. Lying here the last hour pretending to sleep, I've watched your face as they romped in the water. You would like nothing more than to join them. I even suspect that were the children not here, and you were certain of your privacy, you might have taken a plunge yourself."

Bronte said nothing, just reached for a slice of

cinnamon-coated apple, taking little mind of the thick juice that ran down her fingers as she nibbled the confection.

For a long while Brandon said nothing more, just regarded her as if she were some curiosity to be studied at length. Finally, he said, "I'll never forget the night I arrived at Haviland Farms and saw you dancing in the rocket fire. I couldn't believe my eyes, Miss Haviland, that you were the same woman I had met earlier in the day at the prison. I'm not certain I have ever witnessed a more breathtaking spectacle."

"I assume you mean the fireworks."

"Don't play coy, sweetheart."

She ran her tongue down the side of one finger, capturing the oozing drop of golden brown syrup before it dripped onto her skirt. A breeze fluttered with the brim of her hat.

"Take it off," he said in a startling, throaty voice. "The hat. And release your hair. Let it blow in the wind. And turn your face up to the sun as you've been dying to do since we arrived here."

"You're presumptuous, Mr. Tremain."

"And astute. I haven't stayed alive all these years without learning to understand the desires people keep hidden beneath their public facades. You might be surprised what you can learn by watching a person's body, and eyes. They can tell a man or woman's life history in a blink."

With no warning he reached for the bow at her jaw, gave it a quick flick, and flipped the bonnet from her head. Bronte gasped. She made a futile grab for the bonnet, lost her balance, and spilled across his lap.

She should have been outraged at him for his prank, appalled at herself for her clumsiness. Instead she laughed.

Scrambling upright, mentally tamping down the absurd desire to grin at his mischievousness, Bronte sat back on her heels and did her best to look angry.

Grinning, Brandon wagged the bonnet just beyond her reach. "Now the hair," he said. "Come, come, Miss Haviland, it's not as if I've never seen you with your hair down. Remember the night of the fireworks? And the night you came into my room wearing nothing more than a nightgown? Your hair was down then, and it was beautiful."

"Absolutely not."

"Very well, I'll make you a deal."

Setting her chin stubbornly, crossing her arms over her breasts, she focused her sights on the splashing children, and Wang, who laughed uproariously at their antics.

"Just talk to me," Tremain said softly. "Be my friend, Bronte."

She frowned, lowered her eyes, felt suddenly . . . depleted and shockingly close to tears. "I can't be your friend, Mr. Tremain."

"Since when are there laws against friendship? It's not as if I've asked you to marry me, you know."

"No, I suppose not."

"Simple concession," he said again.

Bronte opened and closed her mouth, the horrible realization occurring to her that she really had no earthly idea where to begin or what to say. "Odd," she said, more to herself than to him. "It's been so long since I've discussed anything but business with anyone but my father that I don't know how or where to begin. I was never one to dabble much with chitchat."

"I know your ideals regarding the children. What about the prison system?"

Bronte looked at him hard. "Forgive my hesitance, but I'm more accustomed to being told to keep my nose out of prison business. Very well." She took a deep breath. "I'm for educating the prisoners—requiring them to attend school at least two days a week. That way, they've an education, of sorts, to rely on once they're freemen again. However, convincing educators to come to New South Wales to instruct is another problem. Sydney has little to offer. Most of the businesses have shut down because shopkeepers felt they would strike it rich with gold. Most of the free immigrants who arrive head immediately for the hills. There are few farmers who are successful enough to afford the luxury of prison labor, therefore perpetuating the failure of their crops, not to mention the few languishing businesses."

"You don't like it here."

"It is not an unlikable country. Look about us, Mr. Tremain—the sky, the trees, the flowers, the wildlife . . . I sometimes imagine that this is how Eden must have appeared."

"But . . ."

With a deep sigh, Bronte plucked a white wildflower from the grass and held it up to her nose. She closed her eyes, concentrating on the sweet, tantalizing perfume of the petals.

"I wish I were as strong as my mother, and as capable of accepting these differences."

"She had your father's shoulder to lean on in times of weakness. You have no one. And correct me if I'm wrong, but from certain things your father has said, I imagine that your mother wasn't so concerned with living up to what others deemed respectable. She was a strong woman."

Twirling the flower back and forth between her fingers, Bronte smiled. "Mmm. And yet . . ." She raised one eyebrow and glanced at Brandon's watchful features. "When she and my father were alone," she said in a softly conspiratorial voice, "she seemed as helpless as a feather on the wind. As gentle. As delicate. His every wish was her command. She was as feminine as a dozen women put together. She told me once that he made her feel that way—like a woman."

"And what did you say?"

She giggled and tucked the flower behind her ear, watched as Wang and the children splashed their way around a bend in the river, their laughter growing dimmer then disappearing completely. Finally she realized they had returned to the house. Falling back on the blanket, her hands pillowing her head, she watched the white clouds scuttle across the azure sky.

Brandon rolled to his side beside her.

He watched her face.

And held his breath.

Little by little, as the sun kissed away the paleness of her face and the breeze teased an occasional curl of dark hair from its moorings of tortoiseshell combs, Bronte began to relax. Her long, dark lashes became lazy. Her lips grew mobile, easily smiling, though somewhat wistfully, as she drifted away on her magic carpet of memory.

She seemed, in that moment, a part of the encompassing nature. As easy with her surroundings as the brightly colored butterflies dancing from flower to flower. Her voice sounded almost dreamy when she spoke again—so softly he was forced to lower his head more closely to hear her amid the melodious songs of the birds.

"I was always envious of their relationship—my father and mother's. They were never truly happy unless they were together. I asked her once what it was like, falling in love."

She closed her eyes and remained silent a long while, her cheeks becoming rosy with sunlight. Her breasts rose and fell gently with each breath. Even as Brandon watched her, not daring to move, a pale yellow butterfly lit amid loose strands of her dark hair and pumped its transparent wings. He wished, in that moment, that he were an artist. He would capture her likeness on canvas, though not with oils. Too heavy and predictable. Watercolors would suit her. Light. Flowing. Merging and blending, easily altered with a change of her whims.

Earth child.

Oh yes, this country suited her—every wild, twisted, and vibrant flower and tree—whether she realized it or not.

"What did she say?" he asked.

"That I would know it when it happens. She said it's a little like being hit by a lightning bolt from the blue. You can't eat. Or sleep. Every minute it seems is occupied with thoughts of him, and you, and what it might be like to be together now, and maybe forever. You find yourself living in this daydream of what ifs:

"What if he feels the same?

"What if we were to get married?

"What if we were to have children together?

"What if there really were happily-ever-afters?

"Then, of course, you have all those confusing physical feelings you must deal with. That's the hard part, my mother explained. Dealing with those feelings . . ."

She rolled her face away from him, exposing her graceful profile. The sun winked off the pearl stud in her ear, and the butterfly took flight.

"Obviously, she was not a stranger to those feelings," she ventured, more to herself than to Brandon. Then more softly, "She called them the splendor." Bronte drifted with the tide of memories flowing through her mind. "Of course, all this is shockingly improper. Every book I've ever read advises against acting in such a free way."

Brandon said nothing.

Bronte looked at him again at last, drowsily, her body stretched and limp, the white dress hugging her in loose folds. "I suppose I should be ashamed for telling you all this."

"Are you?"

"I honestly don't know."

> Some people fall in love with the
> swiftness and force of an electric
> shock, while with others the process
> is so gradual that the fact is not
> discovered until some accident or
> emergency reveals it to the interior
> perception.
>
> —*Talks on Women's Topics*
> JENNIE JUNE, 1864

CHAPTER ELEVEN

BRONTE REFUSED HER DINNER, ALTHOUGH COOK HAD PRE-
pared a few of her favorites, somehow scrounging
up strawberries and rich fresh cream that he'd
whipped until frothy and piled in high little mounds
on top of the sweet fruit. And there was café au lait.
Bronte only managed to drink half a cup before she
shoved her tray away, allowing a white-and-gray
floppy-eared bunny named Sugar to snatch a straw-
berry and scurry under the bed with it. The large
charcoal-gray rabbit she called Dusty happily lapped
up the coffee then sprawled on her side and gazed up
at Bronte in contentment, nose wiggling and ears
drooping.

In months past this would have been a perfect
evening. Now restlessness tugged at her.

How very ironic that she had believed that an
outing where she acted according to whim and
shared confidences would expurgate the unsettling

disquietude that had plagued her the last many days.

If anything, the sentiments had grown worse. And what was worse: she liked them.

Moving to her dressing table, she eased down onto the chair and studied her shadowy reflection in the glass.

Who was this stranger with sun-browned cheeks and hair that more likely than not would feel the full force of the wind in it tomorrow? Oh yes, she had not bothered to wear her bonnet the last few days, conveniently forgetting to grab it as she dashed from the house and hurried to the school, conveniently forgetting even to anchor her hair with combs. With it blowing wild and free, she had felt like a youth again.

Tremain had said that day by the river that it was beautiful flowing loose.

Tremain. Thank God she hadn't seen him since Sunday. She felt totally abashed about her intimate revelations. She'd revealed too much of herself to him—perhaps too much to herself as well.

Heavens, what he must think of her shocking frankness. Her face warmed to recall it.

Still, she was beginning to feel like a prisoner herself—keeping to her room when she wasn't at the hospital or orphanage, venturing out only long enough to speak briefly to Wang or Murray, always keeping a wary eye on Tremain's door and the chair where his guard should have been but wasn't most of the time. That was because Tremain had wormed his way into the guard's favor—just as he had into everyone else's. More than once she'd been forced to summon Wang or Murray from Tremain's room,

where they had been playing cards, or listening
with interest to his gory tales of blood and glory on
the battlefield.

If that weren't enough, her father spent the hour
after dinner with Tremain, instead of her. Imagine!
For twenty-seven years William Haviland had set
aside that important hour of the day to spend with
her, and now he cloistered himself in his study with
Tremain while they discussed God only knew what.

"Well, you've only got yourself to blame," she
told her pouting reflection. "No one's forcing you to
hide in this room like a hermit."

She snatched up her brush and dragged it through
her hair.

"Impossible," she uttered and stared harder into
her eyes. "You're stronger than that, Bronte. You
simply allowed his charm—which he'd no doubt
used to seduce the female populace since he was
old enough to quit his knickers—to overwhelm
your good judgment, thereby leaving you vulnerable to the typical yet disquieting sentiments of any
ninny-minded female. Madam Tristan would not
approve."

Certainly Madam Tristan would not approve of
her hiding away in this room like a monk, keeping
company only with rabbits.

Taking a deep breath, Bronte left the chair and
took up her dressing gown, a flowing Matinee of
mull silk dyed *tilleul* and with ruches of soft white
lace about the wrists. She swept up Sugar and
cradled the violet-eyed rabbit close to her heart.

Upon leaving the room, Bronte tiptoed down the
dark hall, thinking to herself that should she come
upon Wang or Murray, she would simply request

them to bring a tray to her room—then she would beat a hasty retreat back to her monasterial existence and stay there until she could convince her father that it was time for Tremain to return to the barracks.

A light shone from under her father's office door. No doubt he was up again poring over the books—crediting this and debiting that—making certain his workers were being sufficiently rewarded for their laborious tasks by depositing their pay into each of their safe boxes—to be given to them at the end of the month, when they would be allowed to wagon into Sydney and waste it on rum and fallen women.

"By Jove, old man, have you no pity?" came an urgent voice from the room.

Father?

"Scoundrel! I should've known not to trust you." Had he dared . . . ?

Bronte burst into the room, slamming the door back against the wall with enough force to shake the windows.

William jumped to his feet. "Good God, girl, what the blazes are you about?"

Bronte glared at the back of Tremain's dark head, which was still bent over the chess board, not the least bit rattled by her unexpected entrance.

Sugar squirmed furiously in her arms.

Heat crept into her cheeks as she forced her eyes back to her father's. "I thought . . . I heard . . ." She sighed. "I do beg your pardon, Father. I didn't realize you had company."

William smiled. "That's quite all right, Pumpkin. Please, come and join us for a brandy. By golly, it's good to see you up and about again."

Her eyes went back to Tremain. He hadn't so much as moved, but continued to study his chess pieces as if he were Galileo contemplating the universe.

"I don't think so." She turned back for the door.

William hurried across the room and gently took her arm. "Please. For me. It's been a very long time since we've enjoyed a toddy together."

"You're busy. We'll talk tomorrow."

"Of course we will. About business." He ushered her and the panting rabbit toward his chair. "It has recently occurred to me that we spend far too little time in lighthearted banter."

Frowning, Bronte glanced up at her father's twinkling eyes. "Are you in your cups, sir?"

William laughed heartily and eased her down in the same comfortable leather chair in which he had bounced her on his knees years before—the very chair he had occupied before her entry, placed directly across the chess board from Tremain.

"Perhaps a bit," he replied, tossing a fringed knitted shawl across her lap. She tucked it around the rabbit. "Captain Tremain and I have been at this game a good while. I suppose we have indulged in a few more brandies than necessary."

As William hurried to fetch her snifter, Bronte stared down at the placement of rooks and pawns and knights and, once again, experienced the same discomposing changes in her mental and physical being as she always did when in Tremain's presence. Her face felt hot. Her spine grew rigid. Her fingers and toes curled inward until they ached.

Her father kept jabbering something in the background—some nonsense about how wonderful it had been of late to have a man as well educated and refined as the Captain to spend the evening hours with.

"Were you aware, Pumpkin, that Brandon grew up not far from Kent?"

Bronte stared down at the brandy her father offered her, refusing yet to raise her eyes for fear of meeting Tremain's—which probably weren't looking at her anyway. He obviously had chosen to ignore her presence completely. The unmitigated clod hadn't even stood when she entered the room.

William pulled up another chair and sat down between them. "He's one hell of a chess player, too, Bronte. I've always prided myself on being capable enough to defeat the best, but, by gosh, I haven't won a single game in the last three nights."

Bronte cleared her throat and raised the snifter to her lips. Speaking into the brandy, she said, "Perhaps Mr. Tremain would be wise to allow his warden to win occasionally."

"Hypothetically speaking," came Tremain's quiet response, "if I were playing you, would you like it if I allowed you to win?"

"Certainly not. But then, I don't control your fate, sir."

"You don't say. That's not the impression I've been given."

At last her angry eyes went to his, only to discover him gazing at her from beneath his long black lashes. The unexpected image affected her like a blow. Gone was the unkempt, unshaven miscreant. In his place postured a man with the elegance of a prince, the bearing of the well bred, and the perfect sculptured features of a god. Elbow resting on the chair arm, he propped his clean-shaven jaw in his open hand and rewarded her with a slow half tilt of a smile that made her lungs compress.

How at ease he appeared, as if he were a guest in her house instead of a prisoner. In truth, he looked like no felon who had ever passed through the doors of New South Wales Prison.

William, having poured himself another drink, relaxed back in his chair and savored the much cherished brandy, sniffing it, holding it to the light, rolling it slightly in the glass before turning it up to his mouth. "I suppose, of all the material things I miss about civilization, good conversation and fine liquor would top the list. Specifically brandy. By golly I do look forward to the new shipment. I'm down to my last bottle, you know."

Tremain lifted the tulip-shaped glass gently, balancing it between his second and third finger, while he continued to regard Bronte and her fidgeting rabbit with so lazy a look she wondered if he had heard her father at all.

"Do your shipments arrive directly from England?" he finally replied, shifting his knight diagonally two places.

"Occasionally. Mostly they come by way of Calcutta, as do most of our supplies."

"I suppose there's a great deal of rationing."

William shrugged and gulped at his drink more deeply than Bronte approved. She frowned and raised one eyebrow in a warning he obviously intended to ignore.

"Yes, yes," he responded. "Much rationing, I'm sorry to say. But mostly there's the little problem of taxes and tariffs on liquor and tobacco. No working man can afford the luxury of drinking or smoking. I'm fortunate, however, to be very close to the captain of the *Sirius*."

"Oh?" Tremain put his drink aside and sat back in his chair, at last centering his attention on Bronte's father instead of her. Thank God. Melting into her chair in relief, she gripped the rabbit in one hand, the snifter in another, and turned it up to her mouth while Tremain said to her father with a teasing smile, "Don't tell me you're into smuggling, Mr. Haviland."

"A bit, I must confess. I—"

"Father." Bronte cleared her throat and put aside her drink. "I fear it's getting dreadfully late."

"Poppycock. She treats me like I'm an old man, Captain Tremain. Or a child. I can't decide which."

"Perhaps she simply needs a child of her own." Tremain looked at her again, a slow smile stretching over his unabashedly handsome features.

"That would be very nice," William replied a bit wistfully, "if I could ever get her to settle on a man."

"Really, Father—"

"It isn't as if she hasn't had the offers, Captain. There are at least a dozen men working for me who have attempted to win her affections." William retreated his bishop and, in the process, captured one of Tremain's pawns. "But dash it all, she spends all her time at the hospital and school—not to mention pandering to those." He pointed to the rabbit in Bronte's lap.

Tremain held out one hand toward Bronte. "May I see her?"

She gripped the rabbit more tightly to her bosom.

"I wouldn't advise it. She doesn't fancy strangers. She is liable to bite your finger off, and then we'll be forced to extend your recuperation."

"I have a way with furry things. She won't bite. I promise."

Reluctantly, Bronte plopped the rabbit in the middle of the chess board, scattering pieces in all directions, bringing a groan from her father and little more than a lift of one eyebrow from Tremain. "She won't like you," she said, sounding like a belligerent child even to her own ears. "Rabbits are extremely loyal to their owners. Anyone else constitutes a threat and—"

The rabbit leapt into his lap and proceeded to climb up to his shoulder. Taking a deep swallow of the brandy, feeling it slither like a burning coal down the back of her throat, to explode in her chest, Bronte watched with tearing eyes as Sugar began to lick the lobe of Tremain's ear. Causing him to laugh.

She had never heard him laugh.

The sound flowed through her like warm treacle, making the effort of taking a breath feel impossibly difficult.

Bronte shoved herself up from her chair, leaned over the table, and grabbed the animal from Tremain's shoulder so suddenly the pet let out a frightened coo and flapped its huge back feet.

His shoulders still shaking, Tremain smiled up at her. "Thank God you saved me, Miss Haviland. I thought for certain the beast would tear my head off at any moment."

"You're contemptible, sir."

He laughed again.

Bronte marched for the door. Her father, finally

shocked out of his complacency, followed her into the hall.

"I was going to bring up the matter with you tomorrow," he began tentatively, "but I suppose tonight is as good a time as any. Pumpkin, if you agree, I think we should offer Tremain a position here at the house."

"He is already working—"

"I don't mean the farm in general terms, as it was before. I mean here. At the house."

Bronte didn't move. She didn't so much as blink.

"As you know, Cook's sentence is done tomorrow. He'll be free to leave. He's mentioned that he'll return to Wales."

"You're suggesting that he take Cook's place." She laughed disbelievingly. "Father, I doubt seriously if the man could boil water."

"The arrangement will only be temporary. Until I can bring in another cook. In the meantime, Brandon's leg can continue to mend properly. Besides, I stand by my conviction that he should be shown a certain amount of consideration considering his character."

Bronte looked hard into her father's eyes. "I fear you've been stricken with a case of hero worship, Father."

Her father stood there, saying nothing, then turned back to his study.

Brandon finished his brandy and set the snifter aside. Months had passed since he'd last spent such enjoyable evenings—civilized nights immersed in educated conversations in pleasant surroundings.

He might well be home in England—at Salin Hall, surrounded by the comfortable and familiar objects of his childhood, occupying the sunlit evenings of his long summer with his mother and sisters.

That, of course, was before the wars, the killing, the plaguing nightmares of dying faces and screams of pain. Another two glasses of brandy and he might manage to forget all that—forget why he was here and enjoy this odd camaraderie that had begun to build between himself and William Haviland. He might even indulge himself into further understanding of the by turns icy and passionate Miss Haviland.

Easing from his chair, he gave his stiff leg a moment to limber up, then he walked over to the desk laden with papers and the rough treasures crafted for Haviland by the children at the orphanage: kangaroo ashtrays, platypus paperweights, emu eggs smeared with blotches of different colored paints.

Picking up the brandy bottle, he held it up to the light. He knew fine brandy when he tasted it, and this was some of the best smuggled brandy he'd ever imbibed.

He put the bottle down. He scanned the desktop, one ear tuned to the distant mumbling of voices while his eyes searched for any clue that might prove that Haviland was involved in smuggling more than good brandy.

Mercenaries, for instance.

Frowning, he moved to the door. They were close by—no chance to investigate further.

But a sick feeling was beginning to squirm in his stomach. While he'd had every intention of moving back to the barracks, he was beginning to believe that the key to the mystery was in this house. The supplier of the cutthroats who would gladly mutiny against the country that had expelled them—the very real possibility existed that he had found him, or her, or them, right here under his nose.

How to be beautiful, and consequently
powerful, is a question of far greater
importance to the feminine mind than
predestination or any other abstract
subject. If women are to govern, control,
manage, influence, and retain the adoration
of husbands, fathers, brothers, lovers, or
even cousins, they must look their prettiest
at all times.

—*Polite Life and Etiquette*
AUTHOR UNKNOWN, 1891

CHAPTER TWELVE

"I CANNOT BEGIN TO TELL YOU HOW THRILLED I WAS TO
receive your invitation to dine, my dear Bronte. I
was beginning to quite despair . . . and now hope!"

Gazing out on the courtyard and the tidy stack of
new bricks placed near the fountain, which grew
closer to completion every day, Bronte pulled herself out of her notions long enough to focus on
Arthur's ramblings. "I suppose," she replied absently.

He moved up behind her. "I see progress is being
made on the fountain."

"Yes."

"Whoever is constructing it is doing a smashing
job. I suppose that would be Wang? Is there nothing
that man can not do?"

Bronte stepped from the parlor into the courtyard, careful not to trip on the discarded spade and
the barrow of mortar, which was beginning to harden
in the late evening sun. "I don't know," she finally

said. "I don't know who's working on the fountain. Yes, I suppose it might be Wang." Bronte nudged the spade with the toe of her shoe, then she looked up at Arthur where he remained by the door. To most he would have appeared quite dashing, actually, the picture of gentry, with his tailored coat and a green vest embroidered with tiny gold horseshoes.

But his image left her cold.

Moving into the yard, he said, "By Jove, but the dinner smells smashing. I assume your father's found a replacement for Cook?"

Bronte retreated from Arthur's closeness by backing to the wall, and somewhat clumsily into the bushes, scattering petals of hibiscus over her shoulders. She wondered how to easily break the news to Arthur that Tremain had taken control of the kitchen.

"I assume your father will be joining us soon," came Arthur's voice through her mental fog.

"No, actually. He's ridden to Sydney."

Looking somewhat bemused, Arthur glanced around the courtyard as if he were some lad contemplating stealing apples from an orchard. "You mean we're alone?"

"Well . . ." She moved around him and to the wrought-iron chair near the blooming mimosa lazily branching over the veranda wall. "There's the help, of course."

"I should think so. You know it's highly irregular for me to be here without a chaperon."

Bronte smiled and spread her skirt evenly over her slippers. "Relax, Arthur; I shan't take advantage of you, I promise."

"I'm only thinking of your reputation, Bronte."

"I shouldn't worry much over my reputation, sir. Need I remind you that we live on a continent made up of malefactors? I hardly believe these expatriots of respectability will write home and decry my breach of decorum, do you?"

"Ah, yes, my dear, but doesn't one strive not to lower one's standards to the substratum, by which one becomes as the plebeian himself, but to uplift oneself to the summit, thereby offering oneself as a fine example of that which is morally and ethically refined?"

Bronte drummed her fingers on the chair arm. "If you're uncomfortable, Arthur, you may leave."

He raised one eyebrow and shrugged. "Of course I'll remain. I wouldn't think of disappointing you."

Wang appeared then and announced dinner.

Arthur offered his arm. Reluctantly, Bronte accepted it.

Her mind felt dazed as they passed through the cool, shadowed corridors of the house. Her heart felt frantic. With any luck Wang would serve the dinner. With any luck this nausea she was experiencing would pass before she fell face-first into her food plate.

The table was exquisitely arranged. Her mother's best china glimmered under the flickering set of candles placed in the center of the table. The maroon velvet curtains had been drawn, giving the room a cozy, rose-lit atmosphere.

But it was the image of Tremain standing in the half shadows near the kitchen door that caught and held her eye—that and his one-sided smile, which turned his partially lit face into that of a satyr's.

Apparently he was far more prepared for this than she.

Arthur stopped abruptly. "Good God, what is he doing here?"

"Didn't she tell you?" Tremain replied, still smiling.

"Tell me what?"

"That her father has hired me as cook."

Bronte looked askance at Arthur. He glowered down his nose at her. "I beg his pardon?" he said.

"Really, Arthur, there's nothing to be concerned about." She moved into the room, focusing straight ahead and not on the fact that both Arthur and Tremain had hurried at once to seat her properly.

"Take your hands off of her chair this moment," Arthur snapped at Tremain. "And I do beg to differ. The whole idea isn't seemly. Besides, what the devil would he know about cooking?"

Indeed, she thought. Indeed, she prayed.

God, what had she been thinking to allow such a debacle?

Arthur dropped into his chair with a grunt, mouth twisted as he watched Tremain snap his fingers, summoning Murray from the kitchen. The stout Scotsman pushed a cart loaded with silver chafing dishes into the room.

Whipping Bronte's napkin from the table, Brandon slung it over the back of one hand and offered it to her. For a moment, Bronte stared at it—or rather his hand beneath it: the crisply starched shirt cuff hugging his wrist and the fine black hairs sprinkled over the backs of his beautifully tapered fingers. She was aware that he was leaning closely enough that she could smell the clear scent of sandalwood on his skin. Had she chosen to lift her hand, she could have easily touched his cheek, which looked incredibly smooth, and close. Clearly it had been a mistake to invite Arthur to distract her thoughts— she was already distracted.

"Bronte!"

Swiftly, she looked back to Arthur.

"I was just informing your domestic that the room is entirely too dark. In fact, this atmosphere isn't appropriate at all."

"No?" She glanced about the room, thinking she had not seen it look so lovely. But before she could say another word, Arthur left his chair, snuffed the candles with his thumb and forefinger, then snatched open the curtains, allowing the last streaks of the meager daylight to brighten the chamber. Then he turned on Tremain.

"Light those sconces on the wall. And those lamps there as well. For the love of all saints, man, one should have adequate illumination to eat, else the digestion is severely impaired."

"Why?" Tremain retorted somewhat sarcastically. "The stomach can't see what it's doing?"

Bronte giggled behind her napkin. Arthur's head spun around with a snap.

Silently Brandon lit the sconces, then the lamps, opened all the curtains, and without another word, or a glance her way, began to serve the food, starting with champagne.

"Champagne?" she whispered, more to herself than to Tremain as he poured the effervescent, golden wine into the goblets.

He glanced down at her and smiled. "Another of your father's little treasures, I assume."

She knew what he meant.

Few times had she ever witnessed such a beautifully prepared display of food. The oysters were followed by a spicy brown soup and sherry. Next came fish with Chablis. There followed an entrée of asparagus, then a slice of succulent pink roast served with claret. Next came a dessert so rich and creamy Bronte's mouth watered just to smell it.

But, as she had the entire meal, she took no more than a bite before she put aside her spoon and sat back in her chair, watching as Arthur stabbed his meat or fish, as if it were still alive, and grumbled about the richness of the sauces and the decadence with which it had been presented. She wasn't certain what put her off her food more: the fact that she was sitting here watching Arthur make a fool of himself, and her, or the fact that Tremain continued to stand at the door, a strong shoulder leaning against the frame, arms crossed over his chest, regarding her as if she were some unusual museum piece.

Occasionally she allowed her eyes to raise to his. The mere sight of him, standing there in the pitiful light of the gasping oil lamps, dressed in a pair of her father's nicest trousers and white shirt, made her feel so . . . odd.

So discomfited.

Unsettled.

It had begun with the first whiff of the sandalwood cologne (borrowed, too, no doubt). Then sometime between the bluefish and the Filet de

Boeuf aux Champignons she had recalled how beautiful he had looked lying in the sunlight, and she remembered how very hard his muscles had been and how smooth his skin. As the evening progressed and the night breeze grew and fluttered the curtains and the lamp flames, she might well have been back at the river, Tremain at her side, coaxing her to admit thoughts and feelings that continued to bother her today. The feelings inside her were the same.

Or perhaps it was simply the champagne. Or the sherry. Maybe the Chablis. She couldn't remember a time when she had felt so garrulous. Even Arthur's trite babblings became less bothersome. Occasionally she laughed—mostly when he hadn't made a joke. By the end of the evening he had become more than a little annoyed.

"I sincerely despise the idea of leaving you so early," he said as they stood on the front porch at the top of the steps. Running his fingers round and round his hat brim, he frowned and shifted his weight back and forth. "But my continued presence isn't proper with your father away from home. Although I can not like you being alone with that convict."

"You've never been concerned about my living in such close contact with Wang or Murray."

"Yes, well, they aren't exactly Tremain, are they?"

Bronte leaned back against the porch balustrade and turned her face into the breeze. The cicadas had begun their nightly serenade, though it was early yet. The Aborigines would say that the premature whirring of the insect wings predicted rain within the next twenty-four hours. Rain, she thought, would be nice.

"Good night, Bronte," Arthur said wearily.

Bronte turned her face toward his, which was little more than a silhouette with the light from the doorway at this back. She could not see his eyes, but she could see the figure of Brandon Tremain standing in the open threshold, leaning there in a proprietary manner.

Later, she would question her sanity for doing what she did—offering her lips to Arthur to kiss. But he merely kissed her cheek. "Good night, Bronte," he repeated, and pressed his mouth chastely to her cheek again. "I'll see you tomorrow."

Without so much as a glance back at the house, Arthur descended the steps and climbed aboard his carriage. Bronte watched until it disappeared into the dark.

"He's an idiot," Tremain finally said.

Bronte wrapped one arm around the porch post and leaned her head against it. The champagne swam behind her eyes.

Tremain moved up behind her and stood not two feet from her—so close she could smell the cologne, now a mélange with the musky scent of his skin.

"Any man who would turn down the opportunity to kiss a beautiful woman on a beautiful night like this has to be out of his mind. No soldier would. Especially when her lips are likely to taste like champagne."

"Your manners, sir. Arthur is merely a gentleman." But her words held no conviction.

He laughed.

She swung partially around to face him. He

seemed much bigger in the dark. Far more intimidating and threatening. He didn't look so much like a prince now, but a pirate—and she had seen plenty of them come and go up and down the river in their skiffs.

"Well?" He propped one big hand on the balustrade.

"My feelings for Arthur are none of your affair, Mr. Tremain."

"I beg to differ. You realize that there is a Chinese custom: when one saves the life of another, the one saved becomes the slave of the one who saved him. Since you saved my life the night Arthur came barreling into my room with an eye for blood, you are my concern."

"Sounds like a lot of foolishness."

He flashed her a white smile and looked off across the lawn, where Hiawatha strutted in the rising moonlight. "There's also another old Chinese saying: kiss a man in the moonlight in the presence of a peacock and you'll bear his child within the year."

She should have been shocked at the impropriety. But looking into his dark face, she took a moment before merely responding, "Liar."

"Seems you'll have to wait another year to have Arthur's baby. What a shame."

She laughed a little and gazed out at Hiawatha, watched as the bird fanned its tail so its scarlet and purple plumage flashed like brief fire in the moonlight.

"So tell me, Princess, aren't you the least bit disappointed that he didn't take the bait?"

"I don't know what you mean."

"Hmm," he said, and propped his shoulder against a pole. "I thought we were friends. Don't friends share secrets?"

Bronte waded into the flowers lining the brick path. Even in the dimness of the moonlight he could tell her color was high, but not so much from anger, as he might have suspected, but from ardor that, in another woman, might have passed for passion. At last, she looked up at him and moistened her lips with her tongue. "I don't think so. After all, we hardly know one another. I suspect friends are those people you've known for years. With whom you've shared life's experiences—the good and bad—secrets, too—a great many secrets." She looked thoughtful. "I suspect that, once, you might have had many friends."

"Not so many."

She tipped her head slightly. The champagne and moonlight caught fire in her eyes. He thought of the miniature in his room, the one of her reposing in flowers, and realized that whoever had painted the likeness had looked upon her in such a way as Brandon was that very moment, with her vulnerability revealed in her magnificent eyes. "And what about you?" he finally said. "Have you many friends, Miss Haviland?"

Lowering her lashes, she brushed the tops of the flowers with her fingertips before replying softly, "No." A tight smile flickered across her mouth. "How could I, living here? There were no other young ladies . . . no tea parties . . . no soirees . . . no giggling gossip sessions . . . So I made friends with the animals. And the children." She moved through the flowers, careful not to trod on them, until she stopped at the foot of the steps and looked up at him, her face in a dim halo of moonlight. "The women, few as they are . . . come and go. Nothing is constant. Nothing is secure. Nothing . . . is safe."

Brandon gripped the balustrade. For several moments they stood, he at the top of the steps looking down into her swimming eyes, she gazing up at him with her truth and pain revealed. The thought occurred to him that if he were to reach out for her in that instant, he would meet with no resistance. For a few hurtling moments he considered it—he wanted to, desperately, more desperately in that instant than he wanted to avenge the death of his men.

At last, her hand resting on the balustrade, she said, "The dinner was very nice."

"How would you know? You didn't eat any of it."

"What a shame. I'm starving now."

"Ah, well . . ." He moved down the steps toward her, watching as she backed away through the bobbing sunflowers—until her better judgment took over and she planted her heels and lifted her chin in a form of challenge, or perhaps surrender.

Gently, slowly, like one outstretching a hand toward a fawn on the verge of fleeing, he reached for her wrist, and eased his fingers around it.

He felt her quiver. Yet she did not bolt. With her lashes veiling her eyes, she hesitantly allowed him to usher her back toward the house, catching his breath slightly as he attempted to maneuver up the steep steps on his sore leg.

"Careful," she reminded him softly, forgetting

momentarily her hesitance in allowing him near her. Then her arm slid around his waist, offering him support.

Her hair, coiled in a braid on the back of her head, smelled faintly of lavender, as did her body, which was soft and fragrant against him. As she bent her head to watch carefully each step he took, her pale nape was exposed, and the downy curls that had escaped the braid. The skin behind her ear looked smooth and slightly moist.

"You mustn't overtax yourself too soon," she told him as they reached the porch landing, just before she slid away like some wisp of smoke and hurried into the house, forcing him to rush the best he was capable to catch her before she escaped again to her room.

Murray had cleared the table of the old dinnerware and—somewhat shockingly—replaced it with fresh. Once having seen Bronte seated, Brandon then reset the candles and dropped the curtains.

"What are you doing?" she asked, her voice tenuous and suddenly suspicious.

"My dear Miss Haviland, I'm going to show you exactly what it's like to be courted by a man who finds you thoroughly entrancing."

"Sir, you aren't suggesting that you—"

"Certainly not, *chérie*. But the next time you go looking for a husband, at least you'll have a vague idea what to expect."

"I never intended to marry Arthur Ellison," she responded. "And I don't understand any of this. Why the table is set again . . ." Her voice trailed off.

"No?"

"Well . . . perhaps . . . I don't know." She sank back into her chair and eyed her empty champagne glass wistfully. Brandon refilled it, and another.

Holding his up to her, he said, "A toast."

Bronte looked surprised. Somewhat hesitantly, she picked up her glass and held it up to his.

"To Saint Bronte," he said softly. "For showing me a little piece of heaven in this hell."

They ate in silence, Brandon at one end of the table, Bronte at the other, with only candlelight to brighten the darkness between them.

She ate as if she were enraptured—with her eyes closed, resting her head back against the chair between mouthfuls, occasionally making little sounds of approval in her throat. When the last bit of custard had been eaten, she put her spoon aside and sighed. "Marvelous. How did you learn to cook like this?"

Brandon relaxed back in his chair, swirling champagne in his glass, enjoying the look of total freedom from strain on Bronte's features. "A requirement of being a soldier. When I was growing up as the only boy with two sisters, at Salin Hall, I never ventured near the kitchen."

"The papers never mentioned—I mean, I didn't realize you had sisters." She looked at him, surprised. "It must have been wonderful having such a large family."

Brandon smiled. "Yes, it was. My sisters, Clarissa and Emily, were my best friends growing up—as was my mother. I suppose because she was little more than a child herself."

"Then she was a young bride?"

"Sixteen when she wed. Eighteen when I was born."

"And your father?"

Brandon held his glass up to the candle and watched the light splinter into rainbow prisms within the champagne. "My father is American. They've lived apart. I was always the man of the family."

"But you were raised in England." She recalled the papers boasting of his roots.

"Not until I was eleven. Until then I was forced to remain in America. Harrison Tremain felt a man's son should learn from his father's example."

"How very sad."

"Infuriating. I ran away. That was while my father was off on a trip. Before he returned home, I went down to the docks and stowed away on a freighter bound for England."

"So you were brave even then."

"No." He smiled. "Simply terrified of dying unloved."

She lowered her eyes. "Certainly, you haven't confronted that problem since you've been grown. There have been all sorts of women in your life who must have loved you. Or so the papers speculated. I understand there was a very special young woman in Meerut."

He watched her fingertip lightly trace the rim of her champagne glass while her eyes continued to search his face for answers.

"Her name was Vishnue," she added quietly.

Another woman might have demurred in her attempt to broach the subject that once had been a source of intense speculation among the populace of England's most refined tongue-waggers. Not she. No downcast eyes. No hint of teasing scandal tingeing the comment.

Only genuine interest. Her eyes—so wide and somber and direct, revealing a new dimension of herself—were an arrow of profoundness that stabbed him in his heart.

A long silence hung between them while he mentally debated whether to avoid the topic of Vishnue—as he had continued to do the last year and a half, since the moment she died in his arms.

"Yes," he heard himself reply. "Her name was Vishnue."

"And you were to be married. I assume you didn't . . . ?"

"She was killed before we could be married."

Her smile died.

Brandon took a last, long drink of his champagne then put down his glass. "Please. Expend no sympathy for either of us. Simply put, I learned too late exactly who and what she was."

"And that was?"

"The enemy. She used our relationship to gather information about our military and their families. She betrayed me."

The champagne bottle was empty, so he refilled his glass with sherry. The normally sweet, mellow drink seemed tasteless, however, which didn't surprise him. His body grew numb when he allowed himself to dwell on those horrifying days and nights of the mutiny.

"There was an uprising. Vishnue had acquainted Nana Sahib, a local Peshwa's adopted son, and his cohorts with the minute-by-minute routine of the British families in Meerut, as well as my own garrison, among others. While most of the regiment

attended a party bestowing another honor on me,
my garrison was being swept upon by butchers.
Men, women, and children were dragged from
their homes and massacred." He swallowed, yet
found himself unable to look away from Bronte's
eyes. "All were my friends. Many as close as
family."

He refilled his glass with the last drab of sherry,
then concentrated hard to keep his hand steady
when he raised the drink to his lips. "I should have
known," he began, then quaffed the entire snifter of
drink. "She was too curious. Too eager to turn her
back on her own traditions. All the signs were there;
I just chose to ignore them because I was too bloody
enamored of her . . . too reckless." A slow smile
crossed his mouth as he sat forward and propped
his forearms on the table. "I executed her."

At last Bronte's gaze wavered, just a subtle
lowering of her lashes before she focused again on
his eyes. Her color slightly paled.

"Then I received a letter from Nana Sahib explaining Vishnue's role in the treachery. She included her own note saying she'd never be back.

"After that I formulated my plan. I took a gun
with a single bullet and returned to Sahib's palace.
I knew the grounds well, since I had been there as
his guest so many times. I hid in a hedge for two
days, until Vishnue left the house. Then I followed
her. A young soldier was killed by mistake."

The room grew silent, and hot, and still.

Murray quietly moved up to the table and put a
new bottle of sherry next to Brandon's empty glass,
then he exited the room as soundlessly as he had
come. Brandon stared down at the decanter a long
while before sitting back in his chair.

"To answer your question, Miss Haviland—yes, there have been women in my life. Many of them. But they loved what I was, not who I was. There's a difference. Take you, for instance."

Her head came up, and her fingers tightened upon the stem of her glass. Obviously she had not been prepared for this sudden and drastic change of topic back to herself—the slight twist of her beautiful mouth still carried a hint of concern; her wide eyes reflected a wealth of distress.

"You wanted me to fit your version of what a hero should be. But the truth of most heroics is a very ugly truth. And sometimes a criminal has an honest hankering for justice in his heart. But I have upset you. I am sorry. Very sorry."

Their eyes held a long moment, before she turned up her glass and finished her sherry. She appeared to lose her breath briefly, as the liquor hit her stomach. Her fingers were trembling as she unsteadily placed the snifter aside and pushed back her chair.

Brandon stood.

"Please don't bother," she said. "It's just that I'm feeling very tired suddenly. Perhaps I should—"

"I'll see you to your room."

"No! That . . . that won't be necessary, Mr. Tremain." Bumping into the chair, Bronte did her best to maneuver her way toward the door. Brandon moved up behind her, caught her arm gently in his fingers, and held her firmly and decidedly as they moved down the dark corridor toward her room, Bronte struggling in her attempt to escape. Yet his fingers were unyielding, and realizing that she could not free herself gracefully, she finally allowed her arm to go slack.

At the threshold to her room, he shoved open the door, spilling light into the hallway, along with the overwhelmingly feminine scent of toilet water and dry lavender potpourri. Her bed, he noted, was a plush refuge of down comforters and immense white pillows covered in crisp ecru lace.

He brought his eyes back to hers, which were wide and watchful, a look of uncertainty. Still, despite her obvious inexperience with men, this was no vaporish miss who intended to fall into a swoon with the mere thought of a man breaching the sanctity of her bedroom. If anything, her look challenged him.

"I apologize if I upset you. I suppose the mutiny doesn't make for pleasant dinner conversation. I really don't know why I told you. Doesn't do much good to dwell on the past, does it? Except to open the door to all the old pain."

"I understand," she said, and put a gentle hand on his arm.

Her fingers felt warm through his shirt; only then did he realize that, despite the intense heat of the night, his body, even to the marrow of his bones, felt cold as death.

"I understand," she repeated as if he had not heard her.

"Do you?" He smiled and released her arm. "Good night, then."

She did nothing for a moment, and the moment seemed to stretch out interminably as, little by little, her face grew hot with color and . . . something else.

Stepping back into the room, she closed the door between them.

He put his hands on the door, then his forehead, and closed his eyes.

He wanted to call her back and kiss her. He wanted to feel pure again. Accepted. Welcomed. He wanted to coax her into her delicious bed with its ecru lace pillows. He wanted to intoxicate himself with the smell and taste of her body—those lips that must taste of champagne—and forget there was ugliness in the world and in himself.

Bronte Haviland had only good intentions, but she was beginning to feel a little desperate. Unmarried. Unloved. And despairingly lonely. Her life alone was beginning to stretch out before her like a yawning chasm of emptiness. There would come a time in the not too distant future when martyring herself for prisoners and orphans would not be enough. She was as well intentioned as he himself. Only she went about her crusade with love, patience, and understanding . . . while he chose guns and killing. He could learn something from her . . . if he allowed himself.

Silence echoed from the other side of the door as Brandon continued to stand there, paralyzed by his infuriating desire to kick open the barrier and assuage the damnable hunger for her that had begun the night she secretly stood by his bedside, her hair loose, her slender body clad only in a semi-transparent nightgown.

But involvement was impossible, of course.

He had a mission to accomplish.

Vengeance to seek.

She might well be the enemy.

* * *

Brandon didn't bother to set flame to the only lamp in his room, but eased closed the door and walked to the bed, dropping onto it with a groan. He felt drained, bothered, and battered.

"Keeping rather late hours these nights, aren't we, old man?"

Raising his head, he stared toward the voice coming from the corner of the room. He could just make out the form of a man in the darkness. "For God's sake. Don't you know how to knock?"

"My, aren't we testy?"

"Go to hell." He ran one hand through his hair.

"Did you enjoy your meal with Miss Haviland?"

"Quite."

"I wasn't aware you were such a connoisseur of fine wine and food."

"We old warriors have to do something to occupy ourselves in the trenches. Beans and hardtack grow a little wearisome after a few years."

"Gracious, but you're sounding a little bitter this evening."

Brandon rolled and buried his face in his pillow. "Just where the hell have you been all these long days while I've been practically dying from injuries?"

Soft laughter. "Asking questions and getting few answers, I'm afraid. How is your leg, Captain?"

"Mending."

"Really, you should try to refrain from your heroic, if not somewhat stupid, tendencies to save the world from its occasional bumps and bruises."

"Are you telling me I should have allowed the boy to fall off that ridgepole and break his neck?"

"I'm simply suggesting you try a bit of caution. Remember who you are supposed to be, and why you are here."

"Tell me something . . . sir."

"Yes, Captain?"

"Are you an example of what happens to loyal officers when they sacrifice most of their lives for the Crown? In short, am I in danger of turning into a coldhearted bastard with no conscience?"

Silence.

"Well?" Brandon said.

"Yes . . . I suppose you are."

Brandon groaned into his pillow. "What the blazes do you want with me tonight?"

"Simply to know that you haven't forgotten your mission."

"Every day that I'm in this hellhole I remember."

"I hardly consider residing in this more than comfortable abode onerous. Unless you reckon spending an evening with a woman as beautiful as Miss Haviland as vexatious."

Brandon sighed wearily. Tomorrow he'd wish like the devil that he hadn't imbibed so freely Haviland's smuggled champagne. Tonight, however, he simply wanted oblivion to banish the unwelcome memories that he'd allowed to surface tonight.

"If I thought you were somehow making progress in learning about our smuggled mercenaries, then perhaps I wouldn't feel quite so nervous. *Are* you making progress, Captain?"

He thought of the mostly empty crates of contra-band liquor he'd discovered buried in the outbuildings. He recalled the way Bronte had efficiently diverted her father's admission of smuggling . . .

"Captain?"

"No," he lied. "Not yet."

"Then I would suggest that you try your best to assuage these bachelor tendencies to seduce Miss Haviland and get focused on the reason why you are here in the first place. You do wish to avoid another mutiny, do you not?"

Growing angry, Brandon rolled from the bed and moved to the window. No light shone from Bronte's room.

"Captain, you're not withholding information, are you?"

"Withholding?"

"We all know what happens to those who suddenly decline to follow orders. The affair can get somewhat messy, I'm sorry to say."

Brandon sensed, rather than heard, his companion move up behind him. He could have turned in that moment and discovered the identity of his contact—but that was against orders as well. Maintaining secrecy was the most assured means of avoiding the possibility of detection—for all concerned.

"I'll remind you that you volunteered for this mission, Captain."

"Thank you."

"Are you certain that by remaining here, working in the house, you'll learn more—"

"Yes."

"And there is the matter of time . . ."

"Yes! Yes! Yes, damn you. Now, leave me alone!"

Silence, then: "Very well. Pleasant dreams, Captain."

Brandon waited a moment before turning to discover the room empty. Right, he thought. Pleasant dreams.

It should be remembered, that the same means which were used to gain affection, are absolutely necessary to preserve it; and I think an indelicate behavior and gross familiarity, if they do not alienate affection, never fail to quench desire . . .

— *The Lover's Instructor: Or The Whole Art of Courtship Rendered Plain and Easy*
AUTHOR UNKNOWN, 1809

CHAPTER THIRTEEN

HER FATHER FROWNED AT BRONTE, LOOKING SLIGHTLY befuddled.

"A companion?" he said. "But, Bronte, you know the rules about allowing women prisoners to participate in the leave program. It's simply not allowed. Bringing a woman onto the premises will throw open the door to all sorts of problems." His voice trailed off.

"She would be a free woman, of course," Bronte stressed as she stood on the threshold of the bedroom piled high with sheet-draped furnishings and trunks of clothes and much cherished objects that had once belonged to her mother.

William glanced about the dusty room, but did not enter. The room reflected a decidedly feminine air, peppered with Bronte's love of horses. On each wall hung glass-framed paintings of magnificent hunters, including Cytduction's dam.

He looked thoughtful. "I suppose a companion is

not beyond the realm of reason," he said. "And in light of how frequently I'm away these days . . ." He almost chuckled. "Arthur would be much relieved."

"I'm not doing this for Arthur's peace of mind, Father."

"Oh?"

Bronte toed the fringed edge of the Persian carpet on the floor. "Only, the idea occurred to me last evening, while Arthur was here and you weren't, that a companion might be appropriate . . . if Arthur intends to press his suit. After all, if we lived in England, I would have one . . ."

William regarded her contemplatively. "By the tone of your voice, I gather you're not altogether certain that you would welcome Arthur's suit."

Bronte shrugged.

"I'll look into it." William turned from the room. "I'll send Tremain to help you with the room, since you seem determined to have it ready in advance."

"That won't be necessary." Bronte hurried after him, hesitating at the open doorway.

"Nonsense. The furniture will need moving and cleaning—"

"I'll get Murray."

"He's riding into Sydney for supplies."

"Then Wang—"

"Has ridden into Parramatta to escort Charles Metcalfe to the farm."

As William disappeared into his office, Bronte said loudly, "Charles Metcalfe is coming here?"

"Seems your letter to Pilot Crenshaw has caught the mayor's attention. Received an urgent missive suggesting that we get together as soon as possible.

I invited him here to dinner." Reappearing in the doorway of his office, William looked down the hall at Bronte and said firmly, "So the Captain will have to do. Really, Bronte, you must try harder to keep an open outlook. He's done an exceptional job these last days—above his responsibilities to help. He's even done a smashing job finishing up that old fountain you fancied."

"He did that?"

"Among a great many other things. In any event, I must be off. I'm late for a meeting at the prison."

"But my companion!" she called, feeling ridiculously anxious at the thought of spending another candlelit dinner—alone—with Brandon Tremain. It wasn't proper, after all. If she found herself alone with him again, she might be forced to acknowledge the unnerving sensations his company had aroused the night before. And *that* would never do!

Hesitating, her father looked back, frowned and shook his head. "I fear employing a girl at this time just wouldn't be practical, Pumpkin. Perhaps later? In a few weeks? Wouldn't hurt to tidy up the room anyway. Just in case."

Bronte watched her father exit the house, slamming the door behind him. However, she had no more than turned back to the room when William reopened the door and poked his head in. "By the way, Lord and Lady Fish will be coming to dinner as well. Inform our new cook."

The room was a far greater task to clean than Bronte had anticipated. Dust lay thick over everything—in each tiny nook and cranny, the baseboards, the windowsills. Trunks were stacked high in each corner, treasure chests of memories.

Frowning, she flung open the lid of a particularly big trunk. "Oh," she gasped softly, and, very gently, she buried her hands in the layers of vapor-thin materials, releasing the scents of lavender and rose sachets buried within the folds of the diaphanous garments. The whispery lingerie poured like air through her fingers.

"Very pretty," Tremain said behind her.

Bronte felt her cheeks grow warm—then warmer still as he knelt behind her and peered over her shoulder into the trunk. She could feel his breath on the back of her neck.

"Your father had exquisite taste," he said quietly.

"My father?" Allowing the silky chemise to fall into her lap, Bronte reached for another in the trunk.

"Of course, your father. One can always tell the garments a man has purchased for the woman he loves, and desires."

"Oh?" Bronte attempted to laugh. She couldn't. This was a highly irregular meeting, and yet little by little her body was turning again into that low flame of unsettlement. His breath burned her and rattled what little composure she had maintained the last two hours of being confined in the room with him.

"Certainly," he said, kneeling down beside her. "A man enjoys being teased a little: a ribbon here, a ruche there, strategically placed, of course. Nothing appeals to a man more than the illusion of innocence."

"I can not imagine—" She tried to sound indignant.

"All men have the same hungers and desires. Some of us are just better at hiding it, *chérie*."

Bronte watched his big, dark hands gently lift a gown from the trunk and raise it up against her, so a blue satin ribbon nestled against the base of her throat. Very slowly, she lifted her eyes up to his.

"Beautiful," his lips said, and gently smiled. "Although it isn't white. But then perhaps white won't always be suitable—or appropriate?"

Her heart turned over in her chest—or so it seemed as she stared up into his exquisite face, which, without the masking of night's shadows, showed the evidence of his past tragedies: subtle lines carved into his sun-darkened skin, between his blacker than black eyebrows and the corners of his blue eyes, around his mouth. Odd that she had not noticed them before, these vestiges of character— the mementos of his life's laughter and pain. Then again, she had never been this close—so very close. Close enough that, if she lifted her mouth, she could kiss him.

She closed her eyes, meaning to subdue the temptation. But then she lifted her mouth and kissed him.

Lightly. She knew no other way.

Briefly. But then she squeezed her eyes shut even tighter. The roaring in her head drowned out all rational thought. She felt abashed. And breathless. And undone. She suddenly longed to crawl into the trunk with her mother's memories and close the lid behind her. Even before her lips left his, her better judgment screamed its recriminations.

She had kissed a man!

And not just any man.

Dear God, she had kissed a man. Not the other way around.

"Bronte." He touched her face with his hand. "Bronte," he said softly. "Open your eyes."

She could not, and averted her head and looked around at the door, her thoughts on escape.

Taking her face gently in both hands, he forced her to look into his deep blue eyes. She felt the strength of his fingers against the heat of her skin. Now he would taunt her. Perhaps ridicule her for succumbing to a girlish temptation—at the ripe age of twenty-seven. And for endangering his well-being, not to mention hers. "I'm sorry," she said to his eyes.

"I'm not."

"I don't know what came over me."

"I'm glad it did."

"I feel so foolish. That wasn't proper of me at all. It was silly, really. If we had been caught—"

He smiled. "Some risks are worth the consequences."

"I . . ."

"Please don't apologize. If you do, I might have to wonder if you enjoyed it. I would hate to think you didn't."

She swallowed and lowered her eyes. Her gaze drifted down to his mouth. Strange that she had never noticed before how fascinating his lips were.

"If you care to do it again, I would be honored."

"No. I . . ." She tried to breathe evenly. "I . . . couldn't. Not proper . . ."

Oh God, she was going to do it again!

The clothing slipped from her hands as she raised her arms and tentatively touched his shoulders. For an instant, she felt his powerful muscles tense. And for an instant she hesitated. But then his eyes became blue flames and his body went still. For a frantic moment she thought that he would flee— perhaps she even prayed a little that he might. Suddenly, looking into his burning eyes, she sensed that she was gazing over an abyss that would send her spiraling into a place she would never be able to escape from—nor would she want to.

His arms wrapped around her, slid slowly up her rigid back until his fingers caressed the smooth nape of her neck, pressing upward slowly, gently tunneling through the soft dark waves of her hair, stroking the curve of her head and cradling it almost possessively as his other arm pulled her close, so close she felt overwhelmed by the heat and strength of his body.

"Kiss me again," he whispered, sounding almost urgent as he wrapped his roughened but gentle fingers in her hair and pulled back her head so she could not look away, so she lay there in his power- ful arms like a captured, quivering bird, his to do with as he wanted. "Quickly, Miss Haviland, before either of us admits how dangerous we are to- gether."

Then his head came down, and his sensual lips touched hers—a spark that stole her breath away, that turned her body into electricity as vibrant as lightning. The intoxicating kiss was cool and de- manding and slow-moving, a drugging wonder that deprived her of all power of thinking or resisting the impulse to kiss him back, to lean her

body into his, to open her lips at the tender prodding of his tongue, to allow him to slide inside her
mouth so his tongue danced against hers in a
rhythm that made her every nerve expand to the
point of pain, until she could not breathe, or move,
or function in any recognizable way. Only allow his
mouth to turn her inside out.

Oh God, this wasn't happening.

This belonged in her most fevered dreams. In her
fantasies. Where she was freed from society's ex-
pectations. And limitations.

So this was what she had longed for.

This was surrender.

Total. Unequivocal.

The splendor.

She kissed him back.

They slid to the floor and lay in a tangle of dusty
sheets and sheer lingerie with pink and blue ribbons. His hungry mouth still kissed her, tongue
tracing her lips, her teeth. She buried her hands in
his dark hair as he moved down to her throat and
up to her ear, kissing, nibbling, stroking in and out
until she heard herself groan, felt herself—this
stranger in her body—wrap her arms and legs
around him until she could feel the whole length
of his body—every swelling, trembling bone and
muscle—strain against her like a famished, furious
leopard on a leash.

They rolled: he on top briefly, she on top briefly;
arms and legs becoming entangled in her skirt and
the sheets while he ravished her mouth and face
and took her breath away with the heat of his
tongue and the intensity of his hunger.

"Oh God," she murmured, as she suddenly realized that he had tugged her blouse and plain cotton chemise up over her white breasts, exposing them to his eyes and hands that, despite the raw need turning his face into stone, touched them with utmost gentleness—as if they were something sacred and mesmerizing.

"My God, you're beautiful," he said softly and breathlessly to her eyes, lightly tracing the pink areola around her nipple with his finger, then lowering his head and taking the nipple into his mouth with an easy tug of his tongue and teeth, so Bronte suddenly found herself whimpering for God only knew what.

Delicious. That's all she could think. Delicious and naughty, and soon she would hate herself for allowing him such liberties, but God oh God oh God, this liberation was sublime.

He groaned, and gasped, and clutched her slender hips with his powerful hands while his mouth continued to smother her. "Tell me to stop, sweetheart," he whispered urgently against her throat. "Tell me to stop," he murmured less urgently into her ear, even as his hand traveled up the inside of her thigh, one finger tracing a mercury-hot path upon the sensitive flesh, up, up, up, until she wanted to scream in denial and amazement and abandoned pleasure.

What sweet wickedness, this.

How deliriously sinful.

Yet her body had never felt so alive.

Closing her eyes and arching her back, she surrendered herself to the unmentionable magic of his hand between her legs, his fingers sliding in and out of her body, which was a stranger even to herself. As if she had somehow left her body, she looked down on herself and the man in her arms, saw her clutching his back with her fingers while his dark hands ran over her shaking white body, tearing at his shirt, which was damp with sweat and clinging to every straining flexing muscle, her drawers down around her calves and her clothes in complete disarray, exposing her to his mouth and hands, which seemed to be everywhere at once— her breasts, her thighs, and in between—flirting with her most sensitive, quivering flesh. And it occurred to her, as she twisted her hands in his thick hair and brought his mouth back up to hers, that this ungovernable torrent of needs was nothing more than the unleashing of all things denied in her life—romance, companionship, sin, and bittersweet madness. For, surely, she must be mad. Brandon Tremain was the epitome of temptation—everything forbidden. And she had succumbed to the temptation, and the forbidden, at long last.

Ah, but it was a thrilling spiral into damnation. She wanted it to go on forever. She wanted— needed—this expanding sensation to fill her up to the fringes of her consciousness, then take her hurdling over the edge into . . .

"Bronte. Bronte. Bronte, for God's sake, love, listen to me."

"No," she gasped.

He took her wrists in his strong hands and pushed them away.

Suddenly her arms were empty. Reality splintered her fog of confusion as she felt herself yanked onto her knees. Blinking, doing her best to breathe evenly, she dumbly watched his hands fumble with her clothing.

"You don't really want this," he said, breathing heavily. "You were overcome with the moment. Hell, we both were. Believe me, you won't like yourself tomorrow if you allow yourself to be taken like this . . . by me. Your ideals are too bloody lofty for that, Miss Haviland."

She touched his face.

He pushed her hand away again and did his best to tuck her hair back into the combs that had earlier anchored it to the back of her head. "Jesus," he said to himself and for a brief moment his eyes flashed with his own desires, and confusion . . . his reluctance to end the dangerous moment.

A door slammed in the distance. Murray began whistling.

On one knee, Brandon took Bronte's chin in the crook of his finger. "Look at me, sweetheart. Remember who I am and what I've done."

"I don't want to," she replied, smiling dreamily.

"The hell you don't." Grabbing her shoulders, he shook her lightly, then harder, until sensibleness took hold and she glared at him angrily.

"You're hurting me."

"Good. Remember that the next time you want to kiss me." Sitting back on his heels, he tugged her skirt down over her shoes.

"You don't like me?"

For a moment, he appeared unsettled, saying nothing, rocked back on his heels with his beautiful hands spread out on his thighs and his mouth a grim line.

He stood and moved quickly and gracefully to

the draped window. "Murray," Brandon called down. "Miss Bronte needs some assistance moving furniture." And without so much as a glance her way, he exited the room, leaving Bronte sitting in a pile of her mother's lingerie.

If their aim and object be to marry, for pity's sake
disguise it. It is disgusting to see it trotted out on
every occasion; besides which, it utterly defeats its
own purpose.

CHAPTER FOURTEEN

BRONTE CONSIDERED FORGOING THAT EVENING'S DINNER.
She wondered what her father would say if she
simply sent her regrets.

*Sorry, but Miss Bronte is occupied by the dreadful
reality that she acted the strumpet with one of her
father's inmates.*

If her own distress were not enough, she remembered that this was the evening that Margorie Fish
would, at last, have the opportunity to see the
former captain. Margorie and her classic worldly
beauty, her exquisite clothes, her slightly scandalous conversation. She, Bronte, would perch on her
own chair in her plain white dress like a dowdy
little mouse and just imagine what it would be like
to tantalize a man with scandalous conversation . . .
not that she ever would, of course—tantalize, that
is. Heavens no.

Had they been lovers, Tremain and Lady Fish?
She would not, could not, think of it.

Bronte ordered a bath. Wang delivered a tub of tepid water. She ordered him to replace it with hot. Very hot. She wanted to sweat Brandon Tremain out of her system—all the longing, the hunger, the ache that remained writhing around inside, refusing to subside, reminding her that the etiquette books were correct. Once such wanton and promiscuous sensitivities were unleashed, a woman was doomed to a life of licentiousness and blemished reputation.

For an hour, she sat in the tub with water steaming off her shoulders, until her skin turned lobster-pink and her stomach felt queasy. With water dripping in puddles off her body, she flung herself across her bed and lay on her back, totally naked.

She had never done that before—lain nude upon her bed, allowing the breeze through the open window to fan the heat from her body.

She lay for another hour, staring at the ceiling, doing her best to ignore the awakening of feelings going on inside her. How dare he do this to her—plant this terrible seed of discontent? How dare she allow him?

At straight up seven, Bronte entered the drawing room, where Charles Metcalfe stood near the French doors with Lord Fish. Arthur had joined Margorie and Bronte's father on the veranda, where Wang was busily filling the newly finished pool and fountain with fresh water syphoned from the nearby stream.

"At any rate," Metcalfe was saying in a low voice, "if we shut down the house, Parramatta would be deserted within a year. Besides, all men need a diversion every now and again." He guffawed.

Bronte cleared her throat.

Startled, Metcalfe and Lord Fish looked around. They stared.

"Gentlemen." She smiled.

"Miss Haviland?" they said in unison.

"Is something wrong?" she asked.

Arthur entered the room, smiling. Then he stopped.

William and Margorie stepped through the doorway. Lady Fish barely hesitated before hurrying forward and allowing Bronte a brush of a kiss on her cheek. "My," Margorie whispered. "I hardly knew you, dear."

She looked down at her costume. "Do you like the dress, Lady Fish?"

Margorie made a moue with her lips, and contemplated. "It is, perhaps, a bit dated, your mother's, perhaps? But it is perfectly beautiful. It suits you, Bronte."

Bronte looked down at the plunging décolletage that revealed a great deal of cleavage—the ruches of pale ivory lace hardly hid her nipples. It had taken a great deal of courage to wear this this evening. But the entire evening would take courage, she knew.

Arthur cleared his throat. "Our styles are not of twenty years past. Decency is one of our most sacred virtues," he said.

Bronte opened her eyes as if surprised. "But I thought you liked indecency," she said. "That's what this dinner is all about, isn't it? For Lord Metcalfe to convince me that prostitutes are necessary?"

Arthur gasped. His face turned white. Lowering

his voice to just above a whisper, he said, "Is that any type of language for a young woman of your breeding to use?" Glaring at William, he declared, "I fear, sir, that you have done your daughter a grave injustice by ignoring her bouts of temperament."

William just chuckled. "Nonsense. My Bronte's just a bit of a reformer. But no matter, I think it's time for dinner."

Bronte smiled brightly and led them into the other room. Though she did not acknowledge it, she was grateful her father had changed the topic. She was feeling a bit out of control—there was no telling what she might have said next.

The Rocks was not mentioned again. The guests appeared to be too entranced with the food to focus on anything other than the occasional comment about the weather, the success of William's wheat crop, and the fact that the *Sirius* from Calcutta was running exceedingly late.

Brandon did not appear. Murray, with his usual Scottish aplomb, whisked away the covers of the steaming, crisply roasted partridges surrounded by brown rice and a scattering of sweet corn. While Bronte breathed a sigh of relief that Brandon was not present, she also sorely regretted having attired herself in a dress befitting a Roman orgy. Lady Fish was obviously disappointed. Repeatedly, Margorie glanced toward the door leading to the kitchen, and as the evening trekked on with no sign of Tremain, her irritation began to show. She said nothing, however, until dessert was served.

"You've discovered yourself a marvelous chef, William. I congratulate you. Who would have thought that our Captain Tremain would prove so invaluable, not only on the battlefield, but in a kitchen?"

William smiled.

Lord Fish sampled his fruit tart topped with sweetened clotted cream. "Excellent! By Jove, Bill, would you consider giving him up?"

Bronte neatly folded her napkin and laid it on the table. Her stomach hurt. The whalebone stays beneath her dress cut into her soft skin like teeth. Had her mother truly worn this uncomfortable garb?

William smiled again. "I haven't given it a thought, my lord. Captain Tremain has been with us such a short time . . ."

Margorie sipped at her burgundy as she sat back in her chair. The rings on her fingers flashed like fire beneath the lit chandelier, as did her eyes. "Seriously, William. As you know, we've recently lost our cook—as well as numerous other men—"

"Let's not get into that, please," Lord Fish declared. "I'm certain William needs no reminders that several of his prisoners have disappeared from our farm without a trace. Besides, I think we all know my main purpose in being here tonight is to once again convince dear Bronte to consider our request for adoption . . ." He looked pointedly at Bronte, who bothered the peas around on her plate.

Charles Metcalfe withdrew a smoking case from his coat pocket, flipped it open, offered William, Arthur, and Lord Fish thin cigars, then took one for himself. Ignoring Fish's attempt to change the subject, he said, "In my opinion, they should all go back to the prison, where they belong. Allow them to languish in the squalor of their own kind."

"Agreed," Arthur chimed in. A moment later, he snapped closed his mouth when Bronte centered him with a dark look.

"I feel the undertaking to rehabilitate the men has been successful," William replied to Metcalf.

"Moderately, old man. Moderately. When one thinks of the scoundrels slipping away the first time opportunity lends itself—forcing us all to divert our time and energy on hunting them down—the idea, though tolerable in concept, soon loses its appeal. I don't know about the rest of you, but I, personally, don't care for the fact that there are men running about free who would like nothing more than to cut our politically conscious throats." He affected a shudder, then added, "I don't envy you at all, William. Every day that you continue to hold the dreadful position of warden, you place your life in jeopardy. They're madmen. Every one of them. Including your Captain Tremain," he muttered, throwing the spellbound guests a pompously knowing look. "Let's face it: any man, or woman, who could, without so much as a blink of an eye, murder a human being is totally without morals and rational compunction."

Bronte could keep silent no longer. "Then I suppose that you oppose war, for any reason," she said. "After all, what is war but a reason to kill the enemy? Is a uniform and a nod from our government just cause to commit murder?"

"I did not come here to discuss the differences between political killing and murder," Margorie said with a dismissive air. Leaning toward William, she smiled. "Seriously, dear. Would you consider allowing Captain Tremain to come to Mill Chase to work for us?"

For the first time, William looked directly at Bronte.

She did not move. Or speak. She felt swallowed up by the ensuing silence as she returned her father's look, which seemed to flow through her like warm sunlight. Could he read her thoughts— her emotions? Did the gentle understanding in his eyes reflect his knowledge and acceptance of her conflicting feelings for Brandon Tremain? No one knew her better than her own father.

Even should he not guess, surely he would not consider such a request—not with Lord Fish's penchant for punishing any convict who wavered the slightest bit from Fish's rules.

Finally, William said politely, "I suppose I would have to give that some thought. He's become quite a valuable member of the household."

Bronte released her breath, only then realizing that she had been holding it. How very ironic that just two days before, she might have instigated the transfer herself. But now . . . she didn't know how she felt.

Lord Fish said, "Certainly he harbors a great deal of resentment toward England, does he not?"

William looked thoughtful. "I suppose he has every right."

"Of course he does," Arthur said, tossing his napkin to the table. "They all do. They would all like nothing more than to cut our throats as we sleep, including your Captain Tremain," he added pointedly to William. "He's a killer, after all."

"I'm certain Mr. Metcalfe didn't come here to

discuss our problem prisoners," William said pointedly.

"Of course not," Lady Fish joined in, flashing Bronte a smile. "He came here to discuss dear Bronte's position on Parramatta's whorehouses."

"Must you be so unceremonious in your manner of speaking, Margorie?" Lord Fish snapped.

Margorie laughed.

Metcalfe gave Bronte a discomfited glance. "I fear our dear Bronte has already made her point on that topic. However, in all fairness, I do wish she might consider giving me fair warning before she dashes off letters, such as the one she wrote to Crenshaw, as well as to Her Royal Highness."

"Good God!" Arthur exclaimed.

William sat back in his chair.

Lady Fish coughed into her napkin, and her husband dropped his lit cigar into his lap.

"Bronte," William said. "Is this true?"

"Yes."

"You wrote Her Highness—"

"I simply made a copy of the letter I wrote to Mr. Crenshaw, then I posted it to Her Highness. I think it only fair that she be aware of the deplorable condition of her colony, and the women who reside there."

The heated debate that followed left Bronte with a pounding head. At another time she might have welcomed the discourse. But as the group moved back into the drawing room, she excused herself and stepped out onto the veranda, thankful the night had turned immeasurably cooler.

God, what a rout. The entire ordeal had drained

her. If only she could fling herself onto Cytduction's back and ride down to the river.

Escape. That's all she wanted. To rid herself of her mind and body's turmoil. To go back to the staid existence that had occupied her life before Brandon Tremain came to uproot every idea and ideal she had ever held as right, when the sum total of her life had been perfecting a home for her father and doing her best to help St. Cluny establish the best hospital, school, and orphanage their meager funds could provide.

Not so long ago she would have stood her ground where The Rocks was concerned. She would have argued heatedly into the night about reformation and education for the lost women, truly believing in those ideals. But perhaps her father was right after all. Try to reform all, but concentrate on those with character.

Character. The word made her think of Tremain and her own behavior that afternoon. She was discovering that the body's desire was in no way related to the mind's better judgment.

Leaving the veranda, she moved off through the garden, wandering the bricked path beyond the surrounding retaining wall, past the thickets of yew trees, which needed thinning, to the tiny one-room house Wang had renovated for her rabbits. The structure, built some fifty years before by England's military, had stood among the reeds and clematis like an old battlement, inviting occupancy.

As always, a single light burned in the hut. The stone floor had been scrubbed spotless. Bronte herself had designed the rabbits' cages, which were not really cages at all, but enclosures of fine-meshed wire dividing the room into separate and equal cubicles roomy enough to allow the rabbits freedom to exercise. Supplying it with old tree stumps, miniature trees, stones, and rich earth formed into hillocks, she had made certain their environment was as close to their natural habitat as possible.

Sugar was the first to materialize from the scrubby brush of her warren. The soft white, floppy-eared rabbit sat up on her back legs and gazed up at Bronte with one long ear cocked forward to better hear her.

Going to her knees, Bronte released the latch on the rabbit's cage and laughed softly as Sugar eagerly leapt into her lap. Cradling the little creature, Bronte wished, not for the first time, that people could be as uncomplicated, unobtrusive, and gentle as her little friends.

A noise.

Bronte looked around. The doorway was empty.

Sugar squirmed furiously in her arms, while within the lair of their hiding places, the other rabbits began thumping their warnings of alarm.

Standing, Bronte moved to the open door. The smell of rain hung heavily in the air, and beyond the roiling clouds in the distance flashed bright spears of static lightning. Then a figure moved up before her suddenly.

Catching her breath, stepping back, Bronte focused on Johnny Turpin's startled features. "Sir, you gave me a fright."

He glanced over his shoulder, into the dark, then back at her, his eyes like dull stones in the dimly lit interior. In one hand he held an evil-looking club. "Sorry, miss. I saw someone movin' round in here.

Thought I ought to check it out. We can't be too careful these days."

Bronte backed toward the cage, holding the slightly panting rabbit up against her. Forcing herself to breathe evenly, she bent and gently returned Sugar to her warren. Then she turned for the door, her step hesitating as Turpin refused to budge out of her way.

"Somethin' wrong?" he asked, looking down at her.

"I have guests waiting. I really should hurry—"

"I hear Tremain has got himself a job in the house."

She nodded and glanced longingly toward the door.

"Then I suppose he won't be returnin' to the building site."

"No."

"Well now, that's a shame, Miss Haviland. A real shame. I reckon his kind gets preferential treatment—'specially when the lady of the house takes a fancy to him."

"You are impertinent, sir."

He grinned and allowed his eyes a leisurely exploration of her bosom. "Whatever you say, Miss Haviland."

Bronte ducked around him for the door, refusing to look back as she hurried up the walk, swiping aside the unkempt branches of bushes and trees in her haste. Silly ninny. What could she have been thinking to wander off like that alone after dark? What could she have been thinking to dress this way, hoping to outshine Margorie Fish? What could she have been thinking to have allowed Tremain to kiss her, to hold her, to touch her? How could she have allowed herself to forget just who and what he was?

The thought of returning to the cramped, smoky drawing room to debate an issue in which she would be far outnumbered, and no doubt ridiculed, didn't appeal to her tonight. Nor did she care to look into Fish's wounded eyes as she again dismissed his request for adoption as kindly as possible. And no doubt she was setting herself up for a good dressing-down from her father over her sadly lacking care and entertainment of their guests. But she didn't care at the moment. She wanted only to bury herself in her room and try her best to forget this horrible day had ever happened.

Bronte hurried through the dark, hoping to escape discovery by entering through a rear door of the house. As she rounded the corner of the house, however, she suddenly stopped, her heart in her throat.

Grateful for a breath of fresh air and a break from the crucifyingly hot kitchen, Tremain leaned back against the rock wall and smoked the cigar he'd won from Haviland the previous evening in a game of whist. Like the brandy, the tobacco product was smuggled and the best he'd enjoyed in years.

Lady Fish lightly ran her hand along his arm. "You can imagine my surprise and distress when I learned of your conviction," she said.

"Really?" He studied the tip of his glowing cheroot. "And what was your husband's view?"

"Such old-fashioned ideals, Brandon," she crooned and leaned slightly against him, close enough that he could detect the rose scent of her pale skin. "Even if I tell you that my husband couldn't care less who I take as . . . a lover?"

"Grown numb to it, has he?"

She laughed throatily. "I see your sense of humor is still as lethal. I had hoped that the years—and the fact that your reputation has fallen into decay—would have humbled you somewhat. You were always so confident of your effect on women. You know we're all weak in the presence of heroes. Even fallen heroes. There is something immensely intriguing about fencing with the devil "

He grinned and drew on his cigar, blowing smoke into the rising wind, where it whipped back and forth before scattering into the dark.

Margorie narrowed her eyes. "So tell me, Sir Galahad, have you indeed mended your ways? Or have you set your sights on the warder's daughter?"

His smile turning brittle, Brandon flicked away his ashes. The bemusement he'd momentarily found in Lady Fish's outrageous behavior vanished like vapor. The woman wanted something from him—and he suspected that seduction was only the prelude.

"Miss Haviland means nothing to me," he snapped.

"No? Why else this special treatment—a comfortable position as cook, a bedroom of your own right here in the house—oh, how convenient. Even William's cigars." Margorie smiled and leaned closer. "If I'm not mistaken that's also William's best brandy I smell on your breath. What service can a convict provide that would merit such treatment?"

"You always did have a very vivid imagination, Lady Fish."

"My dear Brandon, I hardly have to imagine some things. Yet you still don't have the one gift you'd treasure most—your freedom." She ran one finger down his pants. "Perhaps?"

The door opened then. Lord Fish stepped out and stood for a moment with the wind whipping his graying hair and the tail of his thinning dinner jacket while he stared at his wife. "There you are," he finally said.

He lightly took the shallow steps down to the lower landing of the porch. Coming to a stop before Brandon, he squared his shoulders and said, "Has she managed to convince you into coming to work for us, Mr. Tremain?"

Brandon raised one eyebrow. "I didn't realize that was an option."

"Ah. Then I assume she was simply attempting to seduce you."

Brandon didn't comment.

"Bastard," Margorie said with a sneer, then turned on her heels and reentered the house.

Lord Fish chuckled and adjusted his tie, smoothed his hand over his hair, only to have it mussed again by a sudden gust of sea-smelling wind. "By damn, but I grow weary of this godforsaken country—its intolerable bouts of heat and drought, then the damnable rain pummeling everything to muck."

Thunder rumbled, shaking the ground beneath their feet.

"Then go back to England," Brandon suggested.

"Ah, were it only that simple, Captain. But it seems that, like you, I am a prisoner of this wretched existence—doomed, for lack of resources, to wait out my life doing my best to wring crops from this pitiful soil—not to mention dwelling on the impossibility that Margorie will suddenly wake up with wifely instincts. But then I was always a pigeon for the ridiculous. My wife's generosity towards herself doesn't help, which is what sent me into this predicament in the first place—that and other obvious reasons."

Lord Fish grimaced and gazed up at the starless sky. "I'm afraid my creditors would show little tolerance for my sudden resurrection into London society. No doubt I would find myself shipped back over here and working alongside you. Not that you have it so bad . . . working here. They are kind and intelligent people, if not a little too idealistic.

"The truth is, Captain, I could use a man like you at Mill Chase. Quite obviously I have no talent as a gentleman farmer. I need help. William has spoken highly of your capabilities, and, as I understand it, he's not totally disagreeable to the idea of transferring your leave program over to me."

Brandon dropped his cigar to the ground and crushed it with his boot heel.

"If you like, I'll work up a contract. We'll form a partnership, of sorts. Split the profits. Who knows, perhaps we'll eventually make enough money to buy our way out of this mess." A tight smile crossing his features, Lord Fish stepped close enough that Brandon could smell and feel his mephitic breath on his face. "Then we can tell them all to go to hell, can't we, Captain Tremain?"

Tremain looked him in the eye.

All the world loves a lover—but this does not keep the world from watching closely and criticizing severely any breach of good manners . . . Any public display of affection anywhere at any time is grossly unrefined. Love is sacred, and it should not be thrown open to the rude comments of strangers.

—*Book of Etiquette*
LILLIAN EICHLER

CHAPTER FIFTEEN

THE CLOUDS ROILED.

Bothered by the thoughts gnawing at his sleep-deprived conscience, Brandon rolled from his bed and sat for a long while on the edge of it, while thunder trembled the walls of the house and the air grew thicker and hotter—so miserably hot he felt suffocated. He smoked one of William's much cherished, and smuggled, cigars, and cursed under his breath.

Nothing was going as planned. Nothing!

Earlier in the evening, he'd hoped Lord Fish was behind the escapes—that the promises of money he'd offered were evidence of his disloyalty. But there was no avoiding the facts. The Fishes were definitely struggling—only one person Brandon had met was not . . . William.

Brandon had volunteered for this assignment, not out of duty, but out of obligation to his massacred troops, and friends. He'd felt responsible, after all.

He'd come to this godforsaken colony of miscreants with every intention of squashing the cyst of treason that, if not stopped, would rise up and could topple the empire. He'd sacrificed his own reputation toward this end.

He'd expected to unmask an evil man. But now . . .

Hell, nothing was going as planned.

He had not expected the much admired and revered warden of New South Wales to, possibly, be the instigator of the percolating insurrection. Perhaps someone working for him—someone with easy access to the prisoners, someone who needed money to maintain a comfortable lifestyle. Someone—a guard, an employee—with a reason to hate England for committing his or her soul to this purgatory.

Alas, with his own admission of smuggling, and his close friendship with the suspected captain of the *Sirius*, everything pointed to Haviland, except that Haviland and his daughter appeared to adore their mother country—which was the one, and only, piece of evidence for their innocence.

And he was clinging to it like a bloody fool.

Damn . . . Nothing was going as planned.

He liked Haviland. He admired the man's ideals. And as for the daughter . . .

Double damn. He'd originally pursued her as a lark, a way to pass the time. Lately, he couldn't think about anything, or anyone, but her. She obsessed him—had since the moment he'd seen her standing atop that platform with her lovely face and seductive eyes partially hidden by the swooping brim of her hat. The voice of reason in his head had whispered to stay clear of her.

Yet . . . just that morning he had stretched his body out on Bronte Haviland's. He'd tasted her exquisitely beautiful breasts and felt her nipples harden against his tongue. He'd made her quiver, and gasp, and plead to be taken. And, God help him, he would have taken her had Murray not returned home when he did.

Oh yes, he had abandoned his so-called better judgment for the brief ecstasy of knowing her delicious, awakening body.

And now he would pay for it.

He knew her too well to believe that she would consider herself jointly responsible. She was intrigued by him, but did not truly admire him. He had breached her carefully constructed and maintained dignity, had fragmented her prized invulnerability. He had pushed the game beyond her control; therefore she would banish him to Mill Chase, blowing all his carefully laid plans to hell.

Undone by his desire to risk everything yet again.

Christ, how the hell would he explain this to his superiors? How could he forgive himself for letting his country, and countrymen, down—again?

All because of his attraction for a beautiful woman?

He left the bed, stretched his long, naked legs, and moved to the window. How still was the night, and expectant. Black as perdition but for the occasional flash of sheet lightning that shimmered briefly above the treetops.

Shirtless, his body wet with perspiration, Brandon leaned against the window frame and focused on the veranda outside Bronte's dark room, watching the heavy flowers in pots and urns begin their slow dance with the suddenly rising wind. He looked away determinedly. He needed a new plan.

He was about to turn back for his bed, when lightning scattered like sparks across the night sky, briefly illuminating the veranda. Brandon stopped. He focused harder, barely making out the ghostly pale image standing at the waist-high wall, her face turned into the rising wind so it whipped her hair like a black silken flag out behind her.

Bronte wore little more than a thin white chemise that barely covered the tops of her thighs. She stood still as a marble statue . . . as if listening . . . waiting . . .

The thunder rumbled.

As silently and gracefully as a wraith, she slid over the wall, dropping with bare feet onto the dry earth, then disappeared into the night.

For an instant, Brandon neither moved nor blinked. A thousand reasons for her vaporizing into the darkness flashed through his mind—but they all boiled down to one, and though he fought to ignore it, his soldier's mind—that spark of suspicion that had kept him alive long after his comrades had fallen—flared hotly.

She was slipping into the darkness to meet someone. Perhaps responding to a signal. Perhaps Miss Haviland was about to incriminate herself. It was his duty and obligation to find out for certain.

Cursing under his breath, he grabbed for his breeches and yanked them on, wincing as he pulled them up over his injured leg and scrambled out his window, hurrying the best he was capable in the direction of Bronte's disappearance.

What the hell was she doing?

Where was she going?

Most importantly, whom was she meeting?

And what would Brandon do when he found her?

By the time he reached the stables, the wind had grown to a low, menacing howl that frenziedly whipped the spearlike leaves of the wattle trees, scattering them in whirlwind clouds across the ground. Brandon wasn't certain Bronte had come here; he'd only caught brief glimpses of her when the night exploded with lightning.

The horses whinnied and kicked the stall walls, crazed by the typhoon winds barreling inland from the sea. Then he heard her voice—calm amid the terrible building turbulence.

"Easy. Easy," she crooned to the stomping and blowing horse. "There's nothing to be frightened about. It's only the wind, and we love the wind, don't we, Cytduction?"

God, oh God, thank God she was only talking to her horses . . . just her horses . . . no companions in crime.

Brandon eased into the building and stood for a moment in the doorway while his eyes grew accustomed to the dim light of the burning lanterns on the wall. He saw her then, beside the animal, dwarfed by its immense size and barely constrained power. Yet the animal lowered its head into her hands as if finding security there against the magnifying storm.

Almost effortlessly, she leapt onto the horse's back and slid her bare leg over it.

Brandon moved out of the shadows.

Bronte's eyes met his, at first startled.

"What the hell are you doing?" he demanded.

Her long legs gently squeezed the horse, and the animal moved forward, hooves striking noisily against the cobblestone floor, nostrils blowing, and ears pointed straight ahead. Bronte said nothing, just stared down at Brandon with dark, fierce eyes as she moved toward the door.

He grabbed the reins, causing the horse to toss its head and dance in place. Bronte kicked him away.

"Might I remind you, Captain Tremain, your duties do not include me. I might also remind you that while your liberties might include the freedom to wander the house and garden during the day, you are to not to be wandering the grounds after curfew." Her eyes glittered fiercely . . . with alarm? Surprise?

Gripping the reins more tightly, he said, "Get down off that horse before you get killed."

Managing a tight smile, Bronte clutched at the mare's mane. "My goodness, such a show of concern over a woman you care nothing about."

Her meaning struck him like a cudgel. She had overheard his conversation with Lady Fish.

She stared down at him, unmoving, unblinking, her eyes glassy with suppressed emotion, her small white face desperately struggling to remain calm. At last, she whispered, "Bastard," and kicked the nervous animal with all her strength.

Cytduction plunged forward. Brandon jumped back.

"Damn," he hissed through his teeth, then ran for a horse.

He rode forever, it seemed, down one black path after another. He dodged tree limbs that came at him through the dark to claw his head and shoulders and knock him from his mount.

Up ahead, Bronte drove Cytduction forward, a white specter in the tumultuous night that threatened to explode any moment around them. Twice the horses leapt stone-wall hurdles. Three times the animals skidded down the steep sides of the staggered ravines, plunging toward the distant black ribbon of river.

Brandon yelled Bronte's name.

She ignored him.

They hit the wide sandy stretch of strand along the river at a full gallop, and still Brandon's horse could not catch hers, though the gelding, with its ears flattened and its body lathered, did its best, as terrified of Brandon's constant whipping as it was over the ear-shattering crescendo of thunder and lightning overhead.

Then it happened—the inevitable. As lightning struck a distant eucalypt, Cytduction shied and reared. As if time had ground to excrutiating slowness, Brandon watched Bronte slide backward, arms and legs flailing helplessly to grab anything to stop her fall to the ground.

"Ah, Jesus!" he yelled, as she sprawled over the white sand.

He jumped from his horse at a dead run and stumbled over the mostly buried root of a mangrove jutting up out of the river's murky shoal. He splashed through ankle-deep mire that swarmed with something that struck at his pants leg, but missed, and he cursed aloud—as much at his insane fear that he would find her dead, as at his need to kill her himself.

"Bronte!" he yelled as he neared her.

Slowly, she raised her head, her shoulders; she struggled up to her elbows before turning her stark white face up to look at him.

"Stay away," she said hoarsely, and shoved herself to her knees.

Breathing heavily, his heart slamming against his chest and ribs, Brandon slowed, then stopped, bent, with his hands on his knees as he attempted to catch his breath. Relief that—traitor or no—she was apparently not injured made his legs weak.

The first drops of rain spattered the ground as, wobbling, Bronte regained her feet. Her hair, skin, and night shift were coated with damp sand. A rivulet of blood trickled from a cut on her brow.

"I hate you," she said.

"Why?" he replied.

"For doing this."

"For doing what?" he yelled.

"For doing this to me. For not letting me alone. For turning me into the kind of woman who would ride through the night like a lunatic, dressed only in her night rail. Who feels the remotest sense of jealousy over a man who isn't worth a solitary thought in any decent woman's head. Damn you for shattering my every ideal—my stupid, idiotic fantasies. I wasted my entire adult life waiting for a man who, in my own head and heart, you could never, ever live up to!"

Brandon glanced up at the roiling sky, closing his eyes against the big drops of rain that were beginning to fall more forcefully. He was beginning to understand.

Bronte laughed and hugged herself, even as her shoulders began to shake under the impact of her emotions. Tears and rain coursed down her face.

"Do you know you were the epitome of the absolute man? Since I was a young girl, I kept scrapbooks of your exploits. Young, handsome, and brave—and so morally outstanding. You were my knight in shining armor, my substitute for the perfect husband I'll probably never have." Her hands in fists, she screamed at him, "For God's sake, Tremain, you mock me. But look around me. I grew up surrounded by nothing but thieves, murderers, rapists—my life was and is an unending parade of reprehensible and flagitious failures. When it seemed the entire world had gone mad with cruelty and hate for their fellow man, there was you, your name, spread across the *Times* headlines proclaiming your fine, upstanding moral character. You gave me hope . . ."

"I'm sorry," he said through the rain.

"I hate you," she said more softly, the words drowned by the thunder and downpour. "Because I want to forget what you've done. Because I still want you to be perfect. I don't want to give up hope—not yet." Her face in her hands, she looked at him with her bare soul shining through her eyes. "Tell me you're innocent of murder, that you killed that young soldier by accident, and I'll believe you because I want to believe you. Tell me and I'll believe you even if you're lying."

The deluge came, slashing against their shoulders.

She stood before him with her white gown, a thin, transparent film, clinging to her every curve. Her eyes smoldered. Her breasts rose and fell raggedly.

And still he stood before her with the truth imprisoned behind his damned cursed wall of allegiance.

Finally, she turned her back to him and stumbled through the pummeling rain toward her horse.

"Bronte," he called, then again more loudly as he forced himself to move after her, to run when she fled in her attempt to escape him.

Futilely, she attempted to grab Cytduction's reins. Terrified of the crashing thunder and electrified sky, the horse screamed and bolted.

"Damn you!" Bronte cried, tripping in her effort to chase the mare.

Brandon grabbed hold of her arm.

She spun around and hit him across his face with her hand, then against his chest with her fists. "Don't touch me!" she wept. "I hate you," she repeated in a tone almost like a litany—again and again while she struggled against his attempt to haul her out of the rain and under the shelter of a eucalypt.

At last, with her back pressed against the tree, his rain-slicked body against hers, sheltering her from the turbid storm, Brandon took Bronte's face in his hands. He wiped the raindrops away from her face and, very tenderly, kissed the injury on her brow, then her eyelids, her nose, the corner of her trembling little mouth.

She struggled again, briefly, like a butterfly succumbing to its destined death, her eyes almost dreamy, her wet lips a little parted, her hands splayed upon his shirtless chest while a sound of suffering whispered from her throat.

"Don't you understand," she breathed. "I'm lost."

"Bronte, love." He gently cradled her face and touched her rain-heavy black hair where it poured over her white shoulders, and inside he felt his defenses crumbling beneath the weight of his immense desire for Bronte Haviland. In that instant, the doubts and indecisions, all his suspicions and uncertainties, shattered with the cataclysmic force of the storm mounting overhead, shaking the ground and trees, vibrating inside of their bodies, electrifying the night.

"To hell with them," he said through his teeth, and taking her flimsy shift in his two hands, he ripped it down the front.

She did not fight him. He hadn't suspected that she would. He wasn't certain it would have done any good if she had. Bronte stood before him with the ragged remains of her nightgown hanging from her shoulders, her body exposed to his hands and eyes and lips, her head fallen back against the tree as if she were finding some solace in this terrible surrender.

She was exquisite beyond his imagination—her breasts high and perfect, with their cinnamon-dark nipples aroused to hard points, her waist tiny enough that he could easily encompass it with his fingers. And the other—oh God—the other, the dark triangle between her long, tapering legs, the hair like fine silk as dark as the wet waves framing her face.

Dropping to his knees, he pressed his face against it, and felt her quiver, heard her gasp, sensed the sudden tensing of every muscle in her startled, hungry body. He touched her with his tongue— that sweet, wet aphrodisiac of her being. He wanted to devour her, to drink her in and quench, at long last, the insatiable thirst for her that had driven him mad the last many days and nights.

"Oh," she moaned. "Oh God," she wept, and twisted her fingers in his hair. "Wicked man. Oh, wicked, wicked man for doing this. For making me feel so wonderful. Oh, I'm wicked, too. Don't stop. Please don't stop or I shall certainly die."

He didn't, but dove deeper, filling his nostrils with her rich, womanly scent; he stroked her with the tip of his tongue, each petal and bud, until she wept aloud and he couldn't stand another minute of not having her.

Standing, he released his breeches. No time for last chances, second thoughts, regrets. The regrets would come tomorrow, when the storm had subsided, when reality would once again be his responsibility to England—and hers to her reputation—but tonight, ah, tonight he would gladly give her what she needed to feel less hopeless and lost.

"Kiss me," she pleaded, with rain like dewdrops upon her long lashes.

He did, and his arms slid around her slender form and lifted her high, high against him, until she could wrap her legs around his hips and he could easily, and gently, slide her down on his aroused sex.

He knew the moment, the very instant, it happened—her awakening, her flowering, her final declivity from her virginal pedestal. Her body tensed—poised upon the threshold. She might have wept, or pleaded with him to cease the act, the pain, the awful evidence of her moral decline—yet she didn't, but turned her face up into the deluge and laughed, and gasped, and cried aloud, "At last. At long last."

There was still time to end this—to save her from the avalanche of disappointment and heartache that she would face tomorrow. Yet the undisguised magnitude of her surrender crumbled his last resistance. Not even he was man—or hero—enough to deny this supreme supplication.

He kissed her again, more passionately, deeply, while he pressed her back against the tree and allowed her body to, little by little, relax and sink onto him, until the breach was over, until he filled her up to such a level he thought he would explode with the delicious tight heat.

They didn't move.

Just stood there, locked together, hearts pounding against each other, the rain drumming against their faces and shoulders, doing their best to find air amid the flood washing over them, and through them.

Too late for regrets. No chance for second thoughts.

Closing his eyes, Brandon allowed the dam to burst.

A gentleman is always distinguished
by his respectful attention to women.
—*Good Morals and Gentle Manners*
<small>AUTHOR UNKNOWN</small>, 1873

CHAPTER SIXTEEN

BRONTE STARED OUT THE WINDOW OF HER ROOM WATCHING
the last of the storm clouds race across the sky.

When would the regret begin? The shame? The
humiliation for having acted so wantonly? By now,
she should have experienced some remorse, some
modicum of contrition.

Nothing. Nothing but the dizzying race of her
heart each time she recalled her shocking surrender.

Bronte smiled to herself, absorbed in the delicious memory of Brandon's arms around her, his
lips on hers, his body in hers—the heat, the hard-
ness, the sheer magnitude of his passion—equaled
by her own.

She should have been bothered that she had
allowed her fantasies to overwhelm her; yet she
felt . . . free at long last, scrubbed of those terrible
desires that had possessed her since the first moment she'd set eyes on Brandon Tremain.

At long last; she had what she wanted—an end to her miserable dilemma.

She simply would not allow it to happen again. Ever.

The storm having subsided at last, Bronte threw open the window and turned her face into the sunlight. Undoubtedly, she had overslept. She should have made her way to the school long ago, to assess any damage that might have been caused by the winds and rain. The poorly constructed buildings probably had not stood up to such brutal and destructive weather.

Hearing voices, Bronte wandered to the front parlor, unconsciously smoothing her hair and the wrinkles from her skirt. Her father stood just inside the front doorway, his clothes a bedraggled mess. Brandon stood behind him.

Both men turned at her entrance.

Bronte swallowed. "Father, I wasn't aware you'd gone out."

He said nothing for a moment, and there was something in his eyes that disturbed her. "I was just down at St. Cluny's."

"Is everything all right? The children—"

"Are fine." Reaching into his coat pocket, he withdrew an envelope and extended it to her.

She recognized the handwriting immediately. "From Pilot Crenshaw?"

William nodded.

She slipped the missive into her skirt pocket, then looked around her father to Brandon, where he stood in the door, pant legs wet to his knees and shirtsleeves rolled up to his elbows. He did not, however, return her look, but stepped around her

father with a quiet "Excuse me" and headed down
the corridor toward his room.

Not so much as a glance? Bronte thought.

He could so casually ignore her after what had
happened between them the night before?

She stood there awkwardly for a moment.

Finally, she turned back to her father. Having
removed his boots, he wearily walked into the
parlor and dropped into a chair. He closed his eyes.

"The crops took a damnable beating," he announced. "The river frontage was totally flooded.
Blast me, but I should have taken up sheep farming
as your mother suggested."

"It's not too late." Bronte smiled encouragingly.

At last, William looked at her, his face a little gray.
"The livestock were scattered. Tremain helped collect them."

Tremain's name seemed to hang in the air while
her father continued to regard her, his muddy
fingers gribbing the leather chair arms so tightly his
knuckles were white. "Did you sleep well last night,
Pumpkin?"

Bronte swallowed but didn't blink. "Why do you
ask?"

William remained curiously silent for a moment,
then, finally, he closed his eyes and turned his face
away and sat for what seemed to Bronte to be an
eternity before he said quietly, "I'm terribly tired.
Perhaps a nap . . ."

"Of course." She hurried to the settee, grabbed up
a blue-and-white fringed lap blanket, and tucked it
over her father's knees. She kissed his forehead and
said softly, "I love you, Father."

Not until she reached the door did William speak

again. "Regarding Tremain . . ." She froze, stared straight ahead while her heartbeat throbbed in her ears. "It's my feeling that Captain Tremain's position of cook is a thorough waste of his capabilities now, when we're so desperately in need of help during this attempt to save the farm from complete ruin. Therefore, I've decided to send him back to the barracks. Mr. Turpin will need all the help he can get to rebuild this farm . . . The devastation was staggering. I've already spoken to Tremain, and he's assured me that his leg has healed satisfactorily." William laced his hands in his lap and sighed wearily. "He seemed relieved, actually. Perhaps he found living here a bit of a struggle . . ."

"Yes," Bronte said softly, thinking of Brandon sequestered with the prisoners—away from her. Yesterday she would have felt relief . . . but now . . .

"I suspect most of my time will be devoted to the prison. There was a great deal of damage there as well—several prisoners managed to escape during the worst of the storm," her father said. "I fear you'll be forced to deal with the problem here on your own. I'm certain you can manage."

"Of course."

He turned his dark eyes up to hers. "You don't mind?"

"No. I won't mind at all," she managed to reply.

Bronte slipped into the hallway and sank against the wall. Her mouth felt dry, her knees weak. Never had the sense of guilt so overwhelmed her; she wanted to throw herself at her father's feet and beg him to save her from the terrible dilemma in which she was apparently trapped.

How could she have allowed such a thing to happen?

After all, Brandon was a prisoner.

And the punishment for a prisoner taking liberties with a free woman was a hundred lashes with a cat-o'-nine, then transportation to Norfolk Island. As warden of New South Wales Prison, her father could demand any sort of retribution he desired.

But what was done was done, of course.

Once Tremain had returned to the barracks, it would not happen again. How could it?

Taking a deep breath, Bronte moved down the corridor, hesitating outside Brandon's room. The door was not locked. Bronte pushed it open and stood for a moment on the threshold of the room. Sun spilled through the streaked windowpanes and made a harsh yellow pool of light on his bed. Stepping into the room, Bronte quietly closed the door behind her, and leaned there, allowing her knees to steady themselves, her heart to slow down, and her mind to hush its urgent warning to retreat.

He had his back to her, packing up his few belongings.

Hearing her, he turned and found Bronte's eyes. Odd. In that moment, he looked as wretched as he had the first time she saw him at the prison yard those weeks ago—now, however, she thought him spectacular. The sight of his unshaven jaw, dark as a crow's wing, his thick black hair framing his face in unruly waves made something roll over inside her.

Bronte slowly moved over and gazed up at him. His tattered shirt lay open, exposing his chest. He had kicked off his muddy boots and tossed them in a corner.

"It's better that I go," he said softly.

"Agreed," she replied simply, but firmly, proud of her control and just as nervous that the control would shatter with the slightest provocation.

He raised one eyebrow.

"Did you think I had come here to seduce you, Mr. Tremain? To try to concoct some plan to keep you here?"

He said nothing.

"I didn't come here to seduce you," she repeated, despising the breathiness of her voice, knowing what it meant, what it always meant whenever she was around him. In the beginning, she hadn't understood. Now, cursedly, she did. "I'd like to think I'm prouder than that," she said with a touch of her old defiance.

Brandon reached his hand out to her. She stared at it, a sudden shocking hot wave of the previous night's memories washing over her.

What harm would come of just touching him? To experience one last time the feel of his flesh on hers?

She put her hand in his, briefly closing her eyes as his fingers wrapped warmly and tenderly around it.

"Come here," he said.

"No." She shook her head, even as she felt her body slide into his arms.

"My God, I've missed you," he whispered into her hair. "I'll miss you."

She closed her eyes.

"Every minute of the last tortuous hours I've thought about you. I cursed you, because you've altered my priorities."

Closing one hand around her throat, he tipped up her chin with his thumb and stared fiercely into her eyes. "Then I wanted to make love to your mouth, and every place else. I even imagined that we were in love.

"But we're not in love, are we, Bronte?" He shook her. "Are we?" he repeated. "Because we can't be. You are who you are and I'm . . ." He held her tighter, his gaze hot and intense. ". . . I'm not perfect. I'm not the hero you worshipped all those years. What happened between us happened because we are both merely mortal. And I was weak. Too damned weak to fight you any longer.

"It can't happen again." He slid his fingers through her soft black hair. He touched her face lightly with his fingertips—traced her eyebrows, her eyelids, the shape of her lips. "It can't happen again. We can't risk it—I won't risk it, your being discovered. I don't give a damn about what happens to me, but you . . ." He kissed the tip of her nose, her cheek, her closed eyes, then, lightly, the corner of her mouth, allowing his lips to linger, to lightly taste, to breathe slightly upon her cheek as he stroked her ear with his finger. "It's not worth the risk." Twisting his hands in her hair, he pulled back her head so she flinched slightly with the immense pressure upon her scalp. "I won't have you hurt, Bronte. Do you understand?"

"Yes," she breathed, and lowered her lashes, unwilling to allow him to see the emotions there— emotions that she hadn't been aware she felt until that moment.

"Promise me you'll put this behind you," he pleaded in a rough, urgent voice. "Go on with your plans for the children, and . . ."

"And?"

His eyes became bluer, his face tense. For a long moment, he said nothing, as a slow, dark anger built in the line of his flexing jaw. His fingers twisted painfully in her hair. ". . . And consider marrying Arthur."

"Arthur?" she said, her eyes meeting his again.

"He'll be good to you."

"How can you even imagine I would contemplate such a thing?"

Roughly, he gripped her arms and shook her. "Listen to me, sweetheart. The image you've concocted yourself about me is nothing more than fantasy. That Brandon Tremain doesn't exist. He never did. I'm just a man thrust into a position of authority who is obligated to follow orders. The newspapers needed a hero, someone to boost the morale of a war-weary populace, and mine happened to be the name drawn from a hat. There were a thousand other men fighting around me who were just as deserving."

Relaxing, Brandon tipped up her chin and stroked her lower lip with his thumb. "As far as Arthur is concerned . . . he should be given credit for attempting to deal with ruffians like me."

Bronte swallowed, her cheeks growing warm with the unexpected and unwelcome sentiment awakening in her chest: pain. As if her heart were, little by little, beginning to crumble.

"Friends?" he said.

"Of course," she replied.

Brandon slid his arms around her and held her against his chest while she listened to his heart beat and, closing her eyes and breathing deeply, allowed her senses to be filled by his wonderful presence, knowing that she might never hold him again, that what had happened that tumultuous and electrified night would not happen again.

Knowing that, once more, she would be forced to settle for meager dreams and unfulfilled desires. She would learn to deal with it again, as she had in the past.

She had no choice.

Appearing more than a little distraught, Sister Elizabeth stood on the front porch stoop, her glasses spotted with mud. "I think you should come," she said to Bronte. "The children are very upset."

"What's this about?" Bronte stepped from the house.

"It's Mr. Ellison and Mr. Crenshaw and—"

"Crenshaw." Frowning, a sudden flutter of anxiety unsettling her stomach, Bronte reached into her skirt pocket and withdrew the envelope her father had delivered just hours before. She ripped off the seal and withdrew the letter. Her eyes scanned it hurriedly, while her body turned cold as ice.

"Fiend," she said through her teeth, softly, then more loudly as a rush of anger and panic swept through her. Shoving Elizabeth aside, Bronte ran down the rain-washed steps and headed toward the road, stepping over thick mud puddles. Within minutes, steam swallowed her, made her clothes cling to her body, and made her body sweat from the heat and effort of attempting to slog her way down the muddy path.

Crenshaw's coach was parked in front of the school, and even before Bronte flung back the gate and ran up the path toward the building, she heard the boy's cries.

The group congregated in the vestibule turned their white, astonished faces toward Bronte as she threw open the door and stood panting on the threshold, hair damp and twisted over her shoulders. Looking neither left nor right, not at Arthur who stood in the shadows watching with eyes as sharp as a ferret's, or at the unfamiliar couple clinging to each other like unwilling witnesses to a crime, she marched down the hallway to the office door, and with hands fisted at her sides, feet planted firmly apart, she fixed her gaze on Crenshaw, where he stood gripping Sammy's arm like a vise.

"I will give you to three to unhand him," she declared in a hoarse voice.

His features set, Crenshaw gripped the boy more tightly. "Miss Haviland. This is really no concern of yours."

"I beg to differ, sir—"

"He is a ward of this government and therefore belongs to us."

Sammy let loose a howl and squirmed, his face growing red and tears overflowing his dark, frightened eyes. "I won't go!" he cried. "You can't make me."

"I won't allow you to separate Pam and Sam," Bronte said with less vehemence. "They are brother and sister."

"These good people have shown interest in adopting the boy. I'm moving him into Sydney so they might become acquainted." Crenshaw motioned toward the somnolent couple huddled together in the corridor, their bearings stiff as posts as they regarded Bronte with disapproval.

"I won't go!" Sammy yelled, then kicked Crenshaw across the shin, causing the vice-governor to yowl and bare his teeth, releasing his grip on Sammy's arm as he hopped up and down in pain. Sammy ran to Bronte, who dropped to her knees and threw open her arms. Weeping, his hot little body clinging to hers, Sammy whimpered, "I don't want to go, Bronte. I want to stay with you. I don't like those people."

Holding him closely, Bronte swallowed back her emotions. "Hush, now. I'll do my best—"

"I want my sister!" Sammy clutched Bronte more tightly. "I won't leave Pam, I won't! I won't leave you, Bronte. Please don't make me!"

His entire body shook, though the little boy tried to be brave.

Forcing her gaze back to Crenshaw's, Bronte managed to say, "I beg you. Don't separate the boy from his sister. Give us some time to consider the alternatives."

"What alternatives? Would you have him live among this litter of misfits forever? For God's sake, the boy is obviously in need of a disciplined environment."

"What if I were to adopt them, Sammy and his sister?"

"You?" He guffawed. "My dear Miss Haviland, you are a single woman. A boy needs a family."

"But if I were to be married—"

Crenshaw moved across the room. Less than gently he grabbed Sammy's arm and forced him away, mumbling apologies to the watchful couple.

They moved as a group down the corridor with Sammy continuing to struggle, to look back at Bronte. Still on one knee, her gaze frozen on the now empty threshold, Bronte did her best to reason sanely, and calmly. She'd always been so bloody good at that—retaining her equilibrium in the face of any crisis—so why, as she stood and moved woodenly, then hurriedly toward the door did she suddenly feel as if every last thread of self-control had just snapped?

The group had just reached the front gate when Bronte exited the orphanage. She tried to call out; the emotion in her throat would not allow it.

With no warning, someone covered her hand with his and said calmly and firmly in her ear, "Don't do it, Bronte."

Bronte struggled. She heard someone crying and realized it was herself.

"Control," the voice said. "Emotionalism won't help Sammy or your case. Listen to me."

She twisted and stared up into Arthur's smug face, and thought of Brandon. This was all her fault. Her punishment—for succumbing to her own selfish needs when her father and Sammy and the others needed all of her, her body and soul, her loyalty—yes, yes, yes, this was her rod of retribution for being human at last.

"Stand straight," Arthur pronounced with a look of disdain. "Remember your sense of dignity, Bronte." Whipping a kerchief from his pocket, he roughly attempted to cleanse a streak of tears from her face. "Be still and look at me. There. Yes." He allowed her a curl of a smile. "I'm in a position to help you, Bronte. I'll speak with Crenshaw and the prospective parents. Perhaps I can make them listen to reason, or consider your alternative—to adopt the child yourself . . . or rather, for you and your spouse to adopt the child."

Staring into Arthur's emotionless face, Bronte swallowed.

Arthur tucked the mud-streaked kerchief back into his coat pocket and regarded her with one raised eyebrow. "I think I make myself clear, do I not, my dear?"

She nodded, sniffed, and watched the buggy in which the couple and Crenshaw had arrived turn back toward Sydney, Sammy continuing to wail out his displeasure. "I understand perfectly," she finally replied. "Should I expect you to inform my father of our approaching nuptials?"

A gentleman who does not contemplate matrimony
should not pay too exclusive attention to any one lady.
—*Our Deportment, or The Manners, Conduct and
Dress of the Most Refined Society*

CHAPTER SEVENTEEN

BRANDON LAY ON HIS COT IN THE DARK, LISTENING TO A
dozen other men snore and talk in their sleep. His
back ached. So did his head. His hands looked as if
he had run them through a meat grinder. The only
solace he found in recalling his day's grueling work
was the fact that he and the men working with him
had managed to save more of Haviland's crops
than they had first hoped.

The realization occurred to him that he had spent
a great many years lying alone in the dark surrounded by other men with only his thoughts to
occupy the long hours until morning. Hard to
believe that just a few short nights ago he'd made
love to Bronte Haviland.

Bronte. Another mistake to file away in his mind.
No good could come of it.

Besides, at long last, his plans to crack the mercenary smuggling plot were coming together. Working
side by side with the other prisoners, getting to know

them, winning their trust, he had learned of the rumors, whispered conjectures that there might well be a way out of the men's dreary existences . . . for a price.

No doubt about it, holding Bronte Haviland again should have been the last thing on his mind.

He had barely closed his eyes when the whispered voice said, "If our sources have been correct these last many months, then the time is nearly upon us for action. In case you are unaware, the *Sirius* has anchored in Melbourne. She should be docking in Sydney within a fortnight, if not sooner. No, don't move. Don't say a word. Should I be discovered here, I'm afraid I would be hard-pressed to come up with a believable reason why. By golly but you're a hard man to reach these days . . . now that you're back in the trenches . . ."

Brandon covered his face with his hands.

"Captain Dillman should be arriving to see his old friend Haviland in the very near future. Are you aware that Dillman is Bronte's godfather?"

Brandon groaned and rolled toward the wall.

"Did you learn anything before leaving Haviland's house?"

Brandon shook his head no.

"Come, come, Captain. You know something. Don't let any reckless sense of chivalry to a lady blind you."

Brandon remained quiet. He listened to Rossie Rodale grunt and groan in his sleep.

"It's my understanding that the *Sirius* will be anchored in Sydney Harbor for two weeks, and at the end of two weeks she will unfurl her sails and make for Calcutta, no doubt with her belly full of cut-

throats who will do anything to win their freedom—
even massacre innocent men, women, and children.
Do you really believe you could withstand a second
burden of that sort?"

"It's not the girl," he snapped furiously, causing
several men to stir in their bunks. Swinging his feet
from the bed, he stared hard through the dark. "It's
not the girl," he repeated through his teeth.

"Are you certain, Captain?"

He breathed heavily.

"I didn't think so. That's why we chose you for
this mission, Captain. Because the memory of Vishnue's treason would keep you sharp and biting;
you wouldn't trust again easily. Even now, as you
sit there burning, there is that nagging little voice in
the back of your mind that continues to remind you
that . . . she may well be the enemy."

Brandon closed his eyes, depleted of all strength.
He wanted a bottle of whiskey, a cigar, and a bath.
He wanted to turn back the clock a few years, to
when the only memories bothering his long nights
were the faces of the brave young men, barely older
than children, whom he had led to their deaths.

Rossie rolled in his bed, then sleepily sat up.
Brandon looked over his shoulder to discover that
his former companion had swiftly disappeared into
the dark.

Rossie dropped his feet to the floor, rubbed his
hands through his mat of thick red hair, and yawned.

"Can't sleep, eh?" he said to Brandon, who
continued to sit with his elbows on his knees, his
head hanging wearily. "I could use a drink meself,
a nice big bottle of rum. I can't remember when I
last slept the night through." Leaving his cot, he

stumbled over to the barred window overlooking
the dark, deserted grounds. He appeared to contemplate his surroundings before turning back to
Brandon. He stood before the moonlit window like
a paper-doll silhouette.

"Just between you and me, Cap'n, there are times
when I'd sell me soul to the devil 'imself to go home
again. Back to me wife and little children."

At last, Brandon leaned back on his cot. "From
what I hear there are possibilities—"

"There ain't no possibilities," Rossie returned
desperately. "Them tales you hear out there?" He
thumbed out the window over his shoulder. "Fools.
All of 'em, if they think they can leave this place
and go home again. Many's tried, I tell ya, and just
as many have failed. The damned sharks get them
all—and I don't necessarily mean the finned ones."
He lowered his voice. "You'll find, Cap'n, once
you've been here long enough, that there are those
around you who would sell their own mothers to
leave this place. They'd do anything, ya understand."

"So there's a way out," Brandon stated.

For a long moment, Rossie remained silent. Then
he moved to Brandon's cot and stood staring down
at him through the dark, the moonlight occasionally
reflecting off his eyes. At last, in a quieter voice, he
said, "When you first came here, Cap'n, we didn't
like you much, what with the warden bringing you
in before you'd done yer proper time at the hard
labor. Then you got moved into the nice house,
living right there fancy as a king . . . but the last
few days, there are those of us who've come to trust
you, maybe even to like you. Who wouldn't like to

see no harm come to someone who works as hard as us. I guess what I'm saying is, there ain't no way out, Cap'n, no matter what anyone might tell you. If they tell you so, don't trust 'em. Don't listen to 'em. Cause the only freedom you're gonna find across that water is certain death. I don't know about you, sir, but I'm a patient man. When I leave this place, it's gonna be because my time is up. I'm gonna walk off that ship and back into my loving wife's arms . . . and I ain't ever coming back."

She was insane for coming here.

Bronte reined in Cytduction at the edge of the wheat field, which had been mostly flattened by the storm. Men scurried here and there in their attempts to rectify the damage done to the fences and hoisting posts, but dredging water weeped into the postholes the moment they redug them. Bronte's eyes scanned the laboring men, then . . .

He was there, Captain Brandon Tremain—her enemy, her lover—along with several others, his back straining, his brow sweating.

"Miss Haviland . . ."

Cytduction shied, and Bronte collected the loose reins. There was still time to escape, to rethink her insane plan before it was too late . . .

Johnny Turpin moved around her, his club swinging in his hand.

"Mr. Turpin," she replied.

"What brings you way out here?" he asked.

Her eyes drifted toward Tremain, who had not noticed her yet. "I must have a word with the captain," she finally said. "I've a message for him from my father."

Johnny's eyebrows went up. "I'll be happy to deliver him the message—"

"My father preferred that I speak to him myself."

Turpin said nothing, just slapped the club repeatedly against his leg and stared up into her face. Finally, "Tremain!" he barked loudly enough to make Cytduction toss her head and prance in place.

Slowly, slowly, or so it seemed, Brandon turned from his chore and shielded his eyes from the sun. He didn't move.

Hesitantly, without so much as a glance down at Turpin, Bronte nudged her nervous horse forward.

Brandon tossed down his pickax and walked toward her. They met halfway. He placed a skinned and muddy hand on Cytduction's arched neck to quiet the mare, and waited for Bronte to explain her idiotic reason for coming here to see him.

But how could she possibly say what she wished to?

I need you.

I want to hold you one last time, before I sacrifice the rest of my life to duty.

Yet it was a duty he had once scoffed at, then finally encouraged her to perform.

But if it hadn't been for Sammy . . .

"Is there a problem at the house?" his voice said quietly.

She tried to swallow, and nodded. "I . . ." Glancing around at the working men, and once again to a watchful Turpin, who stood in the distance like a sentry atop a tree stump, Bronte did her best to breathe evenly. "I need to see you," she almost whispered.

"When?" he replied calmly, his blue eyes steady,

not even so much as a flicker of surprise crossing his dark features.

"Tonight . . ."

"But how?"

"After the lights go out. I happen to know that once the guards are certain the men are asleep, they meet out back of the kitchen to drink and gamble. By midnight they're oblivious. They'll never know you're gone, as long as you return by dawn."

Bronte glanced back at Turpin and added almost as an afterthought: "There is a trapdoor in the floor of the eating hall . . . The tunnel will bring you out near the river . . ." Then she spurred Cytduction toward the road, leaving Brandon staring after her.

Not bothering to knock, she opened the cottage door and stepped inside.

Lying in a tub of hot water, his wet head resting against the rim, a brandy bottle gripped in one soapy hand and propped on his stomach, Brandon slowly opened his eyes. Upon seeing Bronte standing by the door, he made a sound in his throat.

"Do you like the bath?" she asked nervously. "I had Wang draw it. I told him it was for me . . . that I'd be spending more time here while Father is away . . . He believed me, of course. After all, I'm such a shining example of propriety." She laughed to herself. She was talking much too rapidly.

He moved, sloshing steaming water on the floor, and lifted the bottle to his mouth. She watched his lips caress it, and turned away.

"Do you like my cottage?" She smiled. "I always recline there on the settee and watch the river. In the spring there are white egrets that gather there on the banks and . . ."

"And what?"

"Mate," she replied softly.

The water sloshed again.

"I suppose the floor could use a rug or two."

"No doubt."

"And possibly new curtains for the windows." Her gaze swept the windows on each of the four walls while she did her best to calm the maelstrom of nervousness going on inside her.

She gazed out on the moonlit river and listened to the croaking frogs and the chattering of a bird. The room felt overly warm, what with the steam from Brandon's bath collecting against the low ceiling. The need to cry crept up on Bronte, stuck at the back of her throat so she couldn't swallow, then burned its way to her eyes until tears spilled down her cheeks. It was ridiculous, really, this silly emotionalism.

Slowly, she turned to find Brandon watching her, his eyes deep blue and slightly bloodshot. The idea occurred to her that he looked ridiculously big in the small porcelain tub. The water barely covered his hips. His knees thrust up out of the water like mangrove knobs.

"What's so funny?" he demanded almost in a whisper.

She shook her head and wiped the tears from her face. "We're friends, right?"

He nodded.

Funny how that term "friend" always brought an uncomfortable ache to her chest. "You look ridiculous in that tub."

He raised one eyebrow and rewarded her with a sleepy half smile. "And you look . . ."

"Well?"

"Damn tempting."

What could she say?

"Did you bring me here to seduce me, Miss Haviland?"

"What if I did?"

She moved toward the tub, allowing the gossamer dressing gown to slide from her shoulders, revealing the mull and Mechlin lace peignoir she had dug from an old trunk. A moment passed—an eternity, while her heart beat like that of someone having contemplated jumping over the edge of a black abyss and decided, at the last moment, that she would try one last time to beat life at its own crucifying game.

"I've missed you so," she whispered. "I thought once would be enough, but . . ."

At last, he said, "Then come take me," in soft invitation, and, slowly, he rose up from the bath, allowing the water to flow down his body while the yellow lamplight appeared to catch fire on his golden skin.

She stared at his magnificent body, which seemed to her to be both proud and submissive. In an instant she was drowned by the need to hold him, like a terrible thirst that had to be assuaged. She felt breathless and dizzy, unable to force herself to look away, not wanting to.

"Come here," his lips whispered.

"This is madness," she heard herself respond, even while her body stepped into the warm water.

"We shouldn't be here. I was insane for bringing you here. If we are caught . . ."

"If we are caught," he said, a faint smile on his lips, "we will have our memories to sustain us."

Bronte briefly closed her eyes, absorbing his nearness, the scent of his warm skin, the mellifluous tone of his rich voice, which, as always, touched deep, deep inside her.

"Take it off," he said, meaning her peignoir. "It's much too pretty to ruin."

Her fingers trembling, she untied the satin ribbon at her breasts, allowing the flimsy garment to spill open. With his fingertips, he caught it as it glided from her shoulders, and he dropped it to the floor.

With the steaming water lapping at their shins, they watched each other's eyes. At last, he repeated, "Take me, Miss Haviland."

She swallowed, and when she found herself incapable of moving, he took one of her hands in his and placed it upon his smooth, hard chest, her fingertip pressing upon his firm nipple. "Beautiful," she heard herself murmur. "You're beautiful."

Then, little by little, he slid her hand down his hard stomach, to his magnificent aroused organ, and gently eased her fingers around it. She felt it throb against her palm, and closing her eyes, she allowed herself the infinite joy of learning his most intimate self by stroking and caressing, until his deep groan of pleasure made her open her eyes, to find him a prisoner of his own senses, his dark head back, his eyes closed, his mouth slightly open as he breathed heavily in the quiet.

Oh, that she could cause him such enjoyment.

Emboldened, she allowed her hands the freedom

to explore, finding that the act of bringing him such pleasure intensified her own, and vanquished the remaining thread of hesitance she had had in coming here.

"Nice," he growled. "Yes, oh yes, Miss Haviland. Don't stop. That's good. Very good. Oh God . . ." he breathed. "You learn quickly."

He gasped. He groaned. He lifted the brandy bottle with one hand and took her face in the other. He tipped back her head, touched the rim of the bottle to her lips, and allowed the potent drink to dribble into her mouth, and down her chin, and to drip onto her breasts, where the liquid beaded like an amber raindrop on her nipple. And he bent and flicked it into his mouth with his tongue.

Her breathing quickened.

He poured the brandy down his own body, across his chest, and stomach, and allowed it to run low, and lower, and down the insides of his muscular thighs, where it glistened amid the fine, lacy black hairs that were yet damp from his bath.

A heartbeat passed, and then another while Bronte felt the last of her innocence slide like a yoke from her shoulders. All the while she watched his eyes, like two brilliant blue fires, and his smile, slightly lopsided, enticing, alluring, beckoning her on, perhaps challenging. And it occurred to her that . . . this was no defeat, this surrender. But a plunge from her body's lifelong quiescence into vigor, free at last from her own and society's shackles—at least for the moment, the glorious moment. For the moment, she would not think of what she must ultimately be forced to do.

He whispered her name.

She smiled somewhat tremulously into his eyes, which held an indescribable luster, like low-burning embers.

He took her face in his hands; his eyes were sharp and almost angry. "Why did you really bring me here, Bronte?"

Bronte touched his face, his jaw where his beard had become rough as it always did by the end of the day. In the golden glow of the lantern on the near table, his jet-black hair shimmered with light; his lips looked luscious. "That's obvious, isn't it?" she finally replied.

Going up on her toes, she kissed him. Not timidly. But with her open mouth, and her tongue. Wrapping her arms around him and twisting her hands in his thick hair. Feeding, famished, on his mouth until, with a throaty groan and muttered curse, he wrapped his arms around her and raised her up against his slick body, until their pressing flesh felt as hot and liquid as the water sloshing around his legs.

He swept her aside easily, lifting her from the tub while his hands wrapped her legs around his hips. And still she kept kissing him, tongue dancing with his, in and out, darting and plunging, each fighting for breath as they fell onto their sides on his cot.

The bed ropes creaked. The old, thin mattress sagged under their weight.

Their arms and legs tangled. Their bodies strained against each other, almost frantic with the passion but as yet unwilling to relieve the delicious mounting demand.

She explored him with her fingers and tongue, inhaling his intoxicating scent of man and brandy,

the musky smell of sex that seemed to seep from his
every pore, to make her drunk with this newfound
power to control him. She nipped his budded little
nipples gently between her teeth, and he gasped.
She swirled her tongue round and round his navel,
and his stomach quivered with flirtation, and anticipation. And, finally, when she lowered her head,
and felt his body move against her mouth as if it
were a being unto itself, she knew the ecstasy of
owning him thoroughly—his body, his soul, his
deepest, darkest desire, which made him growl like
a beast, then whimper.

Then, finally, when he could take no more, he
dragged her up his body and rolled to his back,
eased his knee between her thighs and spread her
legs. With his labor-roughened hand, he brushed
her hair back from her face, then gently squeezed
her breasts, possessed their weight in his palms as if
they were treasures.

"Take me, Miss Haviland. Please," he whispered
in a husky, urgent voice.

She smiled into his eyes, which were burning in
the deep, tanned creases of his handsome face.

With his hands, he cupped her buttocks and
lifted her onto him, eased her down so gradually
the sublimity overcame her, and she cried aloud.
Her flesh tingled. Her breathing quickened. Her
body flooded with that familiar delicious pain and
yearning that had started as little more than a
nagging, discomfiting mystery the moment she first
saw him.

She throbbed, there where their bodies cleaved,
his against hers, hot and wet. As she sat there
astride him, filled by him, she found herself mes-

merized by the sight of it, their bodies as one, unable to tell where one quit and the other began.

Except that his body was dark, browned by the sun. And hers was white, like sunlight streaking through shadow.

"Make love to me," he said softly, his mouth slightly open, his breath panting.

"Make love, sir?" She smiled and lowered her lashes, her gaze drifting again to their joined bodies. "Is that what we're doing, Captain? Making love?"

"Are you asking me if I love you, Miss Haviland?"

Her face turned warmer.

His head pressing into his pillow, Brandon murmured, "Will you stop if I say no?"

Briefly, Bronte closed her eyes, acknowledging the reality of his body inside hers. "No," she finally replied, moving her hips, gasping at the instantaneous shock of raw sensation that shot through her. "I couldn't stop now if I wanted to."

And she couldn't. In that moment, she didn't care what he felt. She was being selfish— shockingly so. She would use him, if she must, to know the magic, the temptation, the sweet, illicit pruriency that drove women to such decadence of the soul. This deliverance was what she needed, what she deserved.

She would never know this again.

"Damn you for your innocence," he hissed, and thrust up against her, making her cry out briefly. Then he thrust back, to rock, to grind, to rise up again and again until he was clutching the bed sheet beneath him with both hands and arching under her, until the small bed seemed as if it would shatter any moment and send them crashing to the floor.

On and on he went, while the pressure continued to build and her skin became so hot she thought she might die. His body stretched hers, filled hers, moved into and out of her cleft with almost bruising necessity, born of his leashed need to show her the splendor.

At last it came, sweeping through her unexpectedly, making her body suddenly go stiff and unable to move, helpless—this death, this beautiful momentary death, when the world ceased to be anything but the crash of carnal forces, his and hers at once.

He kissed her brutally, even as she screamed against his mouth, on fire with the white-hot flashes of pleasure that streaked through her. She flailed helplessly against him, arms and legs thrashing, wanting the raw ecstasy to end, wanting it to go on forever. The pleading, whimpering sound of her own voice both shamed and thrilled her, and when she felt his body go rigid, and felt the hot, living fluid pump inside her, felt him shiver, and heard him groan, and sigh, and emit a growl like the purr of a lion, she knew, at long last, the splendor—the glorious, glorious splendor.

Brandon sat in the mouth of the musty tunnel as the first rays of sunlight crept over the watery horizon. He watched the ghostly images of egrets flutter like angels from the dark sky and settle along the muddy banks of the river, and he thought about the last hours he had spent with Bronte.

Bronte . . . who had entranced him from the first moment he saw her.

Bronte . . . who had turned his priorities inside out.

Bronte . . . who had made him want to believe in innocence, and selflessness—and, yes, love—again.

Bronte . . . who was the most beautiful, sensual woman he had ever held.

Who, in a moment of weakness, had revealed a terrible secret.

Around him were stacked the remaining coffin-like crates of smuggled liquor and cigars. He lit a sulfur match, held it to the wood box, and with a tightening of his chest, read aloud: "Calcutta."

Consider not the gift of the lover,
but the love of the giver.

—*"Dame Curtsey's" Book of Novel
Entertainments for Every Day of the Year*
ELLYE HOWELL GLOVER, 1907

CHAPTER EIGHTEEN

ONCE UPON A TIME BRONTE HAD LOVED SYDNEY. TODAY SHE
did not look forward to her trip, aside from visiting
Sammy. The fact that she had sent Arthur a note
agreeing on a wedding date made her head ache.

But all her actions had a reason.

Tipping the parasol toward the sun to shield her
eyes, Bronte sighed and wished she had not allowed Wang to convince her to allow him to drive
her into Sydney. A breakneck ride into town on
Cytduction might have cleared this lethargy from
her heart and mind.

"Whoa!" Wang called and hauled back on the
lines, bringing the horses and the buggy to a quick
stop in the middle of the dusty road. Along the
road, the workers were scattered, working dili-
gently to repair the erosive damage that had been
done by the storm. Her eyes scanning the sweating,
straining men hauling barrows of dirt and rock,
Bronte experienced a sense of panic.

"Why are we stopping?" she asked Wang.

"A message for Turpin from your father," he replied with a quick smile over his shoulder, then he leapt from the buggy and left her staring after him, the heat of the day seeping through her clothes.

"Hello," came the soft voice behind her.

Bronte closed her eyes, sank back in her seat. She twirled the ivory-colored parasol between her hands and refused to look back. Her heart was racing.

"Hello," he repeated, and moved up beside her, close enough to touch.

"Please don't speak," she said desperately. "Please, just go away."

Silence followed, while the men in the distance began a soft, chanting song that helped alleviate the strain of their labor. Bronte watched Wang disappear around a corner in his search for Turpin, and for an insane moment she thought of calling him back.

Gently, Brandon reached for her parasol and, just as gently, pushed it down to her lap. "Look at me, Bronte."

At last, she allowed her gaze to meet his.

His fingers touched her hand, briefly, and his sun-darkened face smiled. "Hello," he said.

"Hello," she replied weakly.

"Friends?"

Swallowing, she toyed with the lace ruching on the parasol.

"Talk to me, Bronte."

"There's nothing to discuss. I've made my decision. We're not to see one another again. I shall, once again, devote my time to the hospital and orphanage—and of course my future husband."

"Time to play the martyr again, love?" Brandon regarded her with heavy-lidded speculative blue eyes, making the countryside and the singsong voices of the workers fade to a blur as Bronte focused on his lips, the rush of memories robbing her of breath and the ability to keep her emotions uninvolved.

Finally, he said, "I know you must admire Flora Tristan. My mother did as well. She was condemned for her decision to leave my father; however, had I not taken the matter into my own hands and returned to England on my own, I might not have seen her until I was grown. Some things should not be wasted through sacrifice. Some things are worth the risk."

She looked up at him. He knew Flora Tristan and her work. She had always imagined meeting a man who could share her ideals.

In an instant, it seemed, the frustration melted from her. Almost weakly, leaning toward him so their faces were inches apart, Bronte said in a soft, sad, and desperate voice, "Do you know what I wish?"

"Tell me."

"That we had met long ago, perhaps at some soiree, or a ride in Hyde Park, or a stroll along the beach in Brighton on a beautiful spring day. We might have eaten cockles from the shells and danced along with the minstrels who roam the seaside singing for coins."

"I would've bought you lace and ribbons for your hair."

She smiled.

Brandon took her hand and gripped it, held her with his eyes and the fierceness of his smile. "I would have courted you with flowers and candy and recited poetry to you."

"Sir." Bronte turned her head and lowered her lashes, feeling caught between the need to laugh at their silliness and the need to cry.

Again, her gaze found his, a growing sense of despondency filling her up. Finally, she said in a whisper, "And yet . . ."

"Tell me, Miss Haviland."

"And yet had we met long ago, then we might have stood a chance . . ."

"A chance at what, love?"

"At forever."

Brandon said nothing, and neither did she, both oblivious to the workers who spread around them, apparently ignoring them, their song growing louder and more animated:

"The very day we landed upon the Fatal Shore,
The planters stood around us, full twenty score or more;
They ranked us up like horses and sold us out of hand,
They chained us up to pull the plough, upon Van
    Diemen's Land."

Bronte pulled away, rested her parasol on her shoulders, and focused on the bend in the road where Wang had disappeared.

And Brandon said good-bye.

Bronte gazed out the window at the bedraggled line of shops up and down the dusty main street, while behind her Pilot Crenshaw shuffled through papers and mumbled directives to his assistant.

"My dear, we've been through this before," Crenshaw said. "This office has not a shilling to spare for the children, I'm sorry to say. While the flooding was tragic, I fear, until approval and funds arrive from Her Majesty, you'll simply have to do with what you have."

"Which is precious little, sir."

"Granted."

Turning from the window, Bronte regarded the more than plush surroundings of the vice-governor's office: the rich paneled walls, plush carpet, objects of fine art decorating the chamber. His home was no less well appointed. "Sir, the Sisters at St. Cluny have, once again, volunteered their own barracks to the children until we can rebuild. However, their accommodations are humble to say the least, and crowded."

Sitting back in his chair, Crenshaw pursed his lips, his gaze roaming the ceiling and walls.

The previous evening, Bronte had rehearsed well-thought-out speeches beseeching him for consideration, but as she stood there before him, regarding his paunchy belly, which threatened to swell between his vest buttons, and thought of the dozen needy children she'd left behind at St. Cluny's, her irritation mounted.

Woman has an incontestable superiority over man, but she must cultivate her intelligence and exercise her self-control in order to retain it, Flora Tristan had written.

Planting her hands on his desk, Bronte leaned toward Crenshaw and offered him a smile cold enough to wipe the condescension from his ruddy features. "Very well, sir. If I must, I'll wait. I have little choice. Now, I would like to see Sammy. Let me rephrase that. I will see Sammy before I leave this building."

Crenshaw said nothing, just regarded her with raised eyebrows before shoving himself from his chair and moving toward the door. He exited the room before her, and lumbered down one hallway after another, leaving the main building to cross an unadorned courtyard, with a marble statue of a rather dignified if not perplexed Captain James Cook, and finally to arrive at a drab brick space with black wrought iron covering the windows.

Inside, the dark hallways smelled musty. The enclosed rooms, though full to capacity with children, were silent as tombs.

Finally, Crenshaw stopped at one of the bleak chambers and rapped hard on the door. A man with heavily oiled hair and pointed chin answered, his eyes bleary behind thick-lensed spectacles.

"The boy Sammy," Crenshaw declared, and his voice echoed in the silence.

The corpse disappeared. Standing in the center of the hallway, gripping her reticule, Bronte did her best to breathe evenly. Comportment, she thought. She would not vent her dissatisfaction over these dreary surroundings.

The door creaked open.

Sammy peered out.

"Hello, Sammy." Bronte greeted him with as little emotion as she was capable. In truth, the lad only vaguely resembled Sammy—this was not her Sammy, whose hair was always tousled, his knees skinned and his nose smudged with dirt. Face red, not a carrot-colored hair out of place, the boy gazed up at her like a freckle-faced puppy. "Good afternoon, Miss Haviland."

Bronte cut her gaze to Crenshaw. "May I walk with the boy briefly outside, perhaps in the courtyard?"

Exchanging glances with the corpse, Crenshaw finally agreed with a sharp nod. "I've a meeting to attend. Shouldn't be long. Ten, fifteen minutes at the most. I'll see the boy back myself.'

Looking at Sammy again, Bronte extended her gloved hand. He took it and gripped it hard with his pudgy fingers. Then, turning their backs to the watchful men, they exited the building into the sunlight.

Staring straight ahead, saying nothing yet, Bronte and Sammy walked to the center yard, to the base of Cook's stone likeness. Then Bronte slowly turned to Sammy. For an instant, they stood there, as motionless as the statue. Then Bronte flung away her reticule and fell to her knees, throwing open her arms so Sammy could fling himself against her with all his strength.

"Take me home," the little boy pleaded.

"Oh, my darling, darling—soon."

"I hate it here. I miss you. I miss Pam."

Bronte closed her eyes. Sammy's tears made a wet blotch on her blouse. Finally, she managed to pry him from her neck so she could hold his little round face in her gloved hands. The child struggled futilely to stem the flow of tears, but his slender shoulders shook. And his nose ran. And his lower lip trembled uncontrollably.

"They give us numbers," he told her. "I'm num-

ber forty-two. They don't even know our names.
They don't let us play. If we speak without permission they wash our mouth out with soap and we
got to go all day without eating, and I'm awful
hungry all the time, Bronte, 'cause they don't feed
us enough, and know what else they call us?"

She shook her head.

"Bastards."

Thumbing the tears from his cheek, Bronte said,
"Perhaps I should wash their mouths out with
soap. Hmm?"

His brown eyes growing round, excitement light-
ing up his face, Sammy smiled and asked eagerly,
"Can I watch?"

"Of course. I'll even let you help."

"Oh boy!" Rubbing his hands together, looking
like his old mischievous self, Sammy hopped up
and down and rewarded her with a snaggletoothed
smile.

Taking his hands in hers, waiting until he settled
down, Bronte stood up. Gazing up at her, Sammy
asked, "Did you come to Sydney alone?"

"I thought it best for Pam to stay home—"

"I thought maybe Mr. Tremain might've come,
too."

"Oh." Bronte picked up her reticule and dusted it
off. "No."

His face crestfallen, Sammy shoved his hands in
his pockets.

"He sends you his love," Bronte told him.

Still, the boy stared at his shoes, looking so
unhappy Bronte felt miserable.

"How long has it been since you last left this
dreadful place?" she asked.

He shrugged.

She chewed her lower lip and glanced toward the distant vine-covered, wrought-iron gate partially obscured between two buildings. Softly, she said, "Give me your hand, Sammy Newman, and promise me you'll behave."

The moment they reached the wharves, Sammy yanked open his cinching starched collar and wiggled out of the heavy woolen coat, flinging it to the dock, so Bronte was forced to run to grab it before the gusty sea wind carried it over the edge and into the water below. He dashed down the planked pier, leaping like her rabbits, arms thrown wide as he scattered a collection of hungry gulls that had lined up along the banister waiting for the frequent handouts from stevedores and sailors. "Sammy!" she cried after him, knowing even as she continually called his name that it would do little good.

Glancing back the way they had come, Bronte frowned. Any moment she expected to see Pilot Crenshaw and his corpse-like assistant come flying down the road after them, but Sammy was not returning to his despairing little prison until he had once again felt the sun on his pale face.

Taking a breath, righting her shoulders, Bronte gripped her reticule in both hands and moved slowly down the plank walk after the rambunctious lad. Only then did she notice the high, spiraling masts of her godfather's ship. The *Sirius*.

With a whoop and squeal, Sammy barreled back up the wharf, leaping ropes and nets, upsetting a stevedore balancing a crate on his shoulder, and flung himself against Bronte, his little body sweating, but his eyes aglitter with happiness. Going to her knees, smoothing down his riot of hair, Bronte gave him a tweak on his freckled nose.

Breathing heavily, smearing the sweat around on his forehead with the back of one hand, Sammy said, "I got an idea. We'll steal aboard one of these ships and escape. But first we'll go home to Hav'land Farm and get Pam. I couldn't leave my sister. I'm responsible for her, you know."

"Of course," Bronte whispered. "We would never go anywhere without Pam."

"And Mr. Tremain."

Bronte sat back on her heels, trying to look stern. "It's not possible. Mr. Tremain is a prisoner—"

"We'll go away. Don't you see, Bronte? Out there, he ain't no prisoner. Out there, we're all free."

He pointed toward the rolling blue-green waves and the watery horizon, his eyes big and full of tears suddenly. "Please," he murmured, a little boy again, lost and afraid.

Her heart in her throat, Bronte gently took his small shoulders in her hands and did her best to smile cheerily. "I was going to tell you later, after . . ." She took a deep breath and forced the tightness from her throat. "I've agreed to marry Mr. Ellison, Sammy."

He didn't move as his tawny brows drew together in a frown. "No," he whispered.

"I've spoken with Mr. Crenshaw—"

"I don't like him."

"And he's assured me—"

"And he don't like me. And he don't like Pammy. He don't like children, Bronte."

"Once I'm married, I can immediately begin adoption proceedings—"

"No!" he shouted and shoved away, stood like a belligerent young man, with his fists clenched at his side while the sea wind whipped his rust-colored hair about his head. "I'll run away. I'll do it. I won't live with nobody but—"

"Listen to me." She reached for him; he stepped away. "Please don't make this any harder for me than it is."

Sammy wiped his nose with his shirtsleeve, his anger subsiding little by little.

"I love you," Bronte said softly. "I only want to see you and your sister happy."

"We won't be happy with Arthur. It's 'cause of him that we're here in the first place."

Bronte frowned. "What do you mean. Sammy?"

"Them people who showed up and say they want to adopt me. Them folk who want to take me away, 'cept they don't really want me. They're just doing Arthur a favor."

Taking Sammy's warm face in her hands, Bronte stared hard into his brown eyes. "The couple who want to adopt you, they're friends of Mr. Ellison? Is that what you're saying, Sammy?"

He nodded, spilling a coil of red hair over his forehead. "I heard 'em arguin', the man and woman. The woman tol' her husband that they should just 'wash their hands,' but the man said they'd told Arthur they'd do what they could to help."

Bronte sat back on her heels, her hands fisted on her knees, her hat brim fluttering in a sudden gust of fish-smelling wind. "You must have misunderstood," she finally said. "It was Arthur's idea that we hurry and marry so we can stop these adoption proceedings."

But as she looked at the boy, she knew he could be telling the truth.

Her eyes moved over the boy's head to the ship bobbing in the water.

Sammy's eyes were still full of hope and pleading as he pointed out to sea and begged for escape . . . for himself, for her, and for Brandon.

There was no escape for her or Sammy . . .

But for Brandon . . .

Bronte eased into Cytduction's stall, making barely a sound. The horse placed its muzzle into her palm and lipped the sugar lump Bronte offered while she cast a cautious look around the dark stable. No one had seen her leave the house or enter the barn. She would saddle Cytduction as quietly as possible, and with any luck, she would arrive at the *Sirius* by midnight, discuss her plan with Captain Dillman, and return home long before sunrise.

She knew the way, of course. Not by the road, certainly. The road was watched constantly. There was the old cleared timber path that ran adjacent to the river, winding its way through Lord Fish's property, then ending near the harbor. Most people avoided the place, finding it too treacherous, what with the rumored quicksand bogs and the ancient Aborigine stake pits, dug years before to dissuade the influx of white trespassers into the land.

She had just gently slid the copper-sweetened bit between the horse's teeth when the voice behind her said, "Had ya called, Miss Haviland, I would have gladly saddled the mare for ya."

Bronte jumped and spun. Rossie Rodale stood in the shadows.

"Mr. Rodale . . . You frightened me out of my wits."

He moved toward her, took the headstall from her hand, and finished sliding the well-oiled leather strap over the horse's ears. Without looking at Bronte, he said, "I've stable duty this week. I enjoy my work here—these are fine horses, yes, ma'am, they are. The finest I've ever seen. You've trained them well . . . I'll be checking this cinch to make certain it's tight enough—you know how she blows out her belly hoping for a little spare room at the first opportunity. There. See, I can take up this cinch another two notches. There now. She's ready. Now, if you'll just wait a minute or two, it won't take me long to get my horse saddled—"

"Your horse?" she said.

He turned his eyes to hers, and the moonlight spilling through the door turned his face ghostly. "Aye," he replied softly. "I won't be having you ride about this place unescorted. I wouldn't be able to sleep at night if something happened to you."

"But—"

"No buts, Miss Haviland. I've a job to do. A responsibility. I don't know who you're meeting or what your reasons are for going there. It's none of my business, and as a man who appreciates the consideration you've shown me the last year of working here, you can rest assured that your secret is good with me. I'm loyal, ma'am, if nothing else. Now, come along, and I'll give ya a leg up."

Captain Dillman, a tall, lean man whose visage had been baked dark and heavily lined by his years in the sun, appeared stunned to greet Bronte on the dimly lit deck of the *Sirius*. It seemed to Bronte that he had aged a decade in the past six months. "My dear Bronte, what a pleasant if not shocking surprise. Good God, has something happened to your father?"

She shook her head, feeling conspicuous and frightfully ridiculous. Nervously, doing her best to gather her courage, she glanced up the towering mast at the tightly furled canvas and taut riggings, which vibrated slightly with each gust of night wind. "My father is well."

"What brings you to Sydney in the middle of the night?"

"I came here to ask for your help. I realize that what I'm about to ask you is rather singular. I only hope that you'll hear me out completely before giving me your final answer."

The man nodded slowly. "This sounds serious."

"What would you say if I told you that I knew someone who wished to leave New South Wales on your vessel?"

"A friend of yours?"

She nodded.

Bronte chewed her lower lip and focused harder on the dark wharves, where an occasional seaman wandered drunkenly amid the crates and pilings of hemp. "What if I tell you that my friend is a prisoner?"

Silence.

Bronte forced herself to look up at her godfather. His dark eyes regarded her sharply. "My dear Bronte," he said. "Are you suggesting that I help a prisoner escape—"

"I realize that what I'm asking you is illegal."

"Agreed."

"But there is someone who loves him desperately. A young free woman—"

"A friend of yours?"

"Yes . . . She's become much too entangled with him. And he . . . doesn't deserve to spend the rest of his life in this place. He's a good and decent man who made a mistake. He is a man of good character who deserves another chance."

"I see."

For a long while, Dillman gazed out at the harbor, his features set. At last, he again looked at Bronte. "Why do you feel that I could help you with this problem?"

"I've no one else to turn to. Whom could I trust?"

"You do realize that if I were caught—"

"I could arrange everything. 'Tis a simple enough plan." Lowering her voice, she met her godfather's gaze directly. "He could stow away on one of the skiffs you bring up the river."

"Skiffs?"

"The liquor and cigars you supply my father."

He smiled. "I wasn't aware your father had shared that information with you, my dear."

"He wouldn't have, of course. But I guessed years ago."

"I see."

"So my plan was this. When your men deliver the next crates of liquor—"

"You could have your friend there, and he could escape down the river to my ship, thereby avoiding customs check. Ingenious plan, Bronte. You've a very sharp mind. Would you mind telling me who this friend is?"

"I would rather not. Not yet, at least."

"You do realize that if I were discovered in this scheme, I would risk losing a great deal more than my position with the East India Company."

"I understand, sir. If you feel the hazard too compromising, I'll tell my friend—"

"You say he's a prisoner?" he said more to himself than to Bronte. "Well . . ." His eyes came back to Bronte's. "You know, you and your father have always been special to me, Bronte. Ever since I attended the university with your father, he's been like a brother to me. When he married your mother, I was there at his side. As you recall, it was my ship that brought the three of you to New South Wales."

"I recall," she replied with a smile.

"I have often told your father that I would do anything to help him, or his, in a time of need."

"You have indeed been a fine friend to my family."

"Yet now you ask me to betray your father, Bronte."

She frowned.

"What if the plan were to go awry and your friend were discovered, my dear? You know the penalty for attempting to escape."

"Norfolk Island."

"An island a thousand miles out in the Pacific Ocean. An impenetrable prison of gale-force winds, rats, and shark-infested bays. Would you have this 'friend' subjected to such terrible circumstances, Bronte?"

"I trust that you would take great care that the gentleman in question is not discovered, sir. As a favor to me."

"I see." He smiled. "Very well, Bronte. I'll do what I can."

Brandon made the same trip he had made many evenings since he had discovered the tunnel. But this was the first night he noticed anything irregular.

From the shadows of the dark stable, he watched Bronte slide from her lathered horse. The hour was near dawn, and Bronte looked haggard and distressed. Her clothes were covered in mud. For a moment, she stood in the nearby swept aisle, her hand gripping the reins so tightly her knuckles looked white.

Brandon didn't move. He didn't speak. But waited, listening, a hot core of anger building. He had been wrong—dead wrong—about this woman.

He'd watched Bronte ride away with Rossie Rodale.

And she had returned, alone.

All airs of mastership, all foolish display of jealousy,
should be avoided . . . Quarrels cannot but impair
mutual respect and diminish love.

— *Good Manners: A Manual of Etiquette
in Good Society*
AUTHOR UNKNOWN, 1870

CHAPTER NINETEEN

SHE DRESSED IN HER MOTHER'S GOWN, A SURPRISE FROM HER
father, who had asked Murray to deposit the trunk
in her room. Along with it, he had included a note.

My Darling Bronte,

*Your mother wore these treasured pieces the night
I proposed marriage to her. I have saved them these
years, hoping you would honor her by wearing them
on your engagement night. I only hope Arthur
realizes what a prize he is winning by marrying
you. Please be happy. I love you.*

Your devoted father

Bronte closed her eyes, dropped into a chair, and
stared at the window.

Her life was a complete shambles. She was about
to commit herself to a man she did not love for the
sake of a child who was hers only by the most
tentative ties. Very soon she would send away the

only man she had ever loved, would ever love. And thanks to her, Rossie Rodale was gone.

She had left him on the verge of town holding their horses, and when she returned, he had disappeared. Only her horse remained. She had searched, desperate and panicked, and turned up nothing.

For hours, she had lain in her bed, finally, reluctantly giving Turpin the lame order to hunt the escaped prisoner. It was her fault that he was gone, yet she prayed that he would not be found and expose her own guilt.

As the clock chimed seven, Bronte eased her feet into the pair of pink satin shoes, then turned to the mirror. The skirt was of pink-coral grosgrain, trimmed with three pink flounces of the same material that extended up the front. The overskirt was of point lace, draped behind *en pannier* by means of two grosgrain ribbons the same shade as the dress, tied in a bow. Between her breasts nestled a basque corsage of pink coral grosgrain, with a vandyked bertha, opening in front over a white lace underwaist and confined by a cluster of pink roses. Having curled and coiled her blue-black hair into a braided chignon, she wore a wreath of pink roses and leaves in it. The soft, fragrant petals brushed her forehead each time she moved.

Dusty scampered out from under the bed and ran to her feet.

Bronte scooped her up and nestled the gray rabbit under her chin just as a light tap, tap, tap sounded on her French door. She slowly turned and stared at the dark glass door, her heartbeat rushing to her throat as she focused on Brandon's image.

Almost in a dream state, she moved to the door and opened it slightly.

Brandon shoved it open and slid in.

Bronte stepped back. Her hands stilled in their tender stroking of her rabbit.

"What do you think you're doing?" was all she could think to say.

"That's obvious, I think. I came to see you."

"You shouldn't be here," she said angrily, her face suddenly flushed with hot color. "If you were discovered . . ."

He watched as she swiftly moved across the room to a dainty upholstered chair before her dressing table. With candlelight spilling softly over her shoulders, she perched there like a colorful bird, staring at her reflection in the dressing table mirror, her hands nervously stroking the rabbit in her lap.

Finally, she shook her head and said breathlessly, "I'm promised to Arthur now. You won't change my mind. You haven't the right to even try."

He moved up behind her and watched her reflection in the silvered glass grow rigid, her eyes round and bright, her cheeks dark red. Her pale breasts, partially exposed by her low décolletage, rose and fell rapidly with her emotions. He lay his big dark hands on her exposed white shoulders, and she closed her eyes, all resistance melting from her body as she leaned back against him and said hoarsely,

"Don't do this to me."

"Do what?" He slid his hand down the inside of her dress, closed his fingers over her breast, and she groaned.

"Someone could come at any moment . . . my

father . . . Wang . . . Murray . . . Arthur's due
to arrive—oh, please, please . . ."

The rabbit jumped from her lap as he slid the
other hand into her dress and cupped both breasts
possessively, forcing the dress to spill down her
arms and torso so it tightly hugged her midriff,
exposing her breasts and his hands in the mirror.
Lifting the soft white mounds, he caressed the pink
nipples with his fingers until they grew erect and
hard. Lowering his lips to her ear, he murmured,
"What did you do with Rossie?"

She gasped and moaned and slid her white hands
over his and closed them more tightly upon her
breasts. "Rossie?" she responded almost incoher-
ently, unable to reason beyond the forbidden thrill
his presence aroused.

"Do you often allow your father's workers to
simply up and disappear?" He moved around her
chair and stood facing her, his legs slightly spread
while his hands trailed up her legs beneath her
skirt, nudging up the petticoats and skirts until they
lay piled high on her pale, slender thighs.

"Stop." She gasped, then shoved him away and
escaped the chair, doing her best to drag up her
gown to cover her breasts, to little avail. He caught
her before she reached the door, spun her around,
and shoved her up against the wall. His hands
moved over her. His warm breath brushed her
cheek.

"Please," she sighed. "Don't do this. Don't make
this any harder for me. It *will* end. I promise! It
must, even if I have to . . ." She groaned and said
in a whisper of desperation, "I can't continue this
way. I want you too badly. I've tried to be good the

last days—to stay away. I thought if I stayed away, these feelings would subside and I could go back to being the kind of woman I used to be. But the moment I saw you, it started again. All these feelings here." She pressed her fist to her heart. "Oh God, it hurts."

She took a breath and willed her shoulders to stop shaking. Brandon said nothing, just continued to pin her body to the wall, feeling every rise and fall of her breasts against his chest. He wanted to kill her . . . to smother her mouth with his. Even now she was confusing his priorities. He'd come here to force her to confess . . . now he wanted only to take her.

Slowly, she raised her head. "How obscene these feelings are," she murmured. "That I should experience them here, in my own bedroom, in my father's house when he waits up the hallway for my fiancé . . ."

She flung herself against him, her face buried in the crook of his neck, her arms thrown around him, clutching him, fingers tearing at the shirt on his back.

"We can't continue like this. I can't . . . live so near you and not touch you, hold you. You have to go, Brandon. I'll help you, if I must. It's the only way, you see, because, as you said, we're dangerous together, you and I. We'll end up destroying one another, destroying those I love. I can't risk that. I can't risk your being hurt because I have no will-power where you're concerned."

She laughed sharply. "How very ironic that I, who pounded my breast and spouted independence, would be driven to my knees by my dreaded dependence on the love of one man. A forbidden love for a forbidden man. There's no help for it. You have to go. Not just from Haviland Farm. I wouldn't send you back into that awful hellhole of a prison. You don't deserve that—no matter what you did. God help us, we all make mistakes despite our better judgment; we're only human. Aren't we, darling? We're only human . . ."

Gripping him tighter, Bronte managed a shaky smile and, in a more resolute voice, said, "I'll help you. I know a way. You can leave this dreadful place and never look back. Promise me you'll never look back."

Pushing herself away, taking his unshaven face in her hands, she stared fiercely into his intense blue eyes. "I've asked my godfather to help you. He'll do anything for me. I told him I have a friend who needs his help. I didn't tell him your name, so he needn't know. Why should it matter? You can return to Calcutta—"

He took her hands from his face; his fingers gripped her severely, yet he said nothing, his blue eyes going black. At last, she turned her face up to his; her lips parted, invited, and he kissed her, pushing her mouth open wider with his tongue, while his hands shoved down her dress, grasped her thighs just beneath her little round buttocks, and lifted her up against the wall—pressed her there with his body, which felt incredibly close to exploding before he ever entered her.

He embraced each subtle, beautiful curve of her body. Kissed her neck. Her face. Her mouth. Her exquisite eyes, the lids of which drooped druggedly with her body's helpless surrender to this inescapable, forbidden, and dangerous passion he aroused in her. Her hands clutched at his back. Arms twisted over his shoulders. Fingers thrust into his hair and gripped like those of someone clinging desperately to some singular thread of life, but knowing the fall was inevitable.

"Damn you, damn you," she murmured over and over, until he clawed at his breeches, released himself, and plunged into the hot core of her, slamming her hard against the wall.

She draped her legs around him and rode with him, gasping and whimpering, sliding her wet mouth over his and dancing her tongue against him until he became breathless.

Then the sounds of voices reached them. Her father's. And Arthur's. Footsteps coming down the corridor. Toward the room.

His eyes holding hers, which were glazed with passion, Brandon ran his hand down the door and fumbled with the key in the lock.

A knock.

"Bronte?" William called. "Arthur has arrived."

They breathed together, into each other's mouths.

"Bronte?" The doorknob turned. "Bronte, are you there?"

"Answer him," Brandon growled in her ear.

Bronte swallowed, closed her eyes, and moved her body harder against his, so his climax teetered on the brink of his ability to control it. "Yes," she finally managed.

"Pumpkin, are you all right?"

Twisting her fingers into his hair, her eyes never leaving his, her face damp with sweat, she allowed a slow smile to cross her red mouth. "I'm fine. I . . . won't be a moment."

Silence followed, then the footsteps headed down the corridor, and Brandon swung her away from the wall and easily slid her to the floor, his body never leaving hers. He started the rhythm again, matched by her own, lifting her hips from the bare floor each time he thrust, until he saw the crash coming, the little death, the spasms that rendered her motionless and helpless beneath him, until the ecstasy opened up and made her thrash, tear his hair, arch her back, and cry out silently while he went on and on, until his own upheaval slammed into him with a force that was far more brutal than anything he had ever experienced before.

Brandon stood amid Bronte's things, the darkness of the cottage interrupted only by the flickering candles he'd lit upon arrival. He felt suffocated by the intense silence and heat of the windless night. The smell of Bronte's passion still burned his nostrils. The sting of her nails clawing his back still burned his flesh.

He had gone to her father's house to confront her—to demand to know the reason for her midnight ride into Sydney, wanting a believable explanation so he could put the demon of doubt from his mind once and for all.

But she had gone to the Sirius. *And she had taken Rossie with her—she'd told him so.*

She had discussed Brandon's escape with Captain Dillman—she had confessed as much just minutes before.

Now Rossie was gone as well.

Shanghaied, no doubt, since Brandon knew Rodale well enough to know he was content to finish out his sentence. Like himself, Rossie had trusted the beautiful Miss Haviland and had unknowingly walked into trouble.

For a long while, Brandon remained there, in the semidark room with its scattering of lit candles making him shiver, the memory of their lovemaking filling him with an insuppressible rage.

Bronte turned away from the table, where she had been vaguely listening to Arthur ramble on about wedding plans.

"A year's engagement is, of course, the normal time period, but considering how long we've known one another." Arthur lit William's cigar then fanned away the smoke with his bandaged hand, injured in a confrontation with an inmate. "What do you say, William? Wouldn't you agree that the sooner we marry the better?"

William smiled his thanks at Wang as he handed him a fresh drink, then he turned his gaze to Bronte. He regarded her intently. "What have you to say on the matter, Bronte?"

She opened and closed her mouth, turned away, and took up a porcelain rabbit from the centerpiece of the table.

William moved up behind her, but did not touch her. "You do realize, Arthur, that I'm hardly typical of most fathers. Perhaps I've been away from England too long, or perhaps I'm overly concerned for my daughter's happiness, but, please understand, that before I give you my approval, I must know beyond any shadow of a doubt that this match is what she wants. Then I'll deal with all that responsibility rubbish—whether or not I think you'll be good for her, etcetera. Will you be good for her, Arthur?"

A pause, a startled silence. "Of course," he finally replied.

"And you would never intentionally do anything to hurt her."

"Far from it, I assure you. My only thought and hope is to gently encourage her down the path of respectability—"

"Predictability, you mean," she said. Finally turning from the table, Bronte looked from her father to Arthur, her chin up and her shoulders squared. "The two of you discuss me as if you were dickering over a sack of corn. I will remind you," she said to Arthur, "that I'm a grown woman with a mind and will of my own. Should you want an object that will be malleable to your ideas of feminine perfection, than I would suggest that you take a jaunt to the seashore. You'll find plenty of clay there that will offer you far less resistance."

Arthur's pale eyes narrowed slightly. His mouth curved. "I think we understand one another perfectly," he finally replied. "I care for you, while I . . . am a means to an end as far as your affections are concerned." Glancing at her frowning father, he added more lightly, "I fear she's still waiting for that knight in shining armor to stroll through the door and sweep her away on his white charger. I assure you, sir, love and respect will come in time. I'll do everything in my power to invite it."

His voice droned on as Bronte gazed out the French doors into the dark, her mind imagining a

movement there, beyond the trees—a man . . .
No. It was just her imagination.

"Bronte?" Arthur said.

Slowly, she turned to face him and her father.

"I was explaining to your father that your attention to the rebuilding of the school and orphanage
simply isn't acceptable as an engaged lady. Therefore, I think you'll agree, William, that, while she
prepares for the wedding, she'll remain away from
the site until the building is completed?"

"No."

"I beg your pardon."

"I said . . ." Bronte took an unsteady breath and,
for the first time in weeks, felt the old fight rear up
inside her. "No. I won't remain home while we are
engaged or once we're married. Those children
depend on me."

Arthur's face turned a slow, molten red, and he
smiled thinly. "You're upset. Understandable, I
suppose, considering the occasion—"

"I'll not leave those children, Arthur."

Silence. Finally, Arthur put down his drink. "It
seems to me that you haven't thought a great deal
about our life together."

"You were well aware of my objectives concerning the children."

"Perhaps I should go and allow you to calm
down a bit. Occasionally I allow my feelings for you
to obscure your tendency toward pugnacity."

"Pugnacity!" Bronte expelled, her hands on her
hips and her chin thrust at Arthur, who looked
down his thin nose at her. "I'll show you pugnacity,
sir."

William stepped forward. "Perhaps we should call it a night, Arthur. There's plenty of time."

"Agreed," he snapped, then turned on his heels for the door.

Bronte followed, closing the door between herself and her father before hurrying down the steps to Arthur's waiting carriage. She called his name; he ignored her, forcing her to grab his arm with a fierceness that startled them both.

"I can't do it," she announced. "I won't do it. Marry you, that is. I don't love you, Arthur. And it's clear you won't make me happy."

No response.

"Please understand—"

"I understand perfectly," he said at last, his voice monotone. His teeth clenched, his eyes sharp as glass, he said, "You do realize that you'll never see your beloved Sammy again."

"I'll fight for him and win," she declared. "I happen to know those people have no interest whatsoever in adopting Sammy. You put them up to it in hopes of blackmailing me into marrying you, but it won't work, Arthur. I may remain a spinster for the remainder of my life, but it's better than sacrificing my dignity by marrying a man I simply pity."

Arthur gasped, and drew back his hand to strike her, yet she did not back away, but squared her shoulders and challenged him with a look.

With a sneer, he spun on his heels and mounted his buggy. With a crack of the whip, he disappeared into the dark.

There is great diversity in the forms of recreation which may be enjoyed . . . That amusement which permits any improper familiarity between the sexes is not in good taste. If the game requires the boys to catch and struggle, and wrestle with the girls, or even to put their hands upon their persons, or to kiss them, it is of very doubtful propriety. Such freedom is not consistent with that respect which the sexes should cultivate for each other.

—*Good Morals and Gentle Manners*
AUTHOR UNKNOWN, 1873

CHAPTER TWENTY

WITH HIS BACK BRACED AGAINST THE TRUNK OF A TREE, Brandon watched Captain Dillman's hired carriage careen down the road toward Haviland Farm. He glanced at Johnny Turpin, who paced the road edge like a big cat on a leash, his strop swinging from one hand as he barked out orders to the bone-weary men.

"Bloody bastard," Jimmy Snipes muttered under his breath and sidled closer to Brandon. "Ever since Rossie up and took off, 'e's been like that, pacin' and cursin' and drivin' us like we was no better'n bleedin' jackasses. I've a good mind to break 'is neck. Wouldn't be no trouble at all, no siree. Not as bleedin' blind as 'e gets when 'e's wagerin'. Quick as a blink it'd be, just like snappin' a wee twig."

"You know and I know Rossie didn't just disappear," Brandon replied as the carriage disappeared around the bend.

"Aye. *They* took him." Snipes drove his shovel

into the hard ground, then swiped the sweat from his brow. "And if that's the case, then I pity his soul, 'cause he won't ever be seein' his blessed wife and little children again."

Brandon looked at him coolly, taking no notice of Turpin, who had discovered Brandon relaxing in the shade. Jimmy Snipes was his new partner, had been since Rossie disappeared. Brandon had learned fairly quickly that, unlike most of the men, who were closemouthed and secretive and reluctant to discuss any goings-on that might land them back in an eight-by-eight prison cell, Jimmy talked too much.

"What do you know about the disappearances?" Brandon asked.

"Not much. Only what I heard some of the men whisper about now and again." Jimmy poked at the bed of rock with his shovel and cursed under his breath. "I reckon there are those who'd welcome the leavin' no matter what waited for 'em out there. Rumor has it only one thing could lure a man into givin' up the life here at the farm for a chance at freedom, and that's a woman."

Brandon looked away, then met Turpin's eyes. A woman. Did Turpin know that at that moment Brandon had a note in his pocket that read, *Sunday afternoon, three o'clock. The cottage. It's imperative that you be there. Promise me.*

For the second time in three days, Bronte stood at her father's side as Pilot Crenshaw faced the agitated and perplexed farmers who had recently discovered workers missing. There were the Higginses, the Bixbys, and the Colberts. And, of course, Lord and Lady Fish. They all watched Crenshaw and sweated in dread as he expounded on his well-recognized opinion that Bronte's father's idea of leniency toward the prisoners, allowing them work leave, was a failed idea.

"Balderdash!" Higgins yelled. "I've not had a single man disappear in the last four years until recently. I tell you, something's afoul."

"Agreed," Colbert joined in. "I find it a little too coincidental that four men disappeared in one night—all from different farms."

J. O. Bixby stood up then and shook his fist at Crenshaw. "I've participated three years in this program and I ain't never had no man up and escape. Never!"

"You can't take this program away from us," Higgins declared. "It'll mean an end to our farms. We can't afford to hire no freemen."

"There ain't no freemen who want to work," Colbert cried. "They all gone up to the mountain to pan gold."

Bronte glanced at her father. His face looked haggard, his eyes nearly glazed from his many nights spent at the prison. And now this. Everything he had worked for for the last years appeared to be crumbling.

A movement at the parlor door caught Bronte's eye. Lady Fish stood there, her eyes slightly hooded, her lips faintly smiling, as if she found amusement in the men's quandary, including her husband's, who had lost three men the night before.

Margorie Fish turned from the room and disappeared into the darker corridor. While the men continued their hot debate, Bronte eased from the room as well, just as Lady Fish exited the front door and headed down the well-worn path toward the distant barracks. By now, the men would have finished their evening meal. They would be allowed the freedom to move around the barracks grounds until lights-out was called.

Her hands gripping the porch balustrade, Bronte watched Margorie glide through the failing light, and knew, with a sick feeling in the pit of her stomach, whom she intended to meet.

At first Brandon had been stunned to discover Lady Fish waiting for him outside the barracks, then slightly bemused. The fact that his barrack mates, not to mention the guards, all grinned and gawked at him, Snipes giving him the thumbs-up signal, made him more than a trifle aggravated. He simply wasn't in the mood for Lady Fish's shenanigans.

"You look shocked to see me," she said when they were out of hearing range.

"It's not every day a lady comes to visit."

She made a slight moue with her lips and tipped her head to one side. The failing sunlight caught fire in her hair. "You really haven't much room to cast stones, you know. This is hardly Buckingham Palace and these men are hardly your well-decorated and adoring young men who followed you so gallantly into heroism's way."

He flashed her an emotionless smile and glanced up the road at the line of carriages parked outside Haviland's house.

"You can't save them now," Margorie declared in a catlike voice.

Frowning, Brandon met her eyes.

"I wouldn't be surprised if William finds himself unemployed by the end of the evening. All the sudden prisoner disappearances seem to have convinced our good political officials that William's work-leave program is a miserable failure. Do you realize what that will mean for you?"

"Why don't you explain it to me?" he replied dryly.

"You'll be returned to prison, of course. Cast back into those filthy little dungeonlike cells to fester right along with the lot of them." She looked toward the barracks and shivered, and managed to look sad. "I simply can't imagine your being forced to live with those horrible, squalid creatures. To spend the rest of your life living like some sewer rat."

"Get to the point," he snapped.

For an instant, she looked slightly surprised. Then her slanted eyes narrowed. Leaning back against a tree, her full-skirted afternoon dress with its color-patterned, plaided double ikat flowing to her feet, she might have made a very pretty subject for some slightly enamored artist. "I'd like you to kill my husband," Lady Fish said, snapping Brandon's attention back to her completely. For an instant, he almost laughed. Almost. Then he realized, by the cold glint in her beautiful, lethal eyes, that she was serious.

"Kill Lord Fish. Is that all? And here I was worried that you wanted me to do something really criminal."

Her face turned ugly. "This is hardly a laughing matter, Captain, so keep your sarcasm to yourself." Whirling away, she paced, furious, along the gravel-packed path. "God, how I loathe this place, these stinking convicts—"

"Don't forget Lord Fish," he said amusedly.

"Yes," she hissed, turning on him again. "Yes, I detest him and his simple-minded ways, his inability to provide for me. For the last five years, he's promised he'd take me away from this wretched place."

"Why not simply leave him?"

In an instant, her look of anger dissolved into one of fear. "Because," she said in a dry voice, "he'd kill me if I ever tried to."

"Lord Fish?" Brandon laughed disbelievingly. He couldn't imagine the pretentiously dignified popinjay raising a finger to swat at a fly, much less a woman.

Margorie, her hands clasped, lowered her eyes. "He . . . frightens me. He blames me for everything—our situation back in England, our indebtedness here. How he hates me."

A burst of activity at the main house momentarily caught Brandon's attention. Several men climbed aboard their carriages, their voices raised at one another.

Damn. He should have found a way to be there, but he'd been too bloody caught up in second guesses—still refusing to believe, despite the evidence, that Bronte and her father were involved in the mercenary smuggling.

None of it made sense. Neither Bronte nor her father would do anything to risk William's losing his position at the prison. Certainly they would do nothing to jeopardize their home.

Still, there were the cold, ugly facts. Bronte had

arranged his escape with her godfather, Captain Dillman, on board the *Sirius*, the very vessel that purportedly would transport mercenaries to Calcutta.

"If I arrange for you to escape this place," came Lady Fish's voice, "will you help me?"

Slowly, he brought his eyes back to hers. "I beg your pardon?"

More urgently, she said, "Please, Brandon. A favor. If you'll help me, I'll find a way to get you out of this miserable country. We'll both leave. The two of us. You'll go your way and I'll go mine, and we'll both be free from our prisons at last."

"And how do you propose to do that?"

"You let me worry about that." She offered him her old seductive smile.

Brandon appeared to give the idea an intense moment of thought, then he nodded, slowly.

"Good." Releasing her breath, Lady Fish rewarded him with a shaky smile.

Throughout Sunday morning Mass, Brandon sat in the back of the chapel with the other prisoners, his head bowed and his eyes closed as the priest rambled on about faith and trust and right and wrong. Occasionally, he looked out the window, down the road toward the cottage, and imagined Bronte at that very moment, perhaps sitting in her sweet-smelling bedroom with its soft bed draped in white coverlets and ecru pillows. No doubt her rabbits would be there with her, preening themselves while she spoke to them as if they were children.

At noon, he returned to the barracks with the

others, sat at the long trestle table, and stared down at his plate of untouched mutton stew while the drone of conversation hummed around him.

Then Wang came, delivering the message: Tremain is wanted at the cottage . . .

He walked along up the road, and when he was out of sight, he slid into the trees and made his way to the river, where he bathed and sat for a long while on the sandy banks. Finally, with his shirt slung across one shoulder, Brandon walked up the faint path to the cottage, hesitated in his step, and considered turning back. If he turned back now, there would be no regrets, no self-recriminations. He might very well avoid making a terrible mistake.

Still, there came a time in every soldier's life when he must make a choice, a sacrifice for a cause in which he truly believed—despite the risks. He had a trunk full of medals to prove that—reminders that the choices he'd made throughout his life and career were right and just and a decided means to an ultimate end.

But never had such a risk meant the possible forfeiting of so much that meant so very much to him personally.

Brandon stepped into the cottage and stopped short. In the center of the room a table had been set with fine china and flickering tapers. Fresh flowers in vases adorned the small tables, and in the corner of the chamber resided a tub of steaming water, from which wafted some familiar fragrant scent.

"Sir," came Bronte's voice from the shadows. "I had almost given you up." Moving into the candle-light, dressed in a soft, flowing breakfast dress of

white organdy with bishop sleeves that pleated
voluminously in a froth of gauze to her wrists, she
smiled tentatively and lowered her lashes, conceal-
ing her eyes. How very pretty she looked, with
white ribbons entwined into her long black hair.
Her lips were like moist ripe fruit. "I'm not much of
a cook. But I thought this once . . . Brandon . . .
I'm so very happy that you came."

Dragging the shirt from his shoulders, frowning,
he said, "Seems I had little choice."

She looked at him with an intense earnestness
that he had not seen in her eyes before. Not even
with her beloved and much cherished children had
her look so openly revealed the tangle of emotions
she was experiencing. Their eyes locked, and though
she said nothing for a long moment, they remained
there, as if they were both hypnotized. There was no
treachery, no suspicion in those wide eyes, but a raw,
open wound of pain, regret, and requited adoration.

"Please." The words were barely audible. "We
haven't much time."

As Bronte took a breath, silence flowed around
them once again. Her hand came out to rearrange a
fork on the table, to nudge a plate, to catch a tear of
soft wax that wept down the side of a melting taper.
It beaded on her fingertip like a tiny opalescent
pearl.

"There is a reason for this madness," she continued. "My madness, I mean my being here now, in
the middle of the day, after everything that has
happened. I'm sure there is, but I've long since
given up the fight to discover what it is just as I
surrendered my attempts to reason why you came
to this dreadful prison in the first place I couldn't

comprehend what would make a man of your upstanding virtue succumb to the barbarousness of murdering another in cold blood . . . until I, the distinguished and well-bred child who had upraised her high ideals onto an ivory tower of superiority, found myself caught within a similar web of moral failure.

"It is simply . . . passions of the heart."

A moment of tense repressed emotions passed, then, slowly, Bronte swept away the tears on her cheeks with the back of her hand and forced a tremulous smile to her lips. "It is, occasionally, very nice to feel human, don't you agree, sir?"

"Yes," he said softly, resignedly, almost sadly. "Very nice."

She sniffed and moved toward him. "If you're not opposed, sir, I would care to feel human once more before you go. Oh yes . . . the arrangements have been made. My godfather is willing to help you. You'll be leaving this place in two nights. You're to meet him at midnight at the river. You know the place . . . where we made love in the sun on the sand . . ."

He closed his eyes and clenched his fists.

"It's for the best, don't you see? We can go on with our lives, devote ourselves to right and just causes without the fear of succumbing to these dreadful and hurtful passions we have for one another."

At last, she turned her drowning eyes up to him, a declaration of supplication and surrender that was so unmistakable that he, in a blink of eternity, disassociated himself entirely from the remote sense of duty that had nagged him since she first mentioned her alliance in such a scheme. He took her in his arms, and she swayed against him. She smelled of lavender water, of fresh baked bread, and of opalescent candle wax. She felt dreadfully small, frail, and tremblingly weak as she clung to him, saying nothing, allowing the silence to speak what she could not.

Then the noise.

He felt her tense.

He gripped her arms, closed his eyes, swallowed back the surge of self-disgust that rose up to choke him. She had been so trusting, not suspecting he'd set them both up. In that instant he wanted to beg her forgiveness. Apologize for the sacrifice she must now make while he went about the sorry business of duty . . . of proving to himself, and to his superiors, that she and her father were not guilty of smuggling mercenaries. God, he hoped his instincts were right.

The door opened behind him.

Her head flew back. Her eyes met his. She fluttered in his arms like a captured, condemned bird caught in a lair.

"Good God," came the quiet gasp of surprise from the door.

He watched her soft mouth open, her eyes question, then he pulled her up against him and buried her face in his chest. As calmly as possible, he kissed the top of her head.

"Forgive me, love," he said quietly, with a catch in his voice. "Please forgive me."

You meet your adversary, you fight
you kill or are killed; and all without
one word or act, which is not characterized
by the most gentlemanly politeness
—*The Illustrated Manners Book*
ROBERT DE VALCOURT, 1855

CHAPTER TWENTY-ONE

ARTHUR ELLISON STOOD INSIDE THE THRESHOLD, HIS FACE A
mask of contempt as he stared at Bronte and
Brandon those eternal seconds without blinking.
Pilot Crenshaw stood to one side, Paramatta's
mayor, Charles Metcalfe, on the other. Lord Fish
was poised, frozen, in the doorway behind them.

Words were passed. Odd, but Bronte couldn't
understand them. They sounded like little more
than angry noises. Ugly tones that roared in her
mind, drowning out all else. The image of Crenshaw's and Metcalfe's faces blazed before her mind's
eye even as she fired her gaze on Brandon's back and
did her best not to allow the excruciating moment to
overwhelm her.

Think rationally.

They had just been discovered committing the
most heinous crime a free woman and prisoner
could commit together.

It would bring shame to her and her father.

Brandon would be whipped and deported to Norfolk Island—oh God, a fate worse than death.

But what terrified her most was the disturbing idea that Brandon had known, had anticipated this horrible blunder and allowed it to happen.

But how could he have known, unless . . .

At last, Brandon turned to her. For what felt like an eternity, she stared up into those intense blue eyes, searching for an answer, finding only a cold wall of steely determination.

"We must leave quickly as possible," he told her in a maddeningly unemotional voice.

She couldn't move.

Arthur and the other witnesses were gone, thank God.

Arthur. The look in his eyes humiliated her. Was love so unkind? Did it turn normally decent, rational human beings into madmen . . . or women?

Yes, she thought numbly. Yes, it did. Obviously she was living proof that no one was above making a fool of herself in the name of love.

Brandon walked her as far as the garden of her father's house, where her attentions focused on her father's buggy parked at the front of the house, just behind Arthur's.

She heard the bell ringing then, a peal of anger, calling in the guards.

Her father exited the house, his face red with a fury she had rarely seen on his features.

Shaking Brandon's hand away, Bronte swiftly moved up the path to meet him. "Father? Father, please—"

Bronte threw herself against him, clutching his coat and suddenly weeping—not out of humilia-

tion, but out of fear for Brandon, and the visible
pain on her father's face.

"It wasn't his fault, Father. Listen to me. Please!"

He gripped her arms fiercely for a moment, then
pushed her aside as if she were nothing but air.

"Wait!" she shouted as he stormed down the path
toward Brandon, who hadn't budged so much as an
inch, even though the armed guards were surrounding him, pointing their loaded weapons his
way. He faced her father with a dauntlessness that
would have caused England's most vile and vicious
foe to question his sanity for confronting Tremain.
Again, Bronte grabbed her father's arm and stared
up into his outraged eyes. "Don't do this. Please
don't do this. Don't make this tragedy any worse
than it already is."

"You've left me little choice."

As Bronte stood rooted to the path, her hands
twisted together, she watched guards flank Brandon and take his arms. Then her father, to Bronte's
mortification, drove his fist into Brandon's jaw.
Brandon sprawled heavily onto the ground.

She expected him to fight. To defend himself. Yet
he didn't so much as resist when her father buried
his trembling hands in his shirt and hauled him to
his feet. Bronte watched it all, and felt her stomach
sink and her heart climb her throat.

Bronte turned back to the house, and sure enough,
there stood Arthur on the stoop, his face a portrait
of malice. Lifting her chin, squaring her shoulders,
she moved up the path as calmly as possible, and
mounted the steps with her knees trembling until
standing toe-to-toe with Arthur.

She tried to speak. Her despondency forbade it

for a long moment. Finally, she took a deep breath and said to his smirking face, "I should despise you for this. But I can't. I can only feel sadness that you should be so lacking in compassion and under-standing. Do you wonder now why I could not love you?"

The smirk slowly slid from his face. "Do you think that I planned this?" he remarked coldly, his lips forming a thin smile of disdain. "Then be informed to the contrary, Miss Haviland. I was only responding to this."

From his coat pocket he produced a letter:

"Imperative that you, along with Crenshaw, Metcalfe, and Lord Fish meet me at the cottage at exactly two o'clock this afternoon. I have informa-tion regarding the recent escapes. Bronte."

Crushing the note in her trembling hand, Bronte slowly met Arthur's eyes. "I didn't write this."

"Obviously."

Letting the paper fall from her hand, she slid by him and into the house, knowing that only Brandon could have written it.

William stood at the window of his office and stared out at the curious crowd gathered near the road. Moments before, he'd asked for privacy, send-ing Ellison, Johnny Turpin, and Charles Metcalfe out into the hallway. Alone with Brandon at last, he slowly turned to face him. William's face looked ashen with distress.

"Why?" he asked in a dry, weary voice. "I brought

you into my home and trusted you with my daughter. Why have you done this to her?"

Brandon said nothing, just stood at military attention in the middle of the room, staring straight ahead. His jaw throbbed where William had hit him earlier.

William moved to him and stood before him, searching Brandon's eyes. "Of course, I suspected. How could I not? Perhaps I've been certain since the dinner party when Lady Fish asked to have you transferred to Mill Chase. I shall never forget Bronte's look of fear when she thought I might actually send you away. Besides Bronte's mother, my daughter has been my best friend for the last twenty-seven years. Only I could have recognized the changes in her since you came here, Captain. I should have stopped it immediately. I should have sent you back to Sydney, but what would that have rectified? She would still love you just as she has since her childhood. But I hold guilt too. I allowed myself to believe in the mythical hero. I honestly thought . . . I wanted to believe that your being here was just some horrible twist of fate. By God, but I thought you would be good for Bronte; I don't want her to always be alone." Clenching his fists, he demanded, "Why did you do it, man? Why did you send that letter to Crenshaw asking him to come to the cottage? How could you hurt Bronte that way? You've ruined her, you bastard, and there you stand as unemotional as a goddamn rock. I could kill you with my bare hands."

For a suspended moment, they stood toe-to-toe, staring into each other's eyes, Brandon not so much as blinking as William's face beaded with sweat in his fury. At last, William turned away, attempted to collect himself, then stepped behind his desk, where he riffled through some papers.

"You do realize what this means," William finally said without looking up. "I shall be forced to administer punishment. The punishment for such a crime as yours is a whipping on the triangles and deportation to Norfolk Island."

At last, William looked up. His features were anguished as he moved around the desk and approached Brandon once more. "If I thought for a moment—" he began, just as a sharp knock sounded on the door. "Yes," he snapped.

The door opened, and several guards pressed forward.

Turning to Brandon, his brow knitted in distress, William said, "For God's sake, man, give me some logical reason why you've done this to Bronte. I want to understand. If I could only believe—"

"That I love her?" Brandon asked softly.

"Yes," William replied as quietly.

Brandon took a deep breath and released it slowly. "I love her more than my life," he finally said.

"William!" called Lord Fish from the door. "A moment, please!"

Lord and Lady Fish moved through the group of men, Lord Fish forcing the guards back out across the threshold and closing the door in their faces. Lady Fish leaned back against the door, one eyebrow raised at Brandon and a smirk on her face.

"I'm sorry to intrude on this unfortunate situation," Lord Fish declared, pressing a damp kerchief to his upper lip, then his temple. "However, I felt it imperative that we speak to you on this matter before any judgment is passed."

"This is none of your business, my lord." William glared at Lord Fish pointedly.

"True," Lady Fish said from the door. Her gaze locked on Brandon, she moved gracefully over the carpeted floor, her day dress making a soft rustling in the stilted quiet. Her floral perfume swirled in the hot air around her. "But think of Bronte," Margorie said in an uncharacteristically concerned voice. "Her reputation would suffer. We can keep this between ourselves, my dear friend."

"Agreed," Lord Fish said. "As I told you not long ago, I need a man like Tremain at Mill Chase. Let me take him, William." Lowering his voice, he added, "You needn't worry that he'll ever bother with Bronte again. I'll make certain of it."

"Yes," William said after a long minute of contemplation. "Yes, of course. Take him. Get him out of my sight before I forget that I once admired him, and that my daughter loved him."

Lord Fish flung open the door and shouted orders to the guards. They poured over the threshold and took Brandon by his arms, turning him for the door while William stood to one side.

Brandon did not look back, but stared straight ahead, his eyes only occasionally straying to the crowd of onlookers who had gathered wide-eyed children and the men he had worked with, broken rock with, and furrowed the earth with. They stared at him with contempt and anger, no doubt disturbed over the fact that he might well have jeopardized their already precarious work program, but mostly, he thought, because he had hurt Bronte.

Bronte. Where was Bronte?

For an instant, he looked around, wanting to see her one last time, wanting to explain but knowing he couldn't.

She emerged through the crowd unexpectedly, Sister Elizabeth at her side, gripping her shoulders although he knew she was stronger than that.

Her shoulders squared, her stubborn chin set, she stepped before Brandon and his burly entourage, her eyes burning and her face flushed with hot color. Shrugging Elizabeth's arm from her shoulder, she moved toward Brandon like a dreamwalker.

Stopping before him, her head tipped back and her fists buried within the folds of her skirt, she stared at him fiercely. Then she slapped his face. "I thought you cared," she said in a husky whisper, "yet you purposefully arranged for those dreadful men to find us together. How could you humiliate me and condemn yourself to exile on that horrible island?"

"Not to worry, Bronte," Lady Fish said behind them. "Brandon will be joining us at Mill Chase. Won't you, darling?" Smiling up at Brandon, Lady Fish moved down the walk to the waiting carriage.

Her face white, Bronte stared after Margorie before turning woodenly to Brandon again. "Did you plan this with her?" she asked, her face stricken with fear.

He might have lied. Probably should have. Sever the thread of fondness completely so he could convince himself that, no matter the outcome of this seemingly ridiculous ploy, he could carry out his orders to the very best of his ability . . . but he couldn't. Not when he found himself drowning in

the pools of her tearing eyes, when her normally
stalwart little chin had begun to tremble ever so
slightly. He wanted to hold her. Console her. Beg for
her forgiveness. "No," he replied gently. "I didn't."
Then, with a breath, he added, "Trust me, Bronte."

Bronte sat in the middle of her bed at the cottage,
her legs crossed beneath her, her attention focused
on the open window, where a sleepy-eyed lizard
reposed on the sill, sunning itself. Dusty and Sugar
lay sprawled across her lap, ears relaxed and eyes
drooping in contentment.

Hard to believe that, just days before, she had
reclined on this bed, lazy and satisfied, with her
lover. With Brandon dozing at her side, his head on
her shoulder and his warm breath falling softly on
her breasts, she had allowed herself that privilege
of daydreaming an imaginary happily ever after for
them.

She'd imagined a lifetime of waking up in his
arms, of raising their children in this very cottage,
once his term was completed, of standing at that
window and watching all the little Brandons and
Brontes frolicking in the river. She, of course, would
continue her work at the hospital and orphanage,
while he—once he had been pardoned by the
Queen—would go about building the greatest empire in this uncivilized world.

But, as always, her thoughts drifted back to this
reality—her sitting on this bed alone but for her
rabbits, listening to earth sounds, finding a sem-
blance of peace, meager as it was, in the affection
and loyalty of her pets. How simple, their lives:

sheltered, pampered, protected . . . predictable day in and day out—as her life used to be.

Yet . . . the thought of going back to that life, when all there was to greet her day in and day out was the company of those darling children in the morning, and rabbits to escort her to sleep at night, suddenly yawned before her as dark and deep as an abyss.

Imagine. Once she had believed that she could survive without a man . . .

Her father stepped into the cottage, his tall frame filling up the threshold. "I take it you were here all night, Pumpkin," he said wearily.

"I intend to move my things in here this afternoon," she replied. "I really should have done so long ago. I've grown too old to be living beneath my father's wing."

"Don't you mean thumb?" he asked with a slight hint of humor.

Bronte said nothing.

His hands in his pockets, William eased into the cottage, his gaze wandering about the cozy, cool interior. "Your mother and I came here frequently after we moved to the main house. She always imagined the cottage to be a little mystical and magical. Damn, but I miss her, Pumpkin."

"As do I," Bronte said softly, hating the sensations going on inside her, because she knew what they meant. She scratched Dusty behind her long, alert ears. Sugar bumped her hand, wanting affection as well.

William poured himself a drink and stared into the liquor a long while. "I've been asked to turn in my resignation at the prison."

Bronte looked at her father at last. His face appeared pale and lined with fatigue and, oddly, a touch of relief.

"I fear I misunderstood, Father."

"No, you didn't. Crenshaw has seen fit to dismiss me. Gave me the old boot. Tossed me out."

She closed her eyes. This wasn't happening. She wanted to cover her ears and beg for him to take the words back—to tell her that this was simply some sick jest to punish her, to make her feel guiltier for having so humiliated and disappointed him.

"'Tis my fault, isn't it? Oh God, I've done this with all my idiotic letters to the Queen, my constant bombardments for money to help the children . . . and my recent behavior. I'm so sorry I've brought you to this."

William sat down beside her on the bed. Hesitantly, Bronte slid her arm around her father's shoulder, and the rabbits leapt to the floor, where they busily began their exploration and rubbing of every stick of furniture throughout the room, their territory. Bronte and William remained silent while the shrieking and chirping of rainbow-colored lorikeets and tiny, seed-eating budgerigars in the surrounding trees filled up the quiet.

Finally, William said, "I'm sorry this terrible thing has happened. I should have stopped Tremain's and your relationship the moment I began to suspect. It went against everything I ever wanted for you, Pumpkin. I allowed the two of you to defy the very laws I, myself, put into effect the moment I took charge of the prison."

"But you loved me," she said softly and sadly, and resignedly.

He squeezed her hand, then withdrew a letter from his coat pocket, slowly unfolded it, and stared at it a while before handing it to Bronte. "A letter from Her Majesty's Parliamentary Select Committee offered me a chair some time ago heading up a council on the reformation of Britain's penal system—thanks to your bombardment of letters. What that means, Pumpkin, is . . . we're going home."

"Home?"

"Back to England."

She stared into her father's eyes, while her own, despite her grandest attempts, overflowed onto her cheeks. William touched her face and forced a smile. "You needn't have to worry what the people here say about you, Bronte. We shall tell them all to go to hell, eh?"

With her father's arms around her, Bronte pressed her face into his strong, broad shoulders and felt the rise of hurt engulf her like a rush of water. "I should be happy for you. For us." She wept against his coat. "But I'm not. Oh, Papa, I'm not."

Sit all day in a moping posture,
sigh, and reply to everything with
a dismal voice, and your melancholy lingers.

—*Psychology: The Briefer Course*
WILLIAM JAMES, 1892

CHAPTER TWENTY-TWO

SWEATING, HIS WRISTS AND ANKLES CHAFED BY MANACLES,
Brandon paced the confined space of his dark cell.
So where the hell were his contacts when he needed
them? Time was running out.

Grabbing the corroded iron bars on the window,
he shook them as hard as he could and yelled at the
top of his voice.

He'd not seen or spoken to Lord Fish since he'd
been dragged from the transport wagon and flung
into this dung heap of a cell the day before. Nor had
he seen Lady Fish, which surprised him. He'd
expected her to come crawling after him with her
skirts hiked and her "I told you so"s purring from
her lips.

For the thousandth time, he thought of Bronte.
Always Bronte. He should have been concerned
about his possibly wreaking havoc on his government's plan to squash another India mutiny, and all
he could think about was Bronte.

He sank against the wall, heat and exhaustion, not to mention thirst and hunger, exaggerating the hollow feeling in his stomach and chest every time he thought of her face the instant she realized that their relationship had been discovered—that he had been the reason for their being discovered.

He hoped like hell that she would forgive him.

No doubt he'd done some stupid things in his life, taken a great many risks, thumbed his nose at fate and laughed in death's face.

Falling for Bronte Haviland had been, undoubtedly, his greatest failing (and grandest reward)— even greater than volunteering for this idiotic assignment. His sacrificing her trust and reputation on a hunch that might well prove to be nothing more than hopeful, if not desperate, seemed, in that instant, to be as absurd. No wonder he'd heard nothing from his contact. The son of a bitch was probably making plans for his court-martial.

He wanted out of this wretched hole. He wanted out of the whole bloody mess. Wanted to tell Haviland, Lord Fish, and the whole of Her Majesty's royal marines to go to hell. He should have done it already—the moment he'd discovered that he'd rather spend the rest of his life eating coconuts on some Pacific island with Bronte.

So why hadn't he?

Duty.

He was sick of the duty.

Guilt.

He was sick of the guilt.

Grabbing the bars in his hands again, he shouted, "Hello! I know you can hear me, you sons of dogs.

Tell Fish that I want to talk to him now or I'm going to take this pit apart with my bare hands!"

Some object slammed against his knuckles with the force of a battering ram.

He threw himself away from the door with an inward groan and a mental howl of anger.

A face, shadowed by night, appeared at the door. "Take it easy, Cap. This ain't no hotel, ya know. Ya might try askin' nicely for a change."

Gritting his teeth, Brandon attempted to move his fingers. Pain forbade it.

"We do things different here at Mill Chase. Not like the Havilands. Lord Fish believes in discipline. An eye for an eye, as the good book says." The voice laughed softly. "Seems you did a bit of naughty with that uppity spinster daughter of the warden's. Who'da thought it, eh?"

Brandon tried to breathe, to block the discomfort from his mind, an old soldier's trick: when injured, focus on some pleasant memory and not on the pain. But the image of Bronte only aggravated the discomfort and fired the anger he was beginning to experience as the man at the window continued to talk.

"Lord Fish don't show no favoritism round here, Cap. Not like Haviland and his daughter. Here a man gets as good as he gives. You give us trouble, you get trouble in return. I suspect Lord Fish has got fine plans for you. He'll want to set an example, make sure you realize that this ain't exactly paradise. Take my advice, if ya know what's good for ya—which apparently ya don't or ya wouldn't be in this predicament now—don't rile him too much or yer liable to find yerself meat for the dingoes.

That's what happens to the mean ones here, Cap. They simply . . . disappear."

They simply disappear.

The words played through his head again and again throughout the sweltering day, and as nightfall encroached, his frustration mounted. He dug at the hard ground with his fingernails in a futile attempt to dig his way out of the dank little cell. He kicked at the walls and threw himself against the door until his shoulders grew numb and ached. Finally, as darkness seeped into the box, he sank to the floor in exhaustion.

A noise. Keys rattled. The lock on the door grated and the door squeaked open. Moonlight flooded into the closet and temporarily blinded Brandon. He threw up his hands to shield his eyes.

"Get up," a scratchy voice said. "Lady Fish wants to see you."

With effort, Brandon slowly stood up, wincing as pain shot up his cramped legs. "Took her long enough," he remarked cryptically.

Hands ushered him out of the building and into the still, hot night. He stumbled along forever, it seemed, tripping over his chains, jutting roots, and loose stones until they came to the rear entry of a squat little house with a few lights burning in the windows. One man shoved open the door. Another shoved him. Brandon landed hard on both knees on the other side of the threshold.

"Welcome to Mill Chase, darling," Lady Fish said in her smooth-as-silk voice.

Brandon looked up into Margorie's emotionless face. In truth, it hardly resembled Margorie at all.

Her face looked lined and pinched. Her normally fastidious hair appeared to have been hastily tied back with a ribbon.

For a long moment, she appeared as stunned over his appearance as he was over hers. A parade of emotions crossed her features—none of which was pleasure. At last, she flashed him a tense smile and quipped with forced humor, "How delightful that you should go to your knees before me so quickly, Captain. God, I do so love an eager man."

"Is this what it's come to?" he responded. "Are you forced to whip and tie your lovers to keep them interested?"

"May I remind you, sir, that you are hardly in a position to insult me with your typical acerbities."

Lady Fish turned, and with a rustle of her blue silk and white flower–brocaded dressing gown, she glided away, down a low-ceilinged, poorly lit, dirt-floored hallway.

Clumsily climbing to his feet, Brandon noted the shabby appearance of the dingy interior—a far cry from Haviland Farm, and certainly a far cry from the pretentious residences Lady Fish had occupied in England—before her marriage to Lord Fish.

He followed Margorie up the corridor and found her waiting in a parlor of sorts, the dirt floor mostly hidden beneath a worn, faded Persian carpet. The scattering of furniture showed wear, as did the once beautiful pianoforte occupying one corner of the cramped room.

Lady Fish regarded him with a slightly raised eyebrow. "You're thinking that I've certainly come down in the world. No servants at my beck and call. No crystal chandeliers. No manse overlooking the

Thames. You're right, of course. I can hardly deny what is so painfully obvious. Then again, I need not point out that your own circumstances leave a great deal to be desired."

"Touché."

"Those really don't suit you, you know." She pointed to his manacles. "Would you like me to remove them?"

Brandon gave her a lazy grin. "That would depend, I suppose."

"On what?"

"What I'm expected to do for you in return."

"Would it matter?"

"Yes," he said mildly.

Lady Fish shook her head. "You're really in no position to annoy me, you know. So be nice, Brandon."

"I'll try, but God knows I'm such a bastard—as you've reminded me through the years."

Lady Fish moved toward him, lashes slightly lowered, her eyes focused on his lips. "So you've been a naughty boy, seducing the warden's daughter. You simply have no willpower when it comes to women."

"I'm going to surprise you, Margorie."

She circled him like a fox sizing up a hare. "The way I see it, Brandon, you tempted fate—as always. And your luck ran out. Again."

"I can hardly argue with that."

She shook her head, and a coil of copper-colored hair spilled over her forehead. "What we endure for love, am I right, Captain?" Sliding the fingers of one hand into the top of her low-cut dress, she eased a tiny key from between her breasts, then moved closer, so close the smell of her toilet water teased his nostrils. "As I recall, you and I made a bargain, dear Captain. Are you willing to go through with it?"

"If I'm not?"

"Then I suppose you would spend the rest of your life in that wretched little hole."

Raising one eyebrow, he smiled dryly.

She continued to hold the key between them while Brandon's mind rushed ahead of the clock that began to strike nine.

Releasing her breath, rewarding him with a shaky smile, Lady Fish slid the key into the manacle's locks. The heavy cuffs clattered to the floor. Dropping to her knees, she unlocked the fetters on his ankles, and he kicked them aside.

The clock struck the quarter hour.

"Where is your husband?" he asked.

"In Parramatta, of course. He won't be home tonight." She tilted her head and gazed at him seductively from beneath her lowered lashes. "You'll have to wait for later to do your dirty work, my darling. Until then, perhaps we should enjoy ourselves."

The insane idea occurred to him that once in his life, he might have found Lady Fish's coy attempts to seduce him charming, if a little silly. Now he found them, quite simply, repugnant.

Lady Fish tugged on the wide silk sash around her waist, and the dressing gown fell open, exposing her heavy breasts. The silk slid from her shoulders and puddled around her ankles.

Then the door opened behind him.

He knew without turning who stood there, on the

threshold. He could see it on her face—the brief
look of shock, then fear, then regret as Lady Fish
met Brandon's eyes.

Slowly, he turned toward the door.

Lord Fish stared at him with emotionless features.

"Damn," Brandon muttered, then his world exploded into blackness and pain.

Bronte paced.

The clock struck eleven.

Would he be there? Brandon? To meet her godfather? It seemed a million years ago that they'd
arranged the time. If he found a way to escape Mill
Chase would he find freedom aboard the *Sirius*?
Would she allow him to sail out of her life without
knowing why he had chosen to disclose their affair?

Why, dear God, was she consumed with this
need to understand? To forgive? To truly believe
that he'd done what he did for a reason and he
hadn't meant to hurt her at all.

She felt . . . desperate to know.

Where was her father? He should have returned
long ago from the prison. After all, his duties were
done. He'd only returned to that dreadful place to
collect his personal belongings.

She looked around. Odd how these walls, which
had been her home for the last many years, seemed
so unwelcoming now. How many days and nights
had she walked these floors fretting over the children's welfare?

The children. With her and her father returning to
England, what would happen to the children? With
her breaking off her engagement to Arthur, what

would become of Sammy and Pam? With her returning to England within days, her slim chances of adopting the children seemed even more hopeless. How could she live with the realization that she had let those dear, sweet children down?

Closing her eyes, she did her best to force the responsibilities from her mind, but the image that reared up in her mind's eye was of Brandon.

"Forgive me," he'd whispered. "Trust me."

She had to see him. She would understand if it was the last thing she ever did.

Stepping out onto the porch, she found that the night was still and hot and silent, reminding her of the evening she and Brandon had finally succumbed to their passion for each other. Yet there were no growling clouds, no spears of lightning. It would be clear, smooth sailing for Captain Dillman and his cohorts as they delivered the smuggled goods to Johnny Turpin, who would return and hide the stores away.

But what was the point now that they were leaving?

Squeezing closed her eyes, she did her best to swallow back her emotions—the same emotions that had overwhelmed her once the realization sank in that she might never see Brandon Tremain again.

There had been love there, in his eyes, just before Lord Fish carted him off to Mill Chase. She was certain of it! Could she be so foolish as to believe, this one last time, that the man she had worshipped all these years for his heroism might prove to be heroic after all?

Bronte frowned and gripped the porch balustrade. "Of course," she said softly to herself.

With one last look back at her father's house, she said softly, "Forgive me, Father, if I'm wrong." Then Bronte fled down the steps into the dark.

Brandon's head hurt like hell. He had trouble focusing his thoughts. Couldn't quite remember where he was or how he had come to be here, facedown in the bottom of some damp pit of slimy seawater.

The floor beneath him rolled. Footsteps thudded above him.

Little by little his memory returned.

Obviously, he was in the bowels of a boat, the hold perhaps. Not a ship. Not large enough for a ship. Some wide, flat vessel, perhaps a barge—

Above him the hatch was suddenly flung open. Lantern light spilled down the hole, then steps dropped in.

Brandon closed his eyes.

Someone descended the stairs, then stopped. The boat rolled again. Voices, spoken in whispers, sounded from above.

"I fear you've killed him. What the blazes could you have been thinking to have hit him that hard? He's worthless to us dead."

"He's worthless to us alive," a familiar feminine voice said—Margorie Fish. Christ, he'd been right, after all. "Surely you didn't think for one moment that Captain Tremain would commit treason and jump willingly into the mutiny. A great many things he might be, but never a traitor."

"Do you think he was on to us?"

"No doubt. I've suspected since learning he was here that he was up to something more than serving time for simple murder. As well respected as he is, or was, in England, he could have cut a dozen esteemed gentlemen's throats and received little more than a slap on the hand. He's simply too valuable to Her Majesty to toss away like refuse. Oh yes, I suspected. I tried like hell to get him to Mill Chase just so I could keep an eye on him, but William and Bronte wouldn't have it. It was most fortuitous that he and Bronte should be discovered together, and that my husband was stupid enough to save him from the triangles."

"What do we do with him now?"

"Make certain he's dead, then dispose of his body, of course."

"Here?"

"Of course not. Wait until the ship's at sea. Now I must hurry back to Mill Chase. Everything is going as planned. Mustn't do anything now to upset our purpose."

"You're certain your men will go along with the plan? They'll vow that we had Tremain delivered to your house, and your husband came home and discovered you together. Lord Fish was killed in the ensuing struggle—"

"And I'll be free at last to leave this miserable place. With the money I've saved from selling these wretched souls to those despicable factions in India I'll be able to return to England and live the life to which I was once accustomed. Are you certain you won't join me, darling?"

"Afraid New Zealand beckons, m'lady."

The footsteps ascended.

Brandon opened his eyes and watched the hatch, waiting for it to close. It didn't.

Struggling, he climbed to his feet, pausing every few seconds to allow his head to stop swimming. Slipping and sliding his way to the stairs, he cautiously pulled himself up, anticipating any moment to be confronted by a guard.

Finally reaching the hatchway, he breathed in the fresh air, allowing it to clear his head a little before venturing a look out.

Two more flat boats were anchored off the point shoal, their decks sparsely lit by torches. Men moved about swiftly, unloading crates and stacking them on the shore.

Aside from the fact that there was contraband being moved, nothing else looked out of the ordinary. Each time a crate of liquor was hoisted off the boat, the sailors replaced it with an empty crate. Except . . . The crates looked a might too heavy to be empty.

Ingenious bastards.

Another time, Brandon might have grabbed up a rifle or two and proceeded to take care of the unseemly matter on his own, but not tonight. He intended to get out of this mess in one piece.

Making certain the coast was clear, he scurried across the empty deck and shimmied over the side of the boat, making hardly a splash as he slid into the water. He headed through the brush growing profusely along the shoal, and, finally, into the trees, pausing long enough to allow his pounding head to stop spinning.

A rustle of leaves to his right. A movement in the dark . . . then a soft whinny.

Cytduction.

Oh, Christ.

Brandon spun around, back toward the point, and stumbled his way through the profuse vegetation, until he came to the clearing where, not so long ago, he had picnicked with Bronte in the bright afternoon sunlight.

What the blazes was she doing here? Damn her, damn her.

Dillman, his eyes sharp, his smile sharper, glanced around the clearing, nodding to a foursome of sailors who hefted a crate over a gangplank and onto the deck of the flat boat. "You shouldn't have come here, Bronte. Were we to be discovered, I fear the ramifications for you would be disastrous. Tell me, did you mention your coming here to your father?"

"No."

"Careful with that crate!" he shouted to a pair of clumsy sailors. Then to Bronte, "Please, my dear, I encourage you to leave this moment. I simply couldn't forgive myself if something untoward happened to you."

Bronte watched the activity a moment longer, her eyes searching each crate. At last, she worked up her courage to say, "My friend . . . did he come?"

Dillman frowned. "Your friend?"

"The man you agreed to help—"

"No," he replied abruptly. "He didn't. Now, I really must insist that you leave, my dear. We wouldn't want to risk the chance that you could somehow be involved in all this nasty smuggling. Your father would never forgive me."

"But are you certain—"

"I said to leave, Bronte," he snapped. "Go. Now. I don't have time for idle chatter."

Bronte stepped back.

There came an excited shout from a group of sailors as they struggled to right a crate that had begun to wobble precariously. Dillman struck out running, as did several others. But the crate careened off the men's shoulders and crashed to the ground, spilling its contents.

Straw.

And a man.

Bronte stared at the shockingly familiar figure as it groaned and tried, despite its tied wrists and ankles, to jump to its feet.

"Ross Rodale," she said numbly.

Confused, she turned her eyes to her godfather, who slowly pivoted on his heels to look at her. Around her, the activity halted stone still—as if everyone, from the oarsmen manning the skiffs, to the men loading the cargo, had suddenly frozen in place, their every eye pinned on her.

A look of despondency crossed Dillman's face, then resignation. "My dear Bronte, I'm so sorry you've seen this."

"That man is a prisoner," she said more to herself than to Dillman, her gaze riveted on Rodale's regretful face as he looked her way.

"Help!" he shouted. "Get help, Miss Haviland. I've been bloody well kidnapped!"

Her gaze flew to the other crates, stacked one atop the other on the deck of two of the skiffs, and realization sank like a stone in her stomach. Every one of the coffinlike boxes were no doubt filled with the prisoners who had gone missing the last weeks. "Why?" was all she could think to say, and she began to back away.

"It's quite simple," Dillman said. "They are expendable treasures. The refuse of humanity—easily annihilated once the deed has been done. No one will miss them and no one will give a damn that they're dead."

"And what, exactly, is the deed?"

"Mutiny, of course. In India. Calcutta this time. I fear they won't fail again, not with this lot of cutthroats, most of whom are willing to dice up their mothers for the opportunity to live as freemen again. Nasty business, this. I'm certain their souls will burn in hell, but I shouldn't care. I'll have taken the profits from my meager efforts and retired to New Zealand."

"But how—"

"Did I arrange for the scum to escape? I was hardly involved with that, although it will seem simple enough if you only allow yourself to think on it."

The coldness of shock and disbelief having turned Bronte's body to ice, she shook her head. What was he insinuating?

A noise sounded behind her—voices barking—and she saw men scattering along her peripheral line of vision. Then, as she stared up into her godfather's face, his features became a mask.

Slowly, Bronte turned.

"Father?"

William stood at the edge of the clearing, his face white as the dozen guns turned his way, his gaze focused on Bronte. "What the devil is going on here?"

"This is terribly regrettable," Dillman said, his voice sounding weary and distressed. "William, you know I would never have involved you in this in any way. Hurting either of you grieves me horribly. If there were some way to spare you this—"

His hands fisted, William took a threatening step toward Dillman. Bronte stepped between them, her hands on her father's chest while her eyes implored him to remain calm.

William shook his head. "I loved you like a brother. Often I entrusted the lives of my family to you. My God, sir, you're Bronte's godfather. Let her go. I beseech you. She'll say nothing about this to anyone, I vow it."

"I wish that I could, William."

Turning on Dillman, Bronte said, "Brandon came here, didn't he?"

"Yes . . . yes, my dear, I'm sorry to say he is here."

"You've killed him, haven't you?"

"Captain!" shouted a deckhand from one of the boats. "The prisoner's escaped!"

Brandon knocked the guard out and eased him to the ground. He grabbed up the unconscious man's rifle and pouch of bullets and powder, tucked the latter into his pocket after making certain the gun was fully loaded, then struck off at a run down the path.

Hiding behind a tree, he looked out on the scene, his gaze going first to Bronte, then to her father—when had William arrived? Damn, that could easily complicate matters—then to the scattering of gun-bearing guards forming a circle around them.

The idea occurred to him that, while he had faced

a great many foes, many times the odds being in the
enemy's favor, he and his meager number of stalwart young marines had bested their opponents by
sheer guts, will, and the determination to succeed.
But he had never faced an army totally alone.
Reckless he might have been in many instances—
but he wasn't a fool. In an instance such as this, he
would normally back off—wait for a more oppor-
tune and vulnerable moment, perhaps pick them
off one by one, a nice sharp blade across the jugular
so their deaths were silent, if not messy.

But there wasn't time for that now.

Dillman, of course, would not, could not, allow
witnesses to attest to his involvement in the mercenary smuggling. As Brandon crouched down behind a mangrove bush and lined the captain up in
his cross hairs, he noted the man's features.

Damn infuriating habit, that. Allowing himself to
read the man's emotions in his face and eyes. No
matter how many times he'd been forced to kill in
the line of duty, he just couldn't shake that flash of
regret before pulling the trigger.

"The prisoner's escaped!" shouted a sailor from
the barge, and in the instant it would have taken
Brandon to pull the trigger, Dillman grabbed Bronte
and, removing a knife from its scabbard, pressed it
to her throat.

As several men jumped to restrain Bronte's father, Dillman frantically searched the dark copse of
trees surrounding the clearing.

"Tremain!" he shouted. "I know you're out there.
You might as well lay down your weapons now, or
I'll kill them both."

Focused on Bronte's face, Brandon lowered his

gun. "Dammit," he cursed under his breath. Then, silent as the wind, he slid into the darkness of the forest.

With the first sound of the alarm ringing, Johnny Turpin stumbled out of his bed and into the yard, gripping his club in one hand, the other holding up his worn woolen underpants. Lights flickered on. Men crashed from their barracks with their breeches around their knees and ankles and their shirts flapping from their hands.

Upon seeing Brandon ringing the bell, a rifle gripped in one hand, Johnny let out a roar and a curse and barreled at him, weapon raised and curses flying. Before Brandon could so much as raise his rifle in defense, he was hit from behind with enough impact to send him facedown into the dirt. A knee pressed into the back of his head, grinding his cheek into the gravel.

"It's that bastard Tremain!" someone shouted.

A chorus of jeers responded as it seemed that a dozen hands twisted into their clothes and pulled him to his feet. Before he could utter a sound, he was shoved and hit and thrown over the water trough where the men bathed twice a week.

Spitting blood and dirt from his mouth, he shielded his face from several kicks and tried his best to make his voice heard over the cacophony of irate cries.

"Hang 'im for what he done to Miss Haviland!" they shouted.

"Whip 'im for what he done to our jobs!"

"Thanks to 'im, we'll be forced back to that bloody prison!"

A gunshot sounded, bringing the melee to an

abrupt and eerie silence. Wang stepped from the dark, as did Murray. Pointing his rifle barrel at Johnny, Wang said calmly, "If you please, Mr. Johnny. Step away from the good Captain."

Johnny did so, narrowing his eyes at the Chinaman and the Scotsman. Brandon struggled to sit up, casting a cautious look at the malevolent men before scrambling to his feet. "I need help," he said. "For Bronte's sake."

This wasn't happening. Bronte told herself over and over that this was all a bad dream. Surely she was safe and sound at home, in her bed with her rabbits, and her father wasn't really bound by his wrists and ankles and tossed like a hogshead on the deck of the boat, near a pile of seaweed-infested rope.

Where was Brandon? He would save her from this.

She struggled to her knees and did her best to see over the rail of the barge. The last of the crates were being loaded. Dillman was shouting orders to the harried men, casting distressed looks toward the trees. Obviously, their time was running out. If Brandon was there, in the dark, he would find a way to save her and her father.

The gag in her mouth cut into her lips and cheeks so fiercely she wanted to cry. But she wouldn't cry. Crying resolved nothing and certainly wouldn't help her or her father. Dillman had every intention of killing them, of tossing their bodies overboard for the sharks just as soon as they were Calcutta-bound . . . if not sooner.

With her heart pounding in her throat, she watched

the last of the crates being hefted onto the barge. Dillman called for the planks to be raised and the oars to be cast immediately.

The figure rose up out of the water with no warning. Giant hands gripping the rail, Johnny Turpin heaved himself up before Bronte's startled eyes, water running in torrents from his face and hair, a knife gripped firmly between his teeth.

She almost screamed. Falling back, her eyes on Johnny's face, she scrambled to her father's side and almost wept in relief.

In the distance, a man cried out. Then another. And another. Until the sudden explosion of activity rang out through the night like shots from a cannon. Within the flickering lights of the torches, bodies dashed here and yonder, scuffling, shouting, screaming out in anger, fear, and pain while Dillman, cursing and barking orders, did his best to encourage his men to "Fight! Fight, damn you, or we are dead men!"

With no warning, Bronte found herself pulled to her feet and her godfather's breath hot on the back of her neck as he dragged her to the center of the bow. She fought him as best she could, even as he pressed the cold barrel of a gun to her temple.

"I'll kill her!" he shouted at the warring men, then shot into the air.

Little by little, the drenched men fell back. There was Johnny and Wang and Murray. She recognized the dozen prisoners who worked for her father—all of whom had slid aboard the boats from the river with hopes of rescuing her and her father.

Bronte closed her eyes and did her best to breathe evenly, while the only sound aside from her own heart beating in her ears was the lapping of water against the sides of the boats.

Then . . .

She heard the pounding, the powerful drumming of a running horse—

They burst through the trees and underbrush, into the gyrating light, Captain Brandon Tremain on her horse, driving the mare toward the water with his heels in her flanks, whipping her haunches with a eucalypt branch so Cytduction was fairly frothing and her nostrils were flared in fear. He drove her straight for the boat, hooves kicking up sand and stones, Brandon's face set in grim determination.

"Holy God," Dillman hissed in her ear, then aimed the gun straight at Brandon and fired.

He missed and Brandon kept coming. Dillman fired again. Missed again. He began backing over the deck, dragging Bronte with him and yelling, "I'll kill her! I'll kill them both if you don't—"

Cytduction hit the plank, the impact splintering the wood with a gunshotlike crack. Then the horse heaved herself and her rider onto the deck and, like some dragon with fire for breath, crashed toward Dillman, who flung Bronte aside and scrambled to escape—to no avail. With one clear swipe of his foot Brandon sent the captain careening to the deck.

Spellbound, not knowing whether to laugh or cry, Bronte watched as Cytduction danced momentarily on her back feet, then spun around, back toward her. For an instant, Bronte's eyes met Brandon's, before he scooped her up and onto the horse and they leapt from the ship, out of harm's way.

Yet the marriage relation is put above the filial, for a man to leave his father and mother, give up his old home with all its sacred ties and memories and cleave to his wife. After marriage, a husband's first and highest duties are to his wife, and a wife's to her husband. The two are to live for each other. Life is to be lost for life.

—*Homemaking*
AUTHOR UNKNOWN, 1882

EPILOGUE

FROM THE TAFFRAIL OF THE HMS *VICTORIAN LADY*, BRANDON watched a gull dive for a fish, then rise again into the silver-blue sky that was, gradually, turning to gray as nightfall crept in. As usual, the Sydney Harbor wharves were alive with activity—fishmongers, stevedores, and sailors who were preparing to pull anchor with the evening's high tide. Freemen and convict laborers moved about the streets, intent on their duties.

"So, Captain, you stand here staring out at sea like a man lost in his deepest thoughts. I needn't ask on what you dwell. 'Tis written on your countenance."

He didn't bother to turn, though he could have, now that his mission was over.

"I must congratulate you on the success of your mission, although I trust luck and coincidence played a great part in your achievement. What a shame that Lady Fish and Captain Dillman will be spending the rest of their lives in that horrid prison. And what a surprise about Arthur, arranging many of those escapes because he wanted Haviland's position as warden. You just never know. Ah, well, be assured that my report will state that you acted on your highly skilled and refined instincts as a much-decorated officer, and gentleman."

Tossing his cigar to the water far below, Brandon straightened and adjusted the red dress jacket of his military uniform. He smoothed the gloves on his hands and cocked his hat over his eyes. The gold epaulets on his shoulders flashed slightly in the failing sunlight. Withdrawing a tiny clay joey from his pocket, a gift from Sammy, he gripped it hard in his hand. "I really don't give a damn what you put in your report . . . sir."

A laugh. "No, I suppose you wouldn't . . . You know, Captain, I've become quite fond of this place. I've given some thought to retiring here, once my commission is up. Might set up sheep farming or some such pastime. Might even apply to the East India Company and try my hand at the import and export business. I have a feeling the gold rush will play out soon enough, people will settle down to the rigors of reality and routine . . . Sydney might well become successful in a few years . . . I could certainly use a partner, should you ever decide to retire your sword . . ."

Slowly, Brandon turned.

"Don't look so surprised, Captain. You should know by now that in our business, you must expect the unexpected."

Brandon grinned.

"Seeing you standing here alone while your

guests gather on yonder deck, I wonder what your thoughts are as you face your next challenge. Oh, please, Captain, you're hardly the sort of man to shy away from a challenge . . . The young woman is, indeed, a handful. I imagine that every day spent with her will be a kind of little war. Loving someone so intensely is a surrendering of the soul, I understand."

"Yes," Brandon replied, and stared out to sea again.

"Your bride is waiting," his companion said softly.

She felt giddy. Like some silly schoolgirl all caught up in her wildest daydreams. Only this was no dream. No fantasy. She was being married aboard the HMS *Victorian Lady*, her decks sparkling clean and England's flag snapping in the wind high above her head. The rails were lined with fresh-faced young seamen and soldiers, who had escorted the dewy-eyed nuns and red-cheeked children on board for the ceremony. Sammy balanced on the windlass, freckled faced beaming. When she saw him and smiled, he squared his small shoulders and saluted, making her heart fill with love and pride, and hope for his—their—future.

On her father's arm, she moved down the honorary, and legendary, arch of swords, past the stalwart officers, who smiled in her wake as she focused on Captain Brandon Tremain's face, his eyes—oh, those beautiful blue eyes that had haunted her from the first moment she opened up that newspaper years before and saw his sketched likeness.

Ah, sweet destiny that they would travel years and thousands of miles to meet and fall in love.

Her father gave her away.

She wore a long white dress and simple lace veil.

Brandon wore his full-dress uniform, and they were accompanied by two dozen Marine and Naval officers also in full dress.

After exchanging vows, they walked together between the line of arched swords, received the well-wishes of their guests. Then, as they were presented a three-tiered cake, Brandon turned to Bronte and smiled.

He presented her with his sword. With trembling hands, she received the gleaming steel treasure with its gilded hilt, the last rays of the day's sunlight reflecting splendidly from the polished blade.

"Sir," she whispered, feeling weak, dizzy, breathless of a sudden. "You have been my hero for years. How does one confront her every dream and fantasy for real? Should I curtsy?"

"I think not." He laughed.

"Then what shall I say? Or do? Tell me how to act in the presence of one whom I've admired—loved—since I was little more than a child."

"Forget, if you can, what I am, and think only of who I am."

"Which is?" She smiled up into his eyes.

"Your husband."

Closing her eyes, she raised the sword to her lips and kissed the hard, sweet blade, and together, his hands enfolding hers, they slid the blue steel through the cake, releasing the cheers of the onlookers, who pressed forward, free at last to congratulate the couple.

Darkness eased gently over Sydney's horizon as the *Victorian Lady* slipped through the waves and out of the harbor. Standing at the rail, watching the image of Sister Elizabeth and the waving children grow dimmer, Bronte swallowed back the tight emotion and did her best to breathe evenly, despite the commotion of anticipation and sadness going on inside her.

Good-byes were never easy.

"Bronte!" came the familiar cry, and suddenly Sammy and his sister burst from the grouping of sailors who were hustling to secure the main sail as the first great gust of wind caught within it and drove them out to sea.

Bronte fell to her knees and opened her arms. The children flung themselves on her, smothering her with hugs and kisses and squeals of delight. But it was Sammy who held her most fiercely.

Sweeping his hair from his brow, Bronte cradled his face in her hands. "Are you happy, darling?" she asked.

"I don't got to be no number no more," he said with an enormous smile. "The Cap'n promised. He said he would never let anybody take me and Pam away from the two of you. I reckon that means I'm yours to keep. Forever and ever."

"Forever and ever," she repeated and hugged Sammy and his sister tightly.

Bronte looked up, above Sammy's head, as he continued to crush close, hugging her fiercely. Brandon stood there, by her father, still in his military uniform, with epaulets and sashes, his sword an-

chored now to his hip, his chest covered in medals.
He watched her with a faint smile, then, slowly,
moved her way, his dark hair slightly blowing in
the sea breeze.

"May I have a moment with your mother?" he
said gently to the children.

They scampered off, Sammy plowing into crates
of Bronte's and her father's belongings, causing her
father and several sailors to shout and scurry to
retrieve the collection of rabbits and birds the
children's rambunctiousness had released to hop,
jump, or flurry over the deck.

Brandon laughed, put his arms around Bronte,
and tenderly turned her toward the sea. In the
distance, Sydney's twinkling lights appeared to be
little more than flickering candles in the dark.

"A final gift from your father," Brandon said
softly in her ear.

In that moment, a rocket speared into the sky.
Then another and another. Red, blue, and green
exploded high above the harbor—great blossoms
of lacy fire that rained toward the white-capped
waves, brightening the night and bringing tears to
Bronte's eyes. Again and again—*Boom! Boom!*—
setting the dark afire with multicolored sparks.

"Catch that rabbit!" someone shouted.

Laughing, Bronte scooped up Sugar and cradled
her close, sighing as the little white and gray lop
proceeded to nuzzle her ear. Baby, a bundle of black
and white fur, scurried one way, Dusty another,
while Hiawatha, her father's prized peacock, strutted,
with green-and-purple plumage presented, over to
Brandon's feet. Somehow all of them would make it
back to England to be together.

Looking up into her husband's twinkling eyes, Bronte smiled. "Sir, as I recall, there is an ancient Chinese belief that—"

"If one is kissed in the presence of a peacock, a baby will be born within the year." Brandon grinned down at her, took the panting rabbit from her hand, and gently dropped it to the deck.

He took Bronte in his arms, his hard body pressed close, then he kissed her, there on the deck of the HMS *Victorian Lady* while the sky lit up behind them in ribbons of bright light.

The sailors cheered, and as Hiawatha flapped his wings and ruffled his expansive, brilliant feathers, Bronte smiled and sighed, "My husband. My happiness . . . My hero."